P9-DEC-431

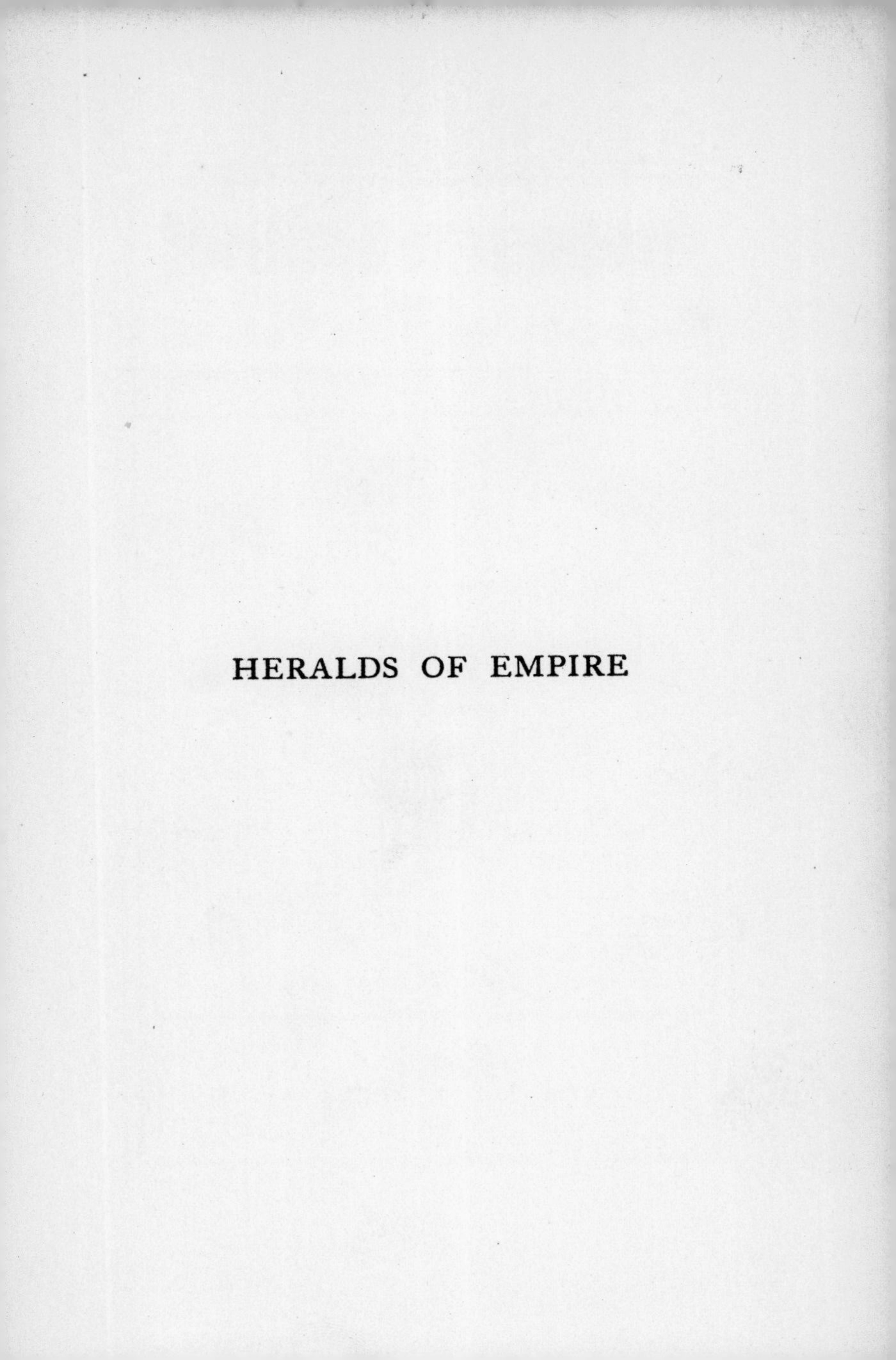

HERALDS OF EMPIRE

Heralds of Empire

BEING

THE STORY OF ONE RAMSAY STANHOPE

LIEUTENANT TO PIERRE RADISSON IN THE NORTHERN FUR TRADE

BY

A. C. LAUT

AUTHOR OF LORDS OF THE NORTH

NEW YORK

D. APPLETON AND COMPANY

1902

Published May, 1902

DEDICATED

TO

THE NEW WORLD NOBILITY

——— Now I learned how the man must have felt when he set about conquering the elements, subduing land and sea and savagery. And in that lies the Homeric greatness of this vast fresh New World of ours. Your Old World victor takes up the unfinished work left by generations of men. Your New World hero begins at the pristine task. I pray you, who are born to the nobility of the New World, forget not the glory of your heritage; for the place which God hath given you in the history of the race is one which men must hold in envy when Roman patrician and Norman conqueror and robber baron are as forgotten as the kingly lines of old Egypt.———

CONTENTS

HERALDS OF EMPIRE

FOREWORD

I SEE him yet—swarthy, straight as a lance, keen as steel, in his eyes the restless fire that leaps to red when sword cuts sword. I see him yet—beating about the high seas, a lone adventurer, tracking forest wastes where no man else dare go, pitting his wit against the intrigue of king and court and empire. Prince of pathfinders, prince of pioneers, prince of gamesters, he played the game for love of the game, caring never a rush for the gold which pawns other men's souls. How much of good was in his ill, how much of ill in his good, let his life declare! He played fast and loose with truth, I know, till all the world played fast and loose with him. He juggled with empires as with puppets, but he died not a groat the richer, which is better record than greater men can boast.

Of enemies, Sieur Radisson had a-plenty, for which, methinks, he had that lying tongue of his to thank. Old France and New France, Old England and New England, would have paid a price for his head; but Pierre Radisson's head held afar too much cunning for any hang-dog of an assassin to try " fall-back, fall-edge " on him. In spite of all the malice with which his enemies fouled him living and dead, Sieur Radisson was never the common buccaneer which your cheap pamphleteers have painted him; though, i' faith, buccaneers stood high enough in my day, when Prince Rupert himself turned robber and pirate of the high seas. Pierre Radisson held his title of nobility from the king; so did all those young noblemen who went with him to the north, as may be seen from M. Colbert's papers in the records *de la marine.* Nor was the disembarking of furs at Isle Percée an attempt to steal M. de la Chesnaye's cargo, as slanderers would have us believe, but a way of escape from those vampires sucking the life-blood of New France—the farmers of the revenue. Indeed, His Most Christian Majesty himself commanded those robber rulers of Quebec to desist from meddling with the northern adventurers. And if some gentleman who has never been farther from city cobblestones than to ride afield with the hounds or take waters at foreign baths, should protest that no maid was ever in so desolate a case as Mistress Hortense, I answer there are to-day many in the same region keeping themselves pure as pond-lilies in a brackish pool, at the forts of their fathers and husbands in the fur-trading country.*

And as memory looks back to those far days, there is another—a poor, shambling, mean-spoken, mean-clad fellow, with the scars of convict gyves on his wrists and the dumb love of a faithful spaniel in his eyes. Compare these two as I may—Pierre Radisson, the explorer with

---

* In confirmation of which reference may be called to the daughter of Governor Norton in Prince of Wales Fort, north of Nelson. Hearne reports that the poor creature died from exposure about the time of her father's death, which was many years after Mr. Stanhope had written the last words of this record.—*Author.*

fame like a meteor that drops in the dark; Jack Battle, the wharf-rat—for the life of me I cannot tell which memory grips the more.

One played the game, the other paid the pawn. Both were misunderstood. One took no thought but of self; the other, no thought of self at all. But where the great man won glory that was a target for envy, the poor sailor lad garnered quiet happiness.

PART I

CHAPTER I

WHAT ARE KING-KILLERS?

My father—peace to his soul!—had been of those who thronged London streets with wine tubs to drink the restored king's health on bended knee; but he, poor gentleman, departed this life before his monarch could restore a wasted patrimony. For old Tibbie, the nurse, there was nothing left but to pawn the family plate and take me, a spoiled lad in his teens, out to Puritan kin of Boston Town.

On the night my father died he had spoken remorsefully of the past to the lord bishop at his bedside.

"Tush, man, have a heart," cries his lordship. "Thou'lt see pasch and yule yet forty year, Stanhope. Tush, man, 'tis thy liver, or a touch of the gout. Take here a smack of port. Sleep sound, man, sleep sound."

And my father slept so sound he never wakened more.

So I came to my Uncle Kirke, whose virtues were of the acid sort that curdles the milk of human kindness.

With him, goodness meant gloom. If the sweet joy of living ever sang to him in his youth, he shut his ears to the sound as to siren temptings, and sternly set himself to the fierce delight of being miserable.

For misery he had reason enough. Having writ a book in which he called King Charles "a man of blood and everlasting abomination"—whatever that might mean—Eli Kirke got himself star-chambered. When, in the language of those times, he was examined "before torture, in torture, between torture, and after torture"—the torture of the rack and the thumbkins and the boot—he added to his former testimony that the queen was a "Babylonish woman, a Potiphar, a Jezebel, a——"

There his mouth was gagged, head and heels roped to the rack, and a wrench given the pulleys at each end that nigh dismembered his poor, torn body. And what words, think you, came quick on top of his first sharp outcry?

"Wisdom is justified of her children! The wicked shall he pull down and the humble shall he exalt!"

And when you come to think of it, Charles

Stuart lost his head on the block five years from that day.

When Eli Kirke left jail to take ship for Boston Town both ears had been cropped. On his forehead the letters S L—seditious libeler—were branded deep, though not so deep as the bitterness burned into his soul.

There comes before me a picture of my landing, showing as clearly as it were threescore years ago that soft, summer night, the harbour waters molten gold in a harvest moon, a waiting group of figures grim above the quay. No firing of muskets and drinking of flagons and ringing of bells to welcome us, for each ship brought out court minions to whip Boston into line with the Restoration—as hungry a lot of rascals as ever gathered to pick fresh bones.

Old Tibbie had pranked me out in brave finery: the close-cut, black-velvet waistcoat that young royalists then wore; a scarlet doublet, flaming enough to set the turkey yard afire; the silken hose and big shoe-buckles late introduced from France by the king; and a beaver hat with plumes a-nodding like my lady's fan. My curls, I mind, tumbled forward thicker than those foppish French perukes.

" There is thy Uncle Kirke," whispers Nurse

Tibbie. "Pay thy best devoirs, Master Ramsay," and she pushes me to the fore of those crowding up the docks.

A thin, pale man with a scarred face silently permitted me to salute four limp fingers. His eyes swept me with chill disapproval. My hat clapped on a deal faster than it had come off, for you must know we unhatted in those days with a grand, slow bow.

"Thy Aunt Ruth," says Tibbie, nudging me; for had I stood from that day to this, I was bound that cold man should speak first.

To my aunt the beaver came off in its grandest flourish. The pressure of a dutiful kiss touched my forehead, and I minded the passion kisses of a dead mother.

Those errant curls blew out in the wind.

"Ramsay Stanhope," begins my uncle sourly, "what do you with uncropped hair and the foolish trappings of vanity?"

As I live, those were the first words he uttered to me.

"I perceive silken garters," says he, clearing his throat and lowering his glance down my person. "Many a good man hath exchanged silk for hemp, my fine gentleman!"

"An the hemp hold like silk, 'twere a fair

exchange, sir," I returned; though I knew very well he referred to those men who had died for the cause.

"Ramsay," says he, pointing one lank forefinger at me, "Ramsay, draw your neck out of that collar; for the vanities of the wicked are a yoke leading captive the foolish!"

Now, my collar was *point-de-vice* of prime quality over black velvet. My uncle's welcome was more than a vain lad could stomach; and what youth of his first teens hath not a vanity hidden about him somewhere?

"Thou shalt not put the horse and the ass under the same yoke, sir," said I, drawing myself up far as ever high heels would lift.

He looked dazed for a minute. Then he told me that he spake concerning my spiritual blindness, his compassions being moved to show me the error of my way.

At that, old nurse must needs take fire.

"Lord save a lad from the likes o' sich compassions! Sure, sir, an the good Lord makes pretty hair grow, 'twere casting pearls before swine to shave his head like a cannon-ball"—this with a look at my uncle's crown—"or to dress a proper little gentleman like a ragged flibbergibbet."

"Tibbie, hold your tongue!" I order.

" Silence were fitter for fools and children," says Eli Kirke loftily.

There comes a time when every life must choose whether to laugh or weep over trivial pains, and when a cut may be broken on the foil of that glancing mirth which the good Creator gave mankind to keep our race from going mad. It came to me on the night of my arrival on the wharves of Boston Town.

We lumbered up through the straggling village in one of those clumsy coaches that had late become the terror of foot-passengers in London crowds. My aunt pointed with a pride that was colonial to the fine light which the townspeople had erected on Beacon Hill; and told me pretty legends of Rattlesnake Hill that fired the desire to explore those inland dangers. I noticed that the rubble-faced houses showed lanterns in iron clamps above most of the doorways. My kinsman's house stood on the verge of the wilds—rough stone below, timbered plaster above, with a circle of bay windows midway, like an umbrella. High windows were safer in case of attack from savages, Aunt Ruth explained; and I mentally set to scaling rope ladders in and out of those windows.

We drew up before the front garden and entered by a turnstile with flying arms. Many a ride have little Rebecca Stocking, of the court-house, and Ben Gillam, the captain's son, and Jack Battle, the sailor lad, had, perched on that turnstile, while I ran pushing and jumping on, as the arms flew creaking round.

The home-coming was not auspicious. Yet I thought no resentment against my uncle. I realized too well how the bloody revenge of the royalists was turning the hearts of England to stone. One morning I recall, when my poor father lay a-bed of the gout and there came a roar through London streets as of a burst ocean dike. Before Tibbie could say no, I had snatched up a cap and was off.

God spare me another such sight! In all my wild wanderings have I never seen savages do worse.

Through the streets of London before the shoutings of a rabble rout was whipped an old, white-haired man. In front of him rumbled a cart; in the cart, the axeman, laving wet hands; at the axeman's feet, the head of a regicide—all to intimidate that old, white-haired man, fearlessly erect, singing a psalm. When they reached the shambles, know you what they did? Go read the old court records and learn what that sentence meant when a man's body was cast into fire before his living eyes! All the while, watching from a window were the princes and their shameless ones.

Ah, yes! God wot, I understood Eli Kirke's bitterness!

But the beginning was not auspicious, and my best intentions presaged worse. For instance, one morning my uncle was sounding my convictions—he was ever sounding other people's convictions—"touching the divine right of kings." Thinking to give strength to contempt for that doctrine, I applied to it one forcible word I had oft heard used by gentlemen of the cloth. Had I shot a gun across the table, the effect could not have been worse. The serving maid fell all of a heap against the pantry door. Old Tibbie yelped out with laughter, and then nigh choked. Aunt Ruth glanced from me to Eli Kirke with a timid look in her eye; but Eli Kirke gazed stolidly into my soul as he would read whether I scoffed or no.

Thereafter he nailed up a little box to receive fines for blasphemy.

"To be plucked as a brand from the burning," I hear him say, fetching a mighty sigh.

But sweet, calm Aunt Ruth, stitching at some spotless kerchief, intercedes.

"Let us be thankful the lad hath come to us."

WHAT ARE KING-KILLERS?

"Bound fast in cords of vanity," deplores Uncle Kirke.

"But all things are possible," Aunt Ruth softly interposes.

"All things are *possible*," concedes Eli Kirke grudgingly, "but thou knowest, Ruth, all things are not *probable!*"

And I, knowing my uncle loved an argument as dearly as merry gentlemen love a glass, slip away leg-bail for the docks, where sits Ben Gillam among the spars spinning sailor yarns to Jack Battle, of the great north sea, whither his father goes for the fur trade; or of M. Radisson, the half-wild Frenchman, who married an English kinswoman of Eli Kirke's and went where never man went and came back with so many pelts that the Quebec governor wanted to build a fortress of beaver fur; * or of the English squadron, rocking to the harbour tide, fresh from winning the Dutch of Manhattan, and ready to subdue malcontents of Boston Town.

Then Jack Battle, the sailor lad from no one knows where, living no one knows how, digs

* Young Stanhope's informant had evidently mixed tradition with fact. Radisson was fined for going overland to Hudson Bay without the governor's permission, the fine to build a fort at Three Rivers. Eli Kirke's kinswoman was a daughter of Sir John Kirke, of the Hudson's Bay Fur Company.—*Author.*

his bare toes into the sand and asks under his breath if we have heard about king-killers.

"What are king-killers?" demands young Gillam.

I discreetly hold my tongue; for a gentleman who supped late with my uncle one night has strangely disappeared, and the rats in the attic have grown boldly loud.

"What are king-killers?" asks Gillam.

"Them as sent Charles I to his death," explains Jack. "They do say," he whispers fearfully, "one o' them is hid hereabouts now! The king's commission hath ordered to have hounds and Indians run him down."

"Pah!" says Gillam, making little of what he had not known, "hounds are only for runaways," this with a sneering look at odd marks round Jack's wrists.

"I am no slave!" vows Jack in crestfallen tones.

"Who said 'slave'?" laughs Gillam triumphantly. "My father saith he is a runaway rat from the Barbadoes," adds Ben to me.

With the fear of a hunted animal under his shaggy brows, little Jack tries to read how much is guess.

"I am no slave, Ben Gillam," he flings back at hazard; but his voice is thin from fright.

"My father saith some planter hath lost ten pound on thee, little slavie," continues Ben. "Pah! Ten pound for such a scrub! He's not worth six! Look at the marks on his arms, Ramsay"—catching the sailor roughly by the wrist. "He can say what he likes. He knows chains."

Little Jack jerked free and ran along the sands as hard as his bare feet could carry him. Then I turned to Ben, who had always bullied us both. Dropping the solemn "thou's" which our elders still used, I let him have plain "you's."

"You—you—mean coward! I've a mind to knock you into the sea!"

"Grow bigger first, little billycock," taunts Ben.

By the next day I was big enough.

Mistress Hortense Hillary was down on the beach with M. Picot's blackamoor, who dogged her heels wherever she went; and presently comes Rebecca Stocking to shovel sand too. Then Ben must show what a big fellow he is by kicking over the little maid's cart-load.

"Stop that!" commands Jack Battle, springing of a sudden from the beach.

For an instant, Ben was taken aback.

Then the insolence that provokes its own punishment broke forth.

"Go play with your equals, jack-pudding! Jailbirds who ape their betters are strangled up in Quebec," and he kicked down Rebecca's pile too.

Rebecca's doll-blue eyes spilled over with tears, but Mistress Hortense was the high-mettled, high-stepping little dame. She fairly stamped her wrath, and to Jack's amaze took him by the hand and marched off with the hauteur of an empress.

Then Ben must call out something about M. Picot, the French doctor, not being what he ought, and little Hortense having no mother.

"Ben," said I quietly, "come out on the pier." The pier ran to deep water. At the far end I spoke.

"Not another word against Hortense and Jack! Promise me!"

His back was to the water, mine to the shore. He would have promised readily enough, I think, if the other monkeys had not followed—Rebecca with big tear-drops on both cheeks, Hortense quivering with wrath, Jack flushed, half shy and half shamed to be championed by a girl.

"Come, Ben; 'fore I count three, promise——"

But he lugged at me. I dodged. With a

splash that doused us four, Ben went headlong into the sea. The uplift of the waves caught him. He threw back his arms with a cry. Then he sank like lead.

The sailor son of the famous captain could not swim. Rebecca's eyes nigh jumped from her head with fright. Hortense grew white to the lips and shouted for that lout of a blackamoor sound asleep on the sand.

Before I could get my doublet off to dive, Jack Battle was cleaving air like a leaping fish, and the waters closed over his heels.

Bethink you, who are not withered into forgetfulness of your own merry youth, whether our hearts stopped beating then!

But up comes that water-dog of a Jack gripping Ben by the scruff of the neck; and when by our united strength we had hauled them both on the pier, little Mistress Hortense was the one to roll Gillam on his stomach and bid us "Quick! Stand him on his head and pour the water out!"

From that day Hortense was Jack's slave, Jack was mine, and Ben was a pampered hero because he never told and took the punishment like a man. But there was never a word more slurring Hortense's unknown origin and Jack's strange wrist marks.

CHAPTER II

I RESCUE AND AM RESCUED

So the happy childhood days sped on, a swift stream past flowered banks. Ben went off to sail the north sea in Captain Gillam's ship. M. Picot, the French doctor, brought a governess from Paris for Hortense, so that we saw little of our playmate, and Jack Battle continued to live like a hunted rat at the docks.

My uncle and Rebecca's father, who were beginning to dabble in the fur trade, had jointly hired a peripatetic dominie to give us youngsters lessons in Bible history and the three R's. At noon hour I initiated Rebecca into all the thrilling dangers of Indian warfare, and many a time have we had wild escapes from imaginary savages by scaling a rope ladder of my own making up to the high nursery window. By-and-bye, when school was in and the dominie dozed, I would lower that timid little whiffet of a Puritan maid out through the window to the turnstile. Then I would ride her round till our heads whirled. If Jack Battle came along, Rebecca would jump down primly and run in, for Jack was unknown in the meeting-house, and the meeting-house was Rebecca's measure of the whole world.

One day Jack lingered. He was carrying something tenderly in a red cambric handkerchief.

"Where is Mistress Hortense?" he asked sheepishly.

"That silly French woman keeps her caged like a squirrel."

Little Jack began tittering and giggling.

"Why—that's what I have here," he explained, slipping a bundle of soft fur in my hand. "It's tame! It's for Hortense," said he.

"Why don't you take it to her, Jack?"

"Take it to her?" reiterated he in a daze. "As long as she gets it, what does it matter who takes it?"

With that, he was off across the marshy commons, leaving the squirrel in my hand.

Forgetting lessons, I ran to M. Picot's house. That governess answered the knocker.

"From Jack Battle to Mistress Hortense!" And I proffered the squirrel.

Though she smirked a world of thanks, she would not take it. Then Hortense came dancing down the hall.

"Am I not grown tall?" she asked, mischievously shaking her curls.

"No," said I, looking down to her feet cased in those high slippers French ladies then wore, "'tis your heels!"

And we all laughed. Catching sight of the squirrel, Hortense snatched it up with caresses against her neck, and the French governess sputtered out something of which I knew only the word "beau."

"Jack is no beau, mademoiselle," said I loftily. "Pah! He's a wharf lad."

I had thought Hortense would die in fits.

"Mademoiselle means the squirrel, Ramsay," she said, choking, her handkerchief to her lips. "Tell Jack thanks, with my love," she called, floating back up the stairs.

And the governess set to laughing in the pleasant French way that shakes all over and has no spite. Emboldened, I asked why Hortense could not play with us any more. Hortense, she explained, was become too big to prank on the commons.

"Faith, mademoiselle," said I ruefully, "an she mayn't play war on the commons, what may she play?"

"Beau!" teases mademoiselle, perking her lips saucily; and she shut the door in my face.

It seemed a silly answer enough, but it put a notion in a lad's head. I would try it on Rebecca.

When I re-entered the window, the dominie still slept. Rebecca, the demure monkey, bent over her lesson book as innocently as though there were no turnstiles.

"Rebecca," I whispered, leaning across the bench, "you are big enough to have a—what? Guess."

"Go away, Ramsay Stanhope!" snapped Rebecca, grown mighty good of a sudden, with glance fast on her white stomacher.

"O-ho! Crosspatch," thought I; and from no other motive than transgressing the forbidden, I reached across to distract the attentive goodness of the prim little baggage; but—an iron grip lifted me bodily from the bench.

It was Eli Kirke, wry-faced, tight-lipped. He had seen all! This was the secret of Mistress Rebecca's new-found diligence. No syllable was uttered, but it was the awfullest silence that ever a lad heard. I was lifted rather than led upstairs and left a prisoner in locked room with naught to do but gnaw my conscience and gaze at the woods skirting the crests of the inland hills.

Those rats in the attic grew noisier, and presently sounds a mighty hallooing outside, with a blowing of hunting-horns and baying of hounds. What ado was this in Boston, where men were only hunters of souls and chasers of devils? The rats fell to sudden quiet, and from the yells of the rabble crowd I could make out only "King-killers! King-killers!" These were no Puritans shouting, but the blackguard sailors and hirelings of the English squadron set loose to hunt down the refugees. The shouting became a roar. Then in burst Eli Kirke's front door. The house was suddenly filled with swearings enough to cram his blasphemy box to the brim. There was a trampling of feet on the stairs, followed by the crashing of overturned furniture, and the rabble had rushed up with neither let nor hindrance and were searching every room.

Who had turned informer on my uncle? Was I not the only royalist in the house? Would suspicion fall on me? But questions were put to flight by a thunderous rapping on the door. It gave as it had been cardboard, and in tumbled a dozen ruffians with gold-lace doublets, cockades and clanking swords.

Behind peered Eli Kirke, pale with fear, his eyes asking mine if I knew. True as eyes can speak, mine told him that I knew as well as he.

I RESCUE AND AM RESCUED

"Body o' me! What-a-deuce? Only a little fighting sparrow of a royalist!" cried a swaggering colt of a fellow in officer's uniform.

"No one here, lad?" demanded a second.

And I saw Eli Kirke close his eyes as in prayer.

"Sir," said I, drawing myself up on my heels, "I don't understand you. I—am here."

They bellowed a laugh and were tumbling over one another in their haste up the attic stairs. Then my blood went cold with fear, for the memory of that poor old man going to the shambles of London flashed back.

A window lifted and fell in the attic gable. With a rush I had slammed the door and was craning out full length from the window-sill. Against the lattice timber-work of the plastered wall below the attic window clung a figure in Geneva cloak, with portmanteau under arm. It was the man who had supped so late with Eli Kirke.

"Sir," I whispered, fearing to startle him from perilous footing, "let me hold your portmanteau. Jump to the slant roof below."

For a second his face went ashy, but he tossed me the bag, gained the shed roof at a leap, snatched back the case, and with a "Lord bless thee, child!" was down and away.

The spurred boots of the searchers clanked on the stairs. A blowing of horns! They were all to horse and off as fast as the hounds coursed away. The deep, far baying of the dogs, now loud, now low, as the trail ran away or the wind blew clear, told where the chase led inland. If the fugitive but hid till the dogs passed he was safe enough; but of a sudden came the hoarse, furious barkings that signal hot scent.

What had happened was plain.

The poor wretch had crossed the road and given the hounds clew. The baying came nearer. He had discovered his mistake and was trying to regain the house.

Balaam stood saddled to carry Eli Kirke to the docks. 'Twas a wan hope, but in a twinkling I was riding like wind for the barking behind the hill. A white-faced man broke from the brush at crazy pace.

"God ha' mercy, sir," I cried, leaping off; "to horse and away! Ride up the brook bed to throw the hounds off."

I saw him in saddle, struck Balaam's flank a blow that set pace for a gallop, turned, and—for a second time that day was lifted from the ground.

"Pardieu! Clean done!" says a low voice. "'Tis a pretty trick!"

And I felt myself set up before a rider.

"To save thee from the hounds," says the voice.

Scarce knowing whether I dreamed, I looked over my shoulder to see one who was neither royalist nor Puritan—a thin, swarth man, tall and straight as an Indian, bare-shaven and scarred from war, with long, wiry hair and black eyes full of sparks.

The pack came on in a whirl to lose scent at the stream, and my rescuer headed our horse away from the rabble, doffing his beaver familiarly to the officers galloping past.

"Ha!" called one, reining his horse to its haunches, "did that snivelling knave pass this way?"

"Do you mean this little gentleman?"

The officer galloped off. "Keep an eye open, Radisson," he shouted over his shoulder.

"'Twere better shut," says M. Radisson softly; and at his name my blood pricked to a jump.

Here was he of whom Ben Gillam told, the half-wild Frenchman, who had married the royalist kinswoman of Eli Kirke; the hero of Spanish fights and Turkish wars; the bold explorer of the north sea, who brought back such wealth from an unknown land, governors and merchant princes were spying his heels like pirates a treasure ship.

" 'Tis more sport hunting than being hunted," he remarked, with an air of quiet reminiscence.

His suit was fine-tanned, cream buckskin, garnished with gold braid like any courtier's, with a deep collar of otter. Unmindful of manners, I would have turned again to stare, but he bade me guide the horse back to my home.

" Lest the hunters ask questions," he explained. " And what," he demanded, " what doth a little cavalier in a Puritan hotbed? "

" I am even where God hath been pleased to set me, sir."

" 'Twas a ticklish place he set thee when I came up."

" By your leave, sir, 'tis a higher place than I ever thought to know."

M. Radisson laughed a low, mellow laugh, and, vowing I should be a court gallant, put me down before Eli Kirke's turnstile.

My uncle came stalking forth, his lips pale with rage. He had blazed out ere I could explain one word.

" Have I put bread in thy mouth, Ramsay Stanhope, that thou shouldst turn traitor? Viper and imp of Satan! " he shouted, shaking his clinched fist in my face. "Was it not enough that thou wert utterly bound in iniquity without persecuting the Lord's anointed?"

I took a breath.

"Where is Balaam?" he demanded, seizing me roughly.

"Sir," said I, "for leaving the room without leave, I pray you to flog me as I deserve. As for the horse, he is safe and I hope far away under the gentleman I helped down from the attic."

His face fell a-blank. M. Radisson dismounted laughing.

"Nay, nay, Eli Kirke, I protest 'twas to the lad's credit. 'Twas this way, kinsman," and he told all, with many a strange-sounding, foreign expression that must have put the Puritan's nose out of joint, for Eli Kirke began blowing like a trumpet.

Then out comes Aunt Ruth to insist that M. Radisson share a haunch of venison at our noonday meal.

And how I wish I could tell you of that dinner, and of all that M. Radisson talked; of captivity among Iroquois and imprisonment in Spain and wars in Turkey; of his voyage over land and lake to a far north sea, and of the conspiracy among merchant princes of Quebec to ruin him. By-and-bye Rebecca Stocking's father came in, and the three sat talking plans for the northern trade till M. Radisson let drop that the English commissioners were keen to join the enterprise. Then the two Puritans would have naught to do with it.

Long ago, as you know, we dined at mid-day; but so swiftly had the hour flown with M. Radisson's tales of daring that Tibbie was already lighting candles when we rose from the dinner table.

"And now," cried M. Radisson, lifting a stirrup-cup of home-brewed October, "health to the little gentleman who saved a life to-day! Health to mine host! And a cup fathoms deep to his luck when Ramsay sails yon sea!"

"He might do worse," said Eli Kirke grimly.

And the words come back like the echo of a prophecy.

I would have escaped my uncle, but he waylaid me in the dark at the foot of the stairs.

"Ramsay," said he gently.

"Sir?" said I, wondering if flint could melt.

"'The Lord bless thee, and keep thee: the Lord make his face shine upon thee, and be gracious unto thee: the Lord lift up his countenance upon thee, and give thee peace!'"

CHAPTER III

TOUCHING WITCHCRAFT

THAT interrupted lesson with Rebecca finished my schooling. I was set to learning the mysteries of accounts in Eli Kirke's warehouse.

"How goes the keeping of accounts, Ramsay?" he questioned soon after I had been in tutelage.

I had always intended to try my fortune in the English court when I came of age, and the air of the counting-house ill suited a royalist's health.

"Why, sir," I made answer, picking my words not to trip his displeasure, "I get as much as I can—and I give as little as I can; and those be all the accounts that ever I intend to keep."

Aunt Ruth looked up from her spinning-wheel in a way that had become an alarm signal. Eli Kirke glanced dubiously to the blasphemy box, as though my words were actionable. There was no sound but the drone of the loom till I slipped from the room. Then they both began to talk. Soon after came transfer from the counting-house to the fur trade. That took me through the shadowy forests from town to town, and when I returned my old comrades seemed shot of a sudden from youth to manhood.

There was Ben Gillam, a giff-gaffing blade home from the north sea, so topful of spray that salt water spilled over at every word.

"Split me fore and aft," exclaims Ben, "if I sail not a ship of my own next year! I'll take the boat without commission. Stocking and my father have made an offer," he hinted darkly. "I'll go without commission!"

"And risk being strangled for't, if the French governor catch you."

"Body o' me!" flouts Ben, ripping out a peck of oaths that had cost dear and meant a day in the stocks if the elders heard, "who's going to inform when my father sails the only other ship in the bay? Devil sink my soul to the bottom of the sea if I don't take a boat to Hudson Bay under the French governor's nose!"

"A boat of your own," I laughed. "What for, Ben?"

"For the same as your Prince Rupert, Prince Robber, took his. Go out light as a cork, come back loaded with Spanish gold to the water-line." Ben paused to take a pinch of snuff and display his new embroidered waistcoat.

"Look you at the wealth in the beaver trade," he added. "M. Radisson went home with George Carteret not worth a curse, formed the Fur Company, and came back from Hudson Bay with pelts packed to the quarter-deck. Devil sink me! but they say, after the fur sale, the gentlemen adventurers had to haul the gold through London streets with carts! Bread o' grace, Ramsay, have half an eye for your own purse!" he urged. "There *is* a life for a man o' spirit! Why don't you join the beaver trade, Ramsay?"

Why not, indeed? 'Twas that or turn cutpurse and road-lifter for a youth of birth without means in those days.

Of Jack Battle I saw less. He shipped with the fishing boats in the summer and cruised with any vagrant craft for the winter. When he came ashore he was as small and eel-like and shy and awkward as ever, with the same dumb fidelity in his eyes.

And what a snowy maid had Rebecca become! Sitting behind her spinning-wheel, with her dainty fingers darting in the sunlight, she seemed the pink and whitest thing that ever grew, with a look on her face of apple-blossoms in June; but the sly wench had grown mighty demure with me. When I laughed over that ending to our last lesson, she must affect an air of injury. 'Twas neither her fault nor mine, I declare, coaxing back her good-humour; 'twas the fault of the face. I wanted to see where the white began and the pink ended. Then Rebecca, with cheeks a-bloom under the hiding of her bonnet, quickens steps to the meeting-house; but as a matter of course we walk home together, for behind march the older folk, staidly discoursing of doctrine.

"Rebecca," I say, "you did not take your eyes off the preacher for one minute."

"How do you know, Ramsay?" retorts Rebecca, turning her face away with a dimple trembling in her chin, albeit it was the Sabbath.

"That preacher is too handsome to be sound in his doctrine, Rebecca."

Then she grows so mighty prim she must ask which heading of the sermon pleases me best.

"I liked the last," I declare; and with that, we are at the turnstile.

Hortense became a vision of something lost, a type of what I had known when great ladies came to our country hall. M. Picot himself took her on the grand tour of the Continent. How much we had been hoping to see more of her I did not realize till she came back and we saw less.

Once I encountered M. Picot and his ward on the wharf. Her curls were more wayward than of old and her large eyes more lustrous, full of deep, new lights, dark like the flash of a black diamond. Her form appeared slender against the long, flowing mantilla shot with gold like any grand dame's. She wore a white beaver with plumes sweeping down on her curls. Indeed, little Hortense seemed altogether such a great lady that I held back, though she was looking straight towards me.

"Give you good-e'en, Ramsay," salutes M. Picot, a small, thin man with pointed beard, eyebrows of a fierce curlicue, and an expression under half-shut lids like cat's eyes in the dark. "Give you good-e'en! Can you guess who this is?"

As if any one could forget Hortense! But I did not say so. Instead, I begged leave to welcome her back by saluting the tips of her gloved fingers. She asked me if I minded that drowning of Ben long ago. Then she wanted to know of Jack.

"I hear you are fur trading, Ramsay?" remarks M. Picot with the inflection of a question.

I told him somewhat of the trade, and he broke out in almost the same words as Ben Gillam. 'Twas the life for a gentleman of spirit. Why didn't I join the beaver trade of Hudson Bay? And did I know of any secret league between Captain Zachariah Gillam and Mr. Stocking to trade without commission?

"Ah, Hillary," he sighed, "had we been beaver trading like Radisson instead of pounding pestles, we might have had little Hortense restored."

"Restored!" thought I. And M. Picot must have seen my surprise, for he drew back to his shell like a pricked snail. Observing that the wind was chill, he bade me an icy good-night.

I had no desire to pry into M. Picot's secrets, but I could not help knowing that he had unbended to me because he was interested in the fur trade. From that 'twas but a step to the guess that he had come to New England to amass wealth to restore Mistress Hortense.

Restore her to what? There I pulled up sharp. 'Twas none of my affair; and yet, in spite of resolves, it daily became more of my affair.

Do what I would, spending part of every day with Rebecca, that image of lustrous eyes under the white beaver, the plume nodding above the curls, the slender figure outlined against the gold-shot mantilla, became a haunting memory. Countless times I blotted out that mental picture with a sweep of common sense. "She was a pert miss, with her head full of French nonsense and a nose held too high in air." Then a memory of the eyes under the beaver, and fancy was at it again spinning cobwebs in moonshine.

M. Picot kept more aloof than formerly, and was as heartily hated for it as the little minds of a little place ever hate those apart.

Occasionally, in the forest far back from the settlement, I caught a flying glimpse of Lincoln green; and Hortense went through the woods, hard as her Irish hunter could gallop, followed by the blackamoor, churning up and down on a blowing nag. Once I had the good luck to restore a dropped gauntlet before the blackamoor could come. With eyes alight she threw me a flashing thanks and was off, a sunbeam through the forest shades; and something was thumping under a velvet waistcoat faster than the greyhound's pace. A moment later, back came the hound in springy stretches, with the riders at full gallop.

Her whip fell, but this time she did not turn.

But when I carried the whip to the doctor's house that night, M. Picot received it with scant grace!

Whispers—gall-midges among evil tongues—were raising a buzz that boded ill for the doctor. France had paid spies among the English, some said. Deliverance Dobbins, a frumpish, fizgig of a maid, ever complaining of bodily ills though her chuffy cheeks were red as pippins, reported that one day when she had gone for simples she had seen strange, dead things in the jars of M. Picot's dispensary. At this I laughed as Rebecca told it me, and old Tibbie winked behind the little Puritan maid's head; for my father, like the princes, had known that love of the new sciences which became a passion among gentlemen. Had I not noticed the mole on the French doctor's cheek? Rebecca asked. I had: what of it?

"The crops have been blighted," says Rebecca; though what connection that had with M. Picot's mole, I could not see.

"Deliverance Dobbins oft hath racking pains," says Rebecca, with that air of injury which became her demure dimples so well.

"Drat that Deliverance Dobbins for a low-bred mongrel mischief-maker!" cries old Tibbie from the pantry door.

"Tibbie," I order, "hold your tongue and drop an angel in the blasphemy box."

"'Twas good coin wasted," the old nurse vowed; but I must needs put some curb on her royalist tongue, which was ever running a-riot in that Puritan household.

It was an accident, in the end, that threw me across M. Picot's path. I had gone to have him bind up a splintered wrist, and he invited me to stay for a round of piquet. I, having only one hand, must beg Mistress Hortense to sort the cards for me.

She sat so near that I could not see her. You may guess I lost every game.

"Tut! tut! Hillary dear, 'tis a poor helper Ramsay gained when he asked your hand. Pish! pish!" he added, seeing our faces crimson; "come away," and he carried me off to the dispensary, as though his preserved reptiles would be more interesting than Hortense.

With an indifference a trifle too marked, he brought me round to the fur trade and wanted to know whether I would be willing to risk trading without a license, on shares with a partner.

"Quick wealth that way, Ramsay, an you have courage to go to the north. An it were not for Hortense, I'd hire that young rapscallion of a Gillam to take me north."

I caught his drift, and had to tell him that I meant to try my fortune in the English court.

But he paid small heed to what I said, gazing absently at the creatures in the jars.

"'Twould be devilish dangerous for a girl," he muttered, pulling fiercely at his mustache.

"Do you mean the court, sir?" I asked.

"Aye," returned the doctor with a dry laugh that meant the opposite of his words. "An you incline to the court, learn the tricks o' the foils, or rogues will slit both purse and throat."

And all the while he was smiling as though my going to the court were an odd notion.

"If I could but find a master," I lamented.

"Come to me of an evening," says M. Picot. "I'll teach you, and you can tell me of the fur trade."

You may be sure I went as often as ever I could. M. Picot took me upstairs to a sort of hunting room. It had a great many ponderous oak pieces carved after the Flemish pattern and a few little bandy-legged chairs and gilded tables with courtly scenes painted on top, which he said Mistress Hortense had brought back as of the latest French fashion. The blackamoor drew close the iron shutters; for, though those in the world must know the ways of the world, worldling practices were a sad offence to New England. Shoving the furnishings aside, M. Picot picked from the armory rack two slim foils resembling Spanish rapiers and prepared to give me my lesson. Carte and tierce, low carte and flanconnade, he taught me with many a ringing clash of steel till beads were dripping from our brows like rain-drops.

"Bravo!" shouted M. Picot in a pause. "Are you son o' the Stanhope that fought on the king's side?"

I said that I was.

"I knew the rascal that got the estate from the king," says M. Picot, with a curious look from Hortense to me; and he told me of Blood, the freebooter, who stole the king's crown but won royal favour by his bravado and entered court service for the doing of deeds that bore not the light of day.

Nightly I went to the French doctor's house, and I learned every wicked trick of thrust and parry that M. Picot knew. Once when I bungled a foul lunge, which M. Picot said was a habit of the infamous Blood, his weapon touched my chest, and Mistress Hortense uttered a sharp cry.

"What—what—what!" exclaims M. Picot, whirling on her.

"'Twas so real," murmurs Hortense, biting her lip.

After that she sat still enough. Then the steel was exchanged for cards; and when I lost too steadily M. Picot broke out: "Pish, boy, your luck fails here! Hillary, child, go practise thy songs on the spinet."

Or: "Hortense, go mull us a smack o' wine!"

Or: "Ha, ha, little witch! Up yet? Late hours make old ladies."

And Hortense must go off, so that I never saw her alone but once. 'Twas the night before I was to leave for the trade.

The blackamoor appeared to say that Deliverance Dobbins was "a-goin' in fits" on the dispensary floor.

"Faith, doctor," said I, "she used to have dumps on our turnstile."

"Yes," laughed Hortense, "small wonder she had dumps on that turnstile! Ramsay used to tilt her backward."

M. Picot hastened away, laughing. Hortense was in a great carved high-back chair with clumsy, wooden cupids floundering all about the tall head-rest. Her face was alight in soft-hued crimson flaming from an Arabian cresset stuck in sockets against the Flemish cabinet.

"A child's trick," began Hortense, catching at the shafts of light.

"I often think of those old days on the beach."

"So do I," said Hortense.

"I wish they could come back."

"So do I," smiled Hortense. Then, as if to check more: "I suppose, Ramsay, you would want to drown us all—Ben and Jack and Rebecca and me."

"And I suppose you would want to stand us all on our heads," I retorted.

Then we both laughed, and Hortense demanded if I had as much skill with the lyre as with the sword. She had heard that I was much given to chanting vain airs and wanton songs, she said.

And this is what I sang, with a heart that knocked to the notes of the old madrigal like the precentor's tuning-fork to a meeting-house psalm:

"Lady, when I behold the roses sprouting,
  Which, clad in damask mantles, deck the arbours,
  And then behold your lips where sweet love harbours,
My eyes perplex me with a double doubting,
Whether the roses be your lips, or your lips the roses."

Barely had I finished when Mistress Hortense seats herself at the spinet, and, changing the words to suit her saucy fancy, trills off that ballad but newly writ by one of our English courtiers:

> "Shall I, wasting in despair,
> Die because—*Rebecca's*—fair?
> Or make pale my cheeks with care
> 'Cause *Rebecca's* rosier are?"

"Hortense!" I protested.

> "Be *he* fairer than the day
> Or the *June-field coils of hay;*
> If *he* be not so to me,
> What care I how *fine* he be?"

There was such merriment in the dark-lashed eyes, I defy Eli Kirke himself to have taken offence; and so, like many another youth, I was all too ready to be the pipe on which a dainty lady played her stops. As the song faded to the last tinkling notes of the spinet her fingers took to touching low, tuneless melodies like thoughts creeping into thoughts, or perfume of flowers in the dark. The melting airs slipped into silence, and Hortense shut her eyes, "to get the memory of it," she said. I thought she meant some new-fangled tune.

"This is memory enough for me," said I.

"Oh?" asked Hortense, and she uncovered

all the blaze of the dark lights hid in those eyes.

"Faith, Hortense," I answered, like a moth gone giddy in flame, "your naughty music wakes echoes of what souls must hear in paradise."

"Then it isn't naughty," said Hortense, beginning to play fiercely, striking false notes and discords and things.

"Hortense," said I.

"No—Ramsay!" cried Hortense, jangling harder than ever.

"But—yes!—Hortense——"

And in bustled M. Picot, hastier than need, methought.

"What, Hillary? Not a-bed yet, child? Ha!—crow's-feet under eyes to-morrow! Bed, little baggage! Forget not thy prayers! Pish! Pish! Good-night! Good-night!"

That is the way an older man takes it.

"Now, devil fly away with that prying wench of a Deliverance Dobbins!" ejaculated M. Picot, stamping about. "Oh, I'll cure her fanciful fits! Pish! Pish! That frump and her fits! Bad blood, Ramsay; low-bred, low-bred! 'Tis ever the way of her kind to blab of aches and stuffed stomachs that were well if left empty. An she come prying into my chemicals, taking fits when she's caught, I'll mix her a pill o' Deliverance!" And M. Picot laughed heartily at his own joke.

The next morning I was off to the trade. Though I hardly acknowledged the reason to myself, any youth can guess why I made excuse to come back soon. As I rode up, Rebecca stood at our gate. She had no smile. Had I not been thinking of another, I had noticed the sadness of her face; but when she moved back a pace, I flung out some foolishness about a gate being no bar if one had a mind to jump. Then she brought me sharp to my senses as I sprang to the ground.

"Ramsay," she exclaimed, "M. Picot and Mistress Hortense are in jail charged with sorcery! M. Picot is like to be hanged! An they do not confess, they may be set in the bilboes and whipped. There is talk of putting Mistress Hortense to the test."

"The test!"

'Twas as if a great weight struck away power to think, for the test meant neither more nor less than torture till confession were wrung from agony. The night went black and Rebecca's voice came as from some far place.

"Ramsay, you are hurting—you are crushing my hands!"

Poor child, she was crying; and the words I would have said stuck fast behind sealed lips. She seemed to understand, for she went on:

" Deliverance Dobbins saw strange things in his house. She went to spy. He hath crazed her intellectuals. She hath dumb fits."

Now I understood. This trouble was the result of M. Picot's threat; but little Rebecca's voice was tinkling on like a bell in a dome.

" My father hath the key to their ward. My father saith there is like to be trouble if they do not confess——"

" Confess!" I broke out. " Confess what? If they confess the lie they will be burned for witchcraft. And if they refuse to confess, they will be hanged for not telling the lie. Pretty justice! And your holy men fined one fellow a hundred pounds for calling their justices a pack of jackasses——"

" Sentence is to be pronounced to-morrow after communion," said Rebecca.

" After communion?" I could say no more. On that of all days for tyranny's crime!

God forgive me for despairing of mankind that night. I thought freedom had been won in the Commonwealth war, but that was only freedom of body. A greater strife was to wage for freedom of soul.

CHAPTER IV

REBECCA AND JACK BATTLE CONSPIRE

'TWAS cockcrow when I left pacing the shore where we had so often played in childhood; and through the darkness came the howl of M. Picot's hound, scratching outside the prison gate.

As well reason with maniacs as fanatics, say I, for they hide as much folly under the mask of conscience as ever court fool wore 'neath painted face. There was Mr. Stocking, as well-meaning a man as trod earth, obdurate beyond persuasion against poor M. Picot under his charge. Might I not speak to the French doctor through the bars of his window? By no means, Mr. Stocking assured. If once the great door were unlocked, who could tell what black arts a sorcerer might use?

"Look you, Ramsay lad," says he, "I've had this brass key made against his witchcraft, and I do not trust it to the hands of the jailer."

Then, I fear, I pleaded too keenly; for, suspecting collusion with M. Picot, the warden of the court-house grew frigid and bade me ask Eli Kirke's opinion on witchcraft.

"'Thou shalt not suffer a witch to live,'" rasped Eli Kirke, his stern eyes ablaze from an inner fire. "'A man also, or woman, that hath a familiar spirit, or that is a wizard, shall surely be put to death.' Think you M. Picot burns incense to the serpent in his jars for the healing of mankind?" he demanded fiercely.

"Yes," said I, "'tis for the healing of mankind by experimentation with chemicals. Knowledge of God nor chemicals springs full grown from man's head, Uncle Eli. Both must be learned. That is all the meaning of his jars and crucibles. He is only trying to learn what laws God ordained among materials. And when M. Picot makes mistakes, it is the same as when the Church makes mistakes and learns wisdom by blunders."

Eli Kirke blinked his eyes as though my monstrous pleadings dazed him.

"'Thou shalt not suffer a witch to live,'" he cried doggedly. "Do the Scriptures lie, Ramsay Stanhope? Tell me that?"

"No," said I. "The Scriptures condemn liars, and the man who pretends witchcraft *is* a liar. There's no such thing. That is why the

Scriptures command burning." I paused. He made no answer, and I pleaded on.

"But M. Picot denies witchcraft, and you would burn him for not lying."

Never think to gain a stubborn antagonist by partial concession. M. Radisson used to say if you give an enemy an inch he will claim an ell. 'Twas so with Eli Kirke, for he leaped to his feet in a fine frenzy and bade me cease juggling Holy Writ.

"'Thou shalt not suffer a witch to live,'" he shouted. "'Tis abomination! It shall utterly be put away from you! Because of this hidden iniquity the colony hath fallen on evil days. Let it perish root and branch!"

But Tibbie breaks in upon his declamation by throwing wide the library door, and in marches a line of pale-faced ascetics, rigid of jaw, cold of eye, and exalted with that gloomy fervour which counts burning life's highest joy. Among them was the famous witch-hanger of after years, a mere youth then, but about his lips the hard lines of a spiritual zeal scarce differing from pride.

"God was awakening the churches by marvellous signs," said one, extending a lank, cold hand to salute Eli Kirke.

"Have we not wrestled mightily for signs

and wonders?" demanded another with jaw of steel. And one description of the generation seeking signs was all but off the tip of my tongue.

"Some aver there be no witches—so fearfully hath error gone abroad," lamented young Mather, keen to be heard then, as he always was. "Brethren, toleration would make a kingdom of chaos, a Sodom, a Gomorrah, a Babylon!"

Faith, it needed no horoscope to forecast that young divine's dark future!

I stood it as long as I could, with palms itching to knock their solemn heads together like so many bowling balls; but when one cadaverous-faced fellow, whose sanctity had gone bilious from lack of sunshine, whined out against "the saucy miss," meaning thereby Mistress Hortense, and another prayed Heaven through his nose that his daughter might "lie in her grave ere she minced her steps with such dissoluteness of hair and unseemly broideries and bright colours, showing the lightness of her mind," and a third averred that "a cucking-stool would teach a maid to walk more shamefacedly," I whirled upon them in a fury that had disinherited me from Eli Kirke's graces ere I spake ten words.

"Sirs," said I, "your slatternly wenches may be dead ere they match Mistress Hortense! As for wearing light colours, the devil himself is painted black. Let them who are doing shameful acts to the innocent walk shamefacedly! For shame, sirs, to cloak malice and jealousy of M. Picot under religion! New England will remember this blot against you and curse you for it! An you listen to Deliverance Dobbins's lies, what hinders any lying wench sending good men to the scaffold?"

At first they listened agape, but now the hot blood rushed to their faces.

"Hold thy tongue, lad!" roared Eli Kirke. Then, as if to atone for that violence: "The Lord rebuke thee," he added solemly.

And I flung from the house dumb with impotent rage.

My thoughts were as the snatched sleep of a sick man's dreams. Again the hideous nightmare of the old martyr at the shambles; but now the shambles were in the New World and the martyr was M. Picot. Something cold touched my hand through the dark, and there crouched M. Picot's hound, whining for its master. Automatically I followed across the commons to the court-house square. It stopped at the prison gate, sniffing and whining and begging in. Poor dog! What could I do? I tried to coax it away, but it lay at the wall like a stone.

Of the long service in the new-built meeting-house I remember very little. Beat of drums, not bells, called to church in those days, and the beat was to me as a funeral march. The pale face of the preacher in the high pulpit overtowering us all was alight with stern zeal. The elders, sitting in a row below the pulpit facing us, listened to the fierce diatribe against the dark arts with looks of approbation that boded ill for M. Picot; and at every fresh fusillade of texts to bolster his argument, the line of deacons below the elders glanced back at the preacher approvingly. Rebecca sat on that side of the congregation assigned to the women with a dumb look of sympathy on the sweet hooded face. The prisoners were not present. At the end of the service the preacher paused; and there fell a great hush in which men scarce breathed, for sentence was to be pronounced. But the preacher only announced that before handing the case to the civil court of oyer and terminer for judgment, the elders wished to hold it in meditation for another day.

The singing of the dismissal psalm began and a smothered cry seemed to break from Rebecca's pew. Then the preacher had raised his hands above bowed heads. The service was over. The people crowded solemnly out, and I was left alone in the gathering darkness—alone with the ghosts of youth's illusions mocking from the gloom. Religion, then, did not always mean right! There were tyrants of souls as well as tyrants of sword. Prayers were uttered that were fitter for hearing in hell than in Heaven. Good men could deceive themselves into crime cloaking spiritual malice, sect jealousy, race hatred with an unctuous text. Here, in New England, where men had come for freedom, was tyranny masking in the guise of religion. Preachers as jealous of the power slipping from their hands as ever was primate of England! A poor gentleman hounded to his death because he practised the sciences! Millions of victims all the world over burned for witchcraft, sacrificed to a Moloch of superstition in the name of a Christ who came to let in the light of knowledge on all superstition!

Could I have found a wilderness where was no human face, I think I had fled to it that night. And, indeed, when you come to think of my breaking with Eli Kirke, 'twas the witch trial that drove me to the wilderness.

There was yet a respite. But the Church

still dominated the civil courts, and a transfer of the case meant that the Church would throw the onus of executing sentence on those lay figures who were the puppets of a Pharisaical oligarchy.

There was no time to appeal to England. There was no chance of sudden rescue. New England had not the stuff of which mobs are made.

I thought of appealing to the mercy of the judges; but what mercy had Eli Kirke received at the hands of royalists that he should be merciful to them?

I thought of firing the prison; but the walls were stone, and the night wet, and the outcome doubtful.

I thought of the cell window; but if there had been any hope that way, M. Picot had worked an escape.

Bowing my head to think—to pray—to imprecate, I lost all sense of time and place.

Some one had slipped quietly into the dark of the church. I felt rather than saw a nearing presence. But I paid no heed, for despair blotted out all thought. Whoever it was came feeling a way down the dark aisle.

Then hot tears fell upon my hands. In the gloom there paused a childlike figure.

"Rebecca!"

She panted out a wordless cry. Then she came closer and laid a hand on my arm. She was struggling to subdue sobs. The question came in a shivering breath.

"Is Hortense—so dear?"

"So dear, Rebecca."

"She must be wondrous happy, Ramsay." A tumult of effort. "If I could only take her place——"

"Take her place, Rebecca?"

"My father hath the key—if—if—if I took her place, she might go free."

"Take her place, child! What folly is this—dear, kind Rebecca? Would 't be any better to send you to the rope than Hortense? No—no—dear child!"

At that her agitation abated, and she puzzled as if to say more.

"Dear Rebecca," said I, comforting her as I would a sister, "dear child, run home. Forget not little Hortense in thy prayers."

May the angel of forgiveness spread a broader mantle across our blunders than our sins, but could I have said worse?

"I have cooked dainties with my own hands. I have sent her cakes every day," sobbed Rebecca.

"Go home now, Rebecca," I begged.

But she stood silent.

"Rebecca—what is it?"

"You have not been to see me for a year, Ramsay."

I could scarce believe my ears.

"My father is away to-night. Will you not come?"

"But, Rebecca——"

"I have never asked a thing of you before."

"But, Rebecca——"

"Will you come for Hortense's sake?" she interrupted, with a little sharp, hard, falsetto note in her baby voice.

"Rebecca," I demanded, "what do you mean?"

But she snapped back like the peevish child that she was: "An you come not when I ask you, you may stay!" And she had gone.

What was she trying to say with her dark hints and overnice scruples of a Puritan conscience? And was not that Jack Battle greeting her outside in the dark?

I tore after Rebecca at such speed that I had cannoned into open arms before I saw a hulking form across the way.

"Fall-back—fall-edge!" roared Jack, closing his arms about me. "'Tis Ramsay himself, with a sword like a butcher's cleaver and a wit like a broadaxe!"

"Have you not heard, Jack?"

"Heard! Ship ahoy!" cried Jack. "Split me to the chin like a cod! Stood I not abaft of you all day long, packed like a herring in a pickle! 'Twas a pretty kettle of fish in your Noah's ark to-day! 'Tis all along o' goodness gone stale from too much salt," says Jack.

I told him of little Rebecca, and asked what he made of it. He said he made of it that fools didn't love in the right place—which was not to the point, whatever Jack thought of Rebecca. Linking his arm through mine, he headed me about.

"Captain Gillam, Ben's father, sails for England at sunrise," vouched Jack.

"What has that to do with Mistress Hortense?" I returned testily.

"'Tis a swift ship to sail in."

"To sail in, Jack Battle?"—I caught at the hope. "Out with your plan, man!"

"And be hanged for it," snaps Jack, falling silent.

We were opposite the prison. He pointed to a light behind the bars.

"They are the only prisoners," he said. "They must be in there."

"One could pass a note through those bars with a long pole," I observed, gazing over the yard wall.

"Or a key," answered Jack.

He paused before Rebecca's house to the left of the prison.

"Ramsay," inquired Jack quizzically, "do you happen to have heard *who* has the keys?"

"Rebecca's father is warden."

"And Rebecca's father is from home to-night," says he, facing me squarely to the lantern above the door.

How did he know that? Then I remembered the voices outside the church.

"Jack—what did Rebecca mean——"

"Not to be hanged," interrupts Jack. "'Tis all along o' having too much conscience, Ramsay. They must either lie like a Dutchman and be damned, or tell the truth and be hanged. Now, ship ahoy," says he, "to the quarter-deck!" and he flung me forcibly up the steps.

Rebecca, herself, red-eyed and reserved, threw wide the door. She motioned me to a bench seat opposite the fireplace and fastened her gaze above the mantel till mine followed there too. A bunch of keys hung from an iron rack.

"What are those, Rebecca?"

"The largest is for the gate," says she with the panic of conscience running from fire. "The brass one unlocks the great door, and—and—the—M. Picot's cell unbolts," she stammered.

"May I examine them, Rebecca?"

"I will even draw you a pint of cider," says Rebecca evasively, with great trepidation, "but come back soon," she called, tripping off to the wine-cellar door.

Snatching the keys, I was down the steps at a leap.

"The large one for the gate, Jack! The brass one for the big door, and the cell unbolts!"

"Ease your helm, sonny!" says Jack, catching the bunch from my clasp. "Fall-back—fall-edge!" he laughed in that awful mockery of the axeman's block. "Fall-back—fall-edge! If there's any hacking of necks, mine is thicker than yours! I'll run the risks. Do you wait here in shadow."

And he darted away. The gate creaked as it gave.

Then I waited for what seemed eternity.

A night-watchman shuffled along with swinging lantern, calling out: "What ho? What ho?" Townsfolks rode through the streets with a clatter of the chairmen's feet; but no words were bandied by the fellows, for a Sabbath hush lay over the night. A great hackney-coach nigh mired in mud as it lumbered through mid-road. And M. Picot's hound came sniffing hungrily to me.

A glare of light shot aslant the dark. Softly the door of Rebecca's house opened. A frail figure was silhouetted against the light. The wick above snuffed out. The figure drew in without a single look, leaving the door ajar. But an hour ago, the iron righteousness of bigots had filled my soul with revolt. Now the sight of that little Puritan maid brought prayers to my lips and a Te Deum to my soul.

The prison gate swung open again with rusty protest. Two hooded figures slipped through the dark. Jack Battle had locked the gate and the keys were in my hand.

"Take them back," he gurgled out with school-lad glee. "'Twill be a pretty to-do of witchcraft to-morrow when they find a cell empty. Go hire passage to England in Captain Gillam's boat!"

"Captain Gillam's boat?"

"Yes, or Master Ben's pirate-ship of the north, if she's there," and he had dashed off in the dark.

When Rebecca appeared above the cellar-way with a flagon that reamed to a beaded top, the keys were back on the wall.

"I was overlong," panted Rebecca, with eyes averted as of old to the folds of her white stomacher. "'Twas a stubborn bung and hard to draw."

"Dear little cheat! God bless you!—and bless you!—and bless you, Rebecca!" I cried. At which the poor child took fright.

"It—it—it was not all a lie, Ramsay," she stammered. "The bung was hard—and—and —and I didn't hasten——"

"Dear comrade—good-bye, forever!" I called from the dark of the step.

"Forever?" asked the faint voice of a forlorn figure black in the doorway.

Dear, snowy, self-sacrificing spirit—'tis my clearest memory of her with the thin, grieved voice coming through the dark.

I ran to the wharf hard as ever heels nerved by fear and joy and triumph and love could carry me. The passage I easily engaged from the ship's mate, who dinned into my unlistening ears full account of the north sea, whither Captain Gillam was to go for the Fur Company, and whither, too, Master Ben was keen to sail, "a pirateer, along o' his own risk and gain," explained the mate with a wink, "pirateer or privateer, call 'em what you will, Mister; the Susan with white sails in Boston Town, and Le Bon Garçon with sails black as the devil himself up in Quebec, ha—ha—and I'll give ye odds on it, Mister, the devil himself don't catch Master Ben! Why, bless you, gentlemen, who's to jail 'im here for droppin' Spanish gold in his own hold and poachin' furs on the king's preserve o' the north sea, when Stocking, the warden, 'imself owns 'alf the Susan and Cap'en Gillam, 'is father, is master o' the king's ship?"

"They do say," he babbled on, "now that Radisson, the French jack-a-boots, hath given the slip to the King's Company, he sails from Quebec in ship o' his own. If him and Ben and the Capiten meet — oh, there'll be times! There'll be times!"

And "times" there were sure enough; but of that I had then small care and shook the loquacious rascal off so that he left me in peace.

First came the servants, trundling cart-loads of cases, which passed unnoticed; for the town bell had tolled the close of Sabbath, and Monday shipping had begun.

The cusp of a watery moon faded in the gray dawn streaks of a muffled sky, and at last came the chairmen, with Jack running alert.

From the chairs stepped the blackamoor,

painted as white as paste. Then a New Amsterdam gentleman slipped out from the curtains, followed by his page-boy and servants.

"Jack," I asked, "where is Hortense?"

The page glanced from under curls.

"Dear Jack," she whispered, standing high on her heels nigh as tall as the sailor lad. And poor Jack Battle, not knowing how to play down, stood blushing, cap in hand, till she laughed a queer little laugh and, bidding him good-bye, told him to remember that she had the squirrel stuffed.

To me she said no word. Her hand touched mine quick farewell. The long lashes lifted.

There was a look on her face.

I ask no greater joy in Paradise than memory of that look.

. . . . . .

One lone, gray star hung over the masthead. The ship careened across the billows till star and mast-top met.

Jack fetched a deep sigh.

"There be work for sailors in England," he said.

In a flash I thought that I knew what he had meant by fools not loving in the right place.

"That were folly, Jack! She hath her station!"

Jack Battle pointed to the fading steel point above the vanishing masthead.

"Doth looking hurt yon star?" asks Jack.

"Nay; but looking may strain the eyes; and the arrows of longing come back void."

He answered nothing, and we lingered heavy hearted till the sun came up over the pillowed waves turning the tumbling waters to molten gold.

Between us and the fan-like rays behind the glossy billows—was no ship.

Hortense was safe!

There was an end-all to undared hopes.

CHAPTER V

M. RADISSON AGAIN

"GOOD-BYE to you, Ramsay," said Jack abruptly.

"Where to, Jack?" I asked, bestirring myself. I could no more go back to Eli Kirke.

But little Jack Battle was squirming his wooden clogs into the sand as he used to dig his toes, and he answered not a word.

"'Tis early yet for the Grand Banks, Jack. Ben Gillam's ship keeled mast over hull from being ice-logged last spring. The spars were solid with frozen sleet from the crosstrees to the crow's nest. Your dories would be ice-logged for a month yet."

"It—it—it aren't the Grand Banks no more," stammered Jack.

His manner arrested me. The honest blue eyes were shifting and his toes at work in the sand.

"There be gold on the high seas for the taking," vouched Jack. "An your fine gentlemen grow rich that way, why mayn't I?"

"Jack," I warned, thinking of Ben Gillam's craft rigged with sails of as many colours as Joseph's coat, "Jack—is it a pirate-ship?"

"No," laughed the sailor lad sheepishly, "'tis a pirateer," meaning thereby a privateer, which was the same thing in those days.

"Have a care of your pirateers—privateers, Jack," said I, speaking plain. "A gentleman would be run through the gullet with a clean rapier, but you—you—would be strangled by sentence of court or sold to the Barbadoes."

"Not if the warden o' the court owns half the ship," protested Jack, smiling queerly under his shaggy brows.

"Oh—ho!" said I, thinking of Rebecca's father, and beginning to understand who supplied money for Ben Gillam's ventures.

"I'm tired o' being a kick-a-toe and fisticuff to everybody. Now, if I'd been rich and had a ship, I might 'a' sailed for M. Picot."

"Or Mistress Hortense," I added, which brought red spots to the sailor lad's cheeks.

Off he went unanswering, leaving me at gaze across an unbroken sea with a heart heavy as lead.

"Poor fellow! He will get over it," said I.

"Another hath need o' the same medicine," came a voice.

I wheeled, expecting arrest.

A tall, wiry man, with coal-black hair and deep-set eyes and a scar across his swarth skin, smiled pleasantly down at me.

"Now that you have them safely off," said he, still smiling, "better begone yourself."

"I'll thank you for your advice when I ask it, sir," said I, suspicious of the press-gang infesting that port. Involuntarily I caught at my empty sword-belt.

"Permit me," proffered the gentleman, with a broader smile, handing out his own rapier.

"Sir," said I, "your pardon, but the press-gang have been busy of late."

"And the sheriffs may be busy to-day," he laughed. "Black arts don't open stone walls, Ramsay."

And he sent the blade clanking home to its scabbard. His surtout falling open revealed a waistcoat of buckskin. I searched his face.

"M. de Radisson!"

"My hero of rescues," and he offered his hand. "And my quondam nephew," he added, laughing; for his wife was a Kirke of the English branch, and my aunt was married to Eli.

"Eli Kirke cannot know you are here, sir——"

"Eli Kirke *need* not know," emphasized Radisson dryly.

And remembering bits of rumour about M. Radisson deserting the English Fur Company, I hastened to add: " Eli Kirke *shall* not know! "

" Your wits jump quick enough sometimes," said he. " Now tell me, whose is she, and what value do you set on her? "

I was speechless with surprise. However wild a life M. Radisson led, his title of nobility was from a king who awarded patents to gentlemen only.

" We neither call our women '*she*' nor give them market value," I retorted.

Thereupon M. de Radisson falls in such fits of laughter, I had thought he must split his baldrick.

" Pardieu! " he laughed, wiping the tears away with a fangled lace thing fit for a dandy, " Pardieu! 'Tis not your girl-page? 'Tis the ship o' that hangdog of a New England captain!"

The thing came in a jiffy. Sieur Radisson, having deserted the English Fur Company, was setting up for himself. He was spying the strength of his rivals for the north sea.

" You praised my wit. I have but given you a sample."

Then I told him all I knew of the ship, and M. de Radisson laughed again till he was like to weep.

"How is she called?" he asked.

"The Prince Rupert," said I.

"Ha! Then the same crew of gentlemen's scullions and courtiers' valets stuffing the lockers full o' trash to trade on their master's account. A pretty cheat for the Company!"

The end of it was, M. Radisson invited me to join his ships. "A beaver-skin for a needle, Ramsay! Twenty otter for an awl! Wealth for a merchant prince," he urged.

But no sooner had I grasped at this easy way out of difficulty than the Frenchman interrupts: "Hold back, man! Do you know the risk?"

"No—nor care one rush!"

"Governor Frontenac demands half of the furs for a license to trade, but M. de la Barre, who comes to take his place, is a friend of La Chesnaye's, and La Chesnaye owns our ships——"

"And you go without a license?"

"And the galleys for life——"

"If you're caught," said I.

"Pardieu!" he laughed, "yes—if we're caught!"

"I'd as lief go to the galleys for fur-trading as the scaffold for witchcraft," said I.

With that our bargain was sealed.

PART II

NOW comes that part of a life which deals with what you will say no one man could do, yet the things were done; with wonders stranger than witchcraft, yet were true. But because you have never lived a sword-length from city pavement, nor seen one man holding his own against a thousand enemies, I pray you deny not these things.

Each life is a shut-in valley, says the jonglière; but Manitou, who strides from peak to peak, knows there is more than one valley, which had been a maxim among the jonglières long before one Danish gentleman assured another there were more things in heaven and earth than philosophy dreamed.

CHAPTER VI

THE ROARING FORTIES

KEEN as an arrow from twanging bowstring, Pierre Radisson set sail over the roaring seas for the northern bay.

'Twas midsummer before his busy flittings between Acadia and Quebec brought us to Isle Percée, at the mouth of the St. Lawrence. Here Chouart Groseillers (his brother-in-law) lay with two of the craziest craft that ever rocked anchor. I scarce had time to note the bulging hulls, stout at stem and stern with deep sinking of the waist, before M. Radisson had climbed the ship's ladder and scattered quick commands that sent sailors shinning up masts, for all the world like so many monkeys. The St. Pierre, our ship was called, in honour of Pierre Radisson; for admiral and captain and trader, all in one, was Sieur Radisson, himself. Indeed, he could reef a sail as handily as any old tar. I have seen him take the wheel and hurl Allemand head-foremost from the pilot-house when that sponge-soaked rascal had imbibed more gin than was safe for the weathering of rocky coasts.

Call him gamester, liar, cheat—what you will! He had his faults, which dogged him down to poverty and ruin; but deeds are proof of the inner man. And look you that judge Pierre Radisson whether your own deeds ring as mettle and true.

The ironwood capstan bars clanked to that seaman's music of running sailors. A clattering of the pawls—the anchor came away. The St. Pierre shook out her bellying sails and the white sheets drew to a full beam wind. Long foam lines crisped away from the prow. Green shores slipped to haze of distance. With her larboard lipping low and that long break of swishing waters against her ports which is as a croon to the seaman's ear, the St. Pierre dipped and rose and sank again to the swell of the billowing sea. Behind, crowding every stitch of canvas and staggering not a little as she got under weigh, ploughed the Ste. Anne. And all about, heaving and falling like the deep breathings of a slumbering monster, were the wide wastes of the sea.

And how I wish that I could take you back with me and show you the two miserable old gallipots which M. de Radisson rode into the roaring forties! 'Twas as if those gods of chance that had held riotous sway over all that watery desolation now first discovered one greater than themselves—a rebel 'mid their warring elements whose will they might harry but could not crush—Man, the king undaunted, coming to his own! Children oft get closer to the essences of truth than older folk grown foolish with too much learning. As a child I used to think what a wonderful moment that was when Man, the master, first appeared on face of earth. How did the beasts and the seas and the winds feel about it, I asked. Did they laugh at this fellow, the most helpless of all things, setting out to conquer all things? Did the beasts pursue him till he made bow and arrow and the seas defy him till he rafted their waters and the winds blow his house down till he dovetailed his timbers? That was the child's way of asking a very old question—Was Man the sport of the elements, the plaything of all the cruel, blind gods of chance?

Now, the position was reversed.

Now, I learned how the Man must have felt when he set about conquering the elements, subduing land and sea and savagery. And in that lies the Homeric greatness of this vast, fresh, New World of ours. Your Old World victor takes up the unfinished work left by generations of men. Your New World hero begins at the pristine task. I pray you, who are born to the nobility of the New World, forget not the glory of your heritage; for the place which God hath given you in the history of the race is one which men must hold in envy when Roman patrician and Norman conqueror and robber baron are as forgotten as the kingly lines of old Egypt.

Fifty ton was our craft, with a crazy pitch to her prow like to take a man's stomach out and the groaning of infernal fiends in her timbers. Twelve men, our crew all told, half of them young gentlemen of fortune from Quebec, with titles as long as a tilting lance and the fighting blood of a Spanish don and the airs of a king's grand chamberlain. Their seamanship you may guess. All of them spent the better part of the first weeks at sea full length below deck. Of a calm day they lolled disconsolate over the taffrail, with one eye alert for flight down the companionway when the ship began to heave.

"What are you doing back there, La Chesnaye?" asks M. de Radisson, with a quiet wink, not speaking loud enough for fo'castle hands to hear.

" Cursing myself for ever coming," growls that young gentleman, scarce turning his head.

" In that case," smiles Sieur Radisson, " you might be better occupied learning to take a hand at the helm."

" Sir," pleads La Chesnaye meekly, " 'tis all I can do to ballast the ship below stairs."

" 'Tis laziness, La Chesnaye," vows Radisson. " Men are thrown overboard for less! "

" A quick death were kindness, sir," groans La Chesnaye, scalloping in blind zigzags for the stair. " May I be shot from that cannon, sir, if I ever set foot on ship again! "

M. de Radisson laughs, and the place of the merchant prince is taken by the marquis with a face the gray shade of old Tibbie's linen a-bleaching on the green.

The Ste. Anne, under Groseillers—whom we called Mr. Gooseberry when he wore his airs too mightily—was better manned, having able-bodied seamen, who distinguished themselves by a mutiny.

Of which you shall hear anon.

But the spirits of our young gentlemen took a prodigious leap upward as their bodies became used to the crazy pace of our ship, whose gait I can compare only to the bouncings of loose timber in a heavy sea. North of Newfoundland we were blanketed in a dirty fog. That gave our fine gentlemen a chance to right end up.

"Every man of them a good seaman in calm weather," Sieur Radisson observed; and he put them through marine drill all that week.

La Chesnaye so far recovered that he sometimes kept me company at the bowsprit, where we watched the clumsy gambols of the porpoise, racing and leaping and turning somersets in mid-air about the ship. Once, I mind the St. Pierre gave a tremor as if her keel had grated a reef; and a monster silver-stripe heaved up on our lee. 'Twas a finback whale, M. Radisson explained; and he protested against the impudence of scratching its back on our keel. As we sailed farther north many a school of rolling finbacks glistened silver in the sun or rose higher than our masthead, when one took the death-leap to escape its leagued foes—swordfish and thrasher and shark. And to give you an idea of the fearful tide breaking through the narrow fiords of that rock-bound coast, I may tell you that La Chesnaye and I have often seen those leviathans of the deep swept tail foremost by the driving tide into some land-locked lagoon and there beached high on naked rock. That was the sea M. Radisson was navigating with cockle-shell boats unstable of pace as a vagrant with rickets.

Even Forêt, the marquis, forgot his dainty-fingered dignity and took a hand at the fishing of a shark one day. The cook had put out a bait at the end of a chain fastened to the capstan, when comes a mighty tug; and the cook shouts out that he has caught a shark. All hands are hailed to the capstan, and every one of my fine gentlemen grasps an ironwood bar to hoist the monster home. I wish you had seen their faces when the shark's great head with six rows of teeth in its gaping upper jaw came abreast the deck! Half the fellows were for throwing down the bars and running, but the other half would not show white feather before the common sailors; and two or three clanking rounds brought the great shark lashing to deck in a way that sent us scuttling up the ratlines. But Forêt would not be beaten. He thrust an ironwood bar across the gaping jaws. The shark tore the wood to splinters. There was a rip that snapped the cable with the report of a pistol, and the great fish was over deck and away in the sea.

By this, you may know, we had all left our landsmen's fears far south of Belle Isle and were filled with the spirit of that wild, tempestuous world where the storm never sleeps and the cordage pipes on calmest day and the beam seas break in the long, low, growling wash that warns the coming hurricane.

But if you think we were a Noah's ark of solemn faces 'mid all that warring desolation, you are much mistaken. I doubt if lamentations ever did as much to lift mankind to victory as the naughty glee of the shrieking fife. And of glee, we had a-plenty on all that voyage north.

La Chesnaye, son of the merchant prince who owned our ships, played cock-o'-the-walk, took rank next to M. Radisson, and called himself deputy-governor. Forêt, whose father had a stretch of barren shingle on The Labrador, and who had himself received letters patent from His Most Christian Majesty for a marquisate, swore he would be cursed if he gave the *pas* to La Chesnaye, or any other commoner. And M. de Radisson was as great a stickler for fine points as any of the new-fledged colonials. When he called a conference, he must needs muster to the quarter-deck by beat of drum, with a tipstaff, having a silver bauble of a stick, leading the way. This office fell to Godefroy, the trader, a fellow with the figure of a slat and a scalp tonsured bare as a billiard-ball by Indian hunting-knife. Spite of many a thwack from the flat of M. de Radisson's sword, Godefroy would carry the silver mace to the chant of a "diddle-dee-dee," which he was always humming in a sand-papered voice wherever he went. At beat of drum for conference we all came scrambling down the ratlines like tumbling acrobats of a country fair. Godefroy grasps his silver stick.

"Fall in line, there, deputy-governor, diddle-dee-dee!"

La Chesnaye cuffs the fellow's ears.

"Diddle-dee-dee! Come on, marquis. Does Your High Mightiness give place to a merchant's son? Heaven help you, gentlemen! Come on! Come on! Diddle-dee-dee!"

And we all march to M. de Radisson's cabin and sit down gravely at a long table.

"Pot o' beer, tipstaff," orders Radisson; and Godefroy goes off slapping his buckskins with glee.

M. Radisson no more takes off his hat than a king's ambassador, but he waits for La Chesnaye and Forêt to uncover. The merchant strums on the table and glares at the marquis, and the marquis looks at the skylight, waiting for the merchant; and the end of it is M. Radisson must give Godefroy the wink, who knocks both their hats off at once, explaining that a landsman can ill keep his legs on the sea, and the sea is no respecter of persons. Once, at the end of his byplay between the two young fire-eaters, the sea lurched in earnest, a mighty pitch that threw tipstaff sprawling across the table. And the beer went full in the face of the marquis.

"There's a health to you, Forêt!" roared the merchant in whirlwinds of laughter.

But the marquis had gone heels over head. He gained his feet as the ship righted, whipped out his rapier, vowed he would dust somebody's jacket, and caught up Godefroy on the tip of his sword by the rascal's belt.

"Forêt, I protest," cried M. Radisson, scarce speaking for laughter, "I protest there's nothing spilt but the beer and the dignity! The beer can be mopped. There's plenty o' dignity in the same barrel. Save Godefroy! We can ill spare a man!"

With a quick rip of his own rapier, Radisson had cut Godefroy's belt and the wretch scuttled up-stairs out of reach. Sailors wiped up the beer, and all hands braced chairs 'twixt table and wall to await M. Radisson's pleasure.

He had dressed with unusual care. Gold braid edged his black doublet, and fine old

Mechlin came back over his sleeves in deep ruffs. And in his eyes the glancing light of steel striking fire.

Bidding the sailors take themselves off, M. Radisson drew his blade from the scabbard and called attention by a sharp rap.

Quick silence fell, and he laid the naked sword across the table. His right hand played with the jewelled hilt. Across his breast were medals and stars of honour given him by many monarchs. I think as we looked at our leader every man of us would have esteemed it honour to sail the seas in a tub if Pierre Radisson captained the craft.

But his left hand was twitching uneasily at his chin, and in his eyes were the restless lights.

"Gentlemen," says he, as unconcerned as if he were forecasting weather, "gentlemen, I seem to have heard that the crew of my kinsman's ship have mutinied."

We were nigh a thousand leagues from rescue or help that day!

"Mutinied!" shrieks La Chesnaye, with his voice all athrill. "Mutinied? What will my father have to say?"

And he clapped his tilted chair to floor with a thwack that might have echoed to the fo'castle.

"Shall I lend you a trumpet, La Chesnaye, or—or a fife?" asks M. Radisson, very quiet.

And I assure you there was no more loud talk in the cabin that day; only the long, low wash and pound and break of the seas abeam, with the surly wail that portends storm. I do not believe any of us ever realized what a frail chip was between life and eternity till we heard the wrenching and groaning of the timbers in the silence that followed M. Radisson's words.

"Gentlemen," continues M. Radisson, softer-spoken than before, "if any one here is for turning back, I desire him to stand up and say so."

The St. Pierre shipped a sea with a strain like to tear her asunder, and waters went sizzling through lee scuppers above with the hiss of a cataract. M. Radisson inverts a sand-glass and watches the sand trickle through till the last grain drops. Then he turns to us.

Two or three faces had gone white as the driving spray, but never a man opened his lips to counsel return.

"Gentlemen," says M. Radisson, with the fires agleam in his deep-set eyes, "am I to understand that every one here is for going forward at any risk?"

"Aye—aye, sir!" burst like a clarion from our circle.

Pierre Radisson smiled quietly.

"'Tis as well," says he, "for I bade the coward stand up so that I could run him through to the hilt," and he clanked the sword back to its scabbard.

"As I said before," he went on, "the crew on my kinsman's ship have mutinied. There's another trifle to keep under your caps, gentlemen —the mutineers have been running up pirate signals to the crew of this ship——"

"Pirate signals!" interrupts La Chesnaye, whose temper was ever crackling off like grains of gunpowder. "May I ask, sir, *how* you know the pirate signals?"

M. de Radisson's face was a study in masks.

"You may ask, La Chesnaye," says he, rubbing his chin with a wrinkling smile, "you may ask, but I'm hanged if I answer!"

And from lips that had whitened with fear but a moment before came laughter that set the timbers ringing.

Then Forêt found his tongue.

"Hang a baker's dozen of the mutineers from the yard-arm!"

"A baker's dozen is thirteen, Forêt," retorted Radisson, "and the Ste. Anne's crew numbers fifteen."

" Hang 'em in effigy as they do in Quebec," persists Forêt.

Pierre Radisson only pointed over his shoulder to the port astern. Crowding to the glazed window we saw a dozen scarecrows tossing from the crosstrees of Groseillers's ship.

" What does Captain Radisson advise? " asks La Chesnaye.

" La Chesnaye," says Radisson, " I never advise. I act! "

CHAPTER VII

M. DE RADISSON ACTS

QUICK as tongue could trip off the orders, eyes everywhere, thought and act jumping together, Pierre Radisson had given each one his part, and pledged our obedience, though he bade us walk the plank blindfold to the sea. Two men were set to transferring powder and arms from the forehold to our captain's cabin. One went hand over fist up the mainmast and signalled the Ste. Anne to close up. Jackets were torn from the deck-guns and the guns slued round to sweep from stem to stern. With a jarring of cranes and shaking of timbers, the two ships bumped together; and a more surprised looking lot of men than the crew of the Ste. Anne you never saw. Pierre Radisson had played the rogues their own game in the matter of signals. They had thought the St. Pierre in league, else would they not have come into his trap so readily. Before they had time to protest, the ships were together, the two captains conferring face to face across the rails, and our sailors standing at arms ready to shoot down the first rebel.

At a word, the St. Pierre's crew were scrambling to the Ste. Anne's decks. A shout through the trumpet of the Ste. Anne's bo'swain and the mutinous crew of the Ste. Anne were marched aboard the St. Pierre.

Then M. Radisson's plan became plain. The other ship was the better. M. de Radisson was determined that at least one crew should reach the bay. Besides, as he had half-laughingly insinuated, perhaps he knew better than Chouart Groseillers of the Ste. Anne how to manage mutinous pirates. Of the St. Pierre's crew, three only remained with Radisson: Allemand, in the pilot-house; young Jean Groseillers, Chouart's son, on guard aft; and myself, armed with a musket, to sweep the fo'castle.

And all the time there was such a rolling sea the two ships were like to pound their bulwarks to kindling wood. Then the Ste. Anne eased off, sheered away, and wore ship for open sea.

Pierre Radisson turned. There faced him that grim, mutinous crew.

No need to try orders then. 'Twas the cat those men wanted. Before Pierre Radisson had said one word the mutineers had discovered the deck cannon pointing amidships. A shout of baffled rage broke from the ragged group. Quick words passed from man to man. A noisy, shuffling, indeterminate movement! The crowd swayed forward. There was a sudden rush from the fo'castle to the waist. They had charged to gain possession of the powder cabin—Pierre Radisson raised his pistol. For an instant they held back. Then a barefoot fellow struck at him with a belaying-pin.

'Twere better for that man if he had called down the lightnings.

Quicker than I can tell it, Pierre Radisson had sprung upon him. The Frenchman's left arm had coiled the fellow round the waist. Our leader's pistol flashed a circle that drove the rabble back, and the ringleader went hurling head foremost through the main hatch with force like to flatten his skull to a gun-wad.

There was a mighty scattering back to the fo'castle then, I promise you.

Pierre Radisson uttered never a syllable. He pointed to the fore scuttle. Then he pointed to the men. Down they went under hatches—rats in a trap!

"Tramp—bundle—pack!" says he, as the last man bobbed below.

But with a ping that raised the hair from my head, came a pistol-shot from the main-masts. There, perched astride of the cross-trees, was a rascal mutineer popping at M. Radisson bold as you please.

Our captain took off his beaver, felt the bullet-hole in the brim, looked up coolly, and pointed his musket.

"Drop that pistol!" said he.

The fellow yelped out fear. Down clattered his weapon to the deck.

"Now sit there," ordered Radisson, replacing his beaver. "Sit there till I give you leave to come down!"

Allemand, the pilot, had lost his head and was steering a course crooked as a worm fence. Young Jean Groseillers went white as the sails, and scarce had strength to slue the guns back or jacket their muzzles. And, instead of curling forward with the crest of the roll, the spray began to chop off backward in little short waves like a horse's mane—a bad, bad sign, as any seaman will testify. And I, with my musket at guard above the fo'scuttle, had a heart thumping harder than the pounding seas.

And what do you think M. Radisson said as he wiped the sweat from his brow?

M. DE RADISSON ACTS

" A pretty pickle,* indeed, to ground a man's plans on such dashed impudence! Hazard o' life! As if a man would turn from his course for them! Spiders o' hell! I'll strike my topmast to Death himself first—so the devil go with them! The blind gods may crush—they shall not conquer! They may kill—but I snap my fingers in their faces to the death! A pretty pickle, indeed! Batten down the hatches, Ramsay. Lend Jean a hand to get the guns under cover. There's a storm!"

And "a pretty pickle" it was, with the "porps" floundering bodily from wave-crest to wave-crest, the winds shrieking through the cordage, and the storm-fiends brewing a hurricane like to engulf master and crew!

In the forehold were rebels who would sink us all to the bottom of the sea if they could. Aft, powder enough to blow us all to eternity! On deck, one brave man, two chittering lads, and a gin-soaked pilot steering a crazy course among the fanged reefs of Labrador.

---

* These expressions are M. de Radisson's and not words coined by Mr. Stanhope, as may be seen by reference to the French explorer's account of his own travels, written partly in English, where he repeatedly refers to a "pretty pickle." As for the ships, they seem to have been something between a modern whaler and old-time brigantine.—AUTHOR.

The wind backed and veered and came again so that a weather-vane could not have shown which way it blew. At one moment the ship was jumping from wave to wave before the wind with a single tiny storms'l out. At another I had thought we must scud under bare poles for open sea.

The coast sheered vertical like a rampart wall, and up—up—up that dripping rock clutched the tossing billows like watery arms of sirens. It needed no seaman to prophecy the fate of a boat caught between that rock and a nor'easter.

Then the gale would veer, and out raced a tidal billow of waters like to take the St. Pierre broadside.

"Helm hard alee!" shouts Radisson in the teeth of the gale.

For the fraction of a second we were driving before the oncoming rush.

Then the sea rose up in a wall on our rear.

There was a shattering crash. The billows broke in sheets of whipping spray. The decks swam with a river of waters. One gun wrenched loose, teetered to the roll, and pitched into the seething deep. Yard-arms came splintering to the deck. There was a roaring of waters over us, under us, round us—then M. de Radisson, Jean, and I went slithering forward like water-rats caught in a whirlpool. My feet struck against windlass chains. Jean saved himself from washing overboard by cannoning into me; but before the dripping bowsprit rose again to mount the swell, M. de Radisson was up, shaking off spray like a water-dog and muttering to himself: "To be snuffed out like a candle —no—no—no, my fine fellows! Leap to meet it! Leap to meet it!"

And he was at the wheel himself.

The ship gave a long shudder, staggered back, stern foremost, to the trough of the swell, and lay weltering cataracts from her decks.

There was a pause of sudden quiet, the quiet of forces gathering strength for fiercer assault; and in that pause I remembered something had flung over me in the wash of the breaking sea. I looked to the crosstrees. The mutineer was gone.

It was the first and last time that I have ever seen a smoking sea. The ocean boiled white. Far out in the wake of the tide that had caught us foam smoked on the track of the ploughing waters. Waters—did I say? You could not see waters for the spray.

Then Jean bade me look how the stays'l had been torn to flutters, and we both set about righting decks.

For all I could see, M. Radisson was simply holding the wheel; but the holding of a wheel in stress is mighty fine seamanship. To keep that old gallipot from shipping seas in the tempest of billows was a more ticklish task than rope-walking a whirlpool or sacking a city.

Presently came two sounds—a swish of seas at our stern and the booming of surf against coast rocks. Then M. de Radisson did the maddest thing that ever I have seen. Both sounds told of the coming tempest. The veering wind settled to a driving nor'easter, and M. de Radisson was steering straight as a bullet to the mark for that rock wall.

But I did not know that coast. When our ship was but three lengths from destruction the St. Pierre answered to the helm. Her prow rounded a sharp rock. Then the wind caught her, whirling her right about; but in she went, stern foremost, like a fish, between the narrow walls of a fiord to the quiet shelter of a land-locked lagoon. Pierre Radisson had taken refuge in what the sailors call "a hole in the wall."

There we lay close reefed, both anchors out, while the hurricane held high carnival on the outer sea.

After we had put the St. Pierre ship-shape, M. Radisson stationed Jean and me fore and aft with muskets levelled, and bade us shoot any man but himself who appeared above the hatch. Arming himself with his short, curved hanger —oh, I warrant there would have been a carving below decks had any one resisted him that day! —down he went to the mutineers of the dim-lighted forehold.

Perhaps the storm had quelled the spirit of rebellion; but up came M. de Radisson, followed by the entire crew—one fellow's head in white cotton where it had struck the floor, and every man jumping keen to answer his captain's word.

I must not forget a curious thing that happened as we lay at anchor. The storm had scarce abated when a strange ship poked her jib-boom across the entrance to the lagoon, followed by queer-rigged black sails.

"A pirate!" said Jean.

But Sieur de Radisson only puckered his brows, shifted position so that the St. Pierre could give a broadside, and said nothing.

Then came the strangest part of it. Another

ship poked her nose across the other side of the entrance. This was white-rigged.

"Two ships, and they have us cooped!" exclaimed Jean.

"One sporting different sails," said M. de Radisson contemptuously.

"What do you think we should do, sir?" asked Jean.

"Think?" demanded Radisson. "I have stopped thinking! I act! My thoughts are acts."

But all the same his thought at that moment was to let go a broadside that sent the stranger scudding. Judging it unwise to keep a half-mutinous crew too near pirate ships, M. Radisson ordered anchor up. With a deck-mop fastened in defiance to our prow, the St. Pierre slipped out of the harbour through the half-dark of those northern summer nights, and gave the heel to any highwayman waiting to attack as she passed.

The rest of the voyage was a ploughing through brash ice in the straits, with an occasional disembarking at the edge of some great ice-field; but one morning we were all awakened from the heavy sleep of hard-worked seamen by the screaming of a multitude of birds. The air was odorous with the crisp smell of woods,

M. DE RADISSON ACTS

When we came on deck, 'twas to see the St. Pierre anchored in the cove of a river that raced to meet the bay.

The screaming gulls knew not what to make of these strange visitors; for we were at Port Nelson—Fort Bourbon, as the French called it.

And you must not forget that we were French on *that* trip!

CHAPTER VIII

M. DE RADISSON COMES TO HIS OWN

THE sea was touched to silver by the rising sun—not the warm, red sun of southern climes, nor yet the gold light of the temperate zones, but the cold, clear steel of that great cold land where all the warring elements challenge man to combat. Browned by the early frosts, with a glint of hoar rime on the cobwebs among the grasses, north, south, and west, as far as eye could see, were boundless reaches of hill and valley. And over all lay the rich-toned shadows of early dawn.

The broad river raced not to meet the sea more swiftly than our pulses leaped at sight of that unclaimed world. 'Twas a kingdom waiting for its king. And its king had come!

Flush with triumph, sniffing the nutty, autumn air like a war-horse keen for battle, stood M. Radisson all impatience for the conquest of new realms. His jewelled sword-hilt glistened in the sun. The fire that always slumbered in the deep-set eyes flashed to life; and, fetching a deep breath, he said a queer thing to Jean and me.

"'Tis good air, lads," says he; "'tis free!"

And I, who minded that bloody war in which my father lost his all, knew what the words meant, and drank deep.

But for the screaming of the birds there was silence of death. And, indeed, it was death we had come to disenthrone. M. Radisson issued orders quick on top of one another, and the sailors swarmed from the hold like bees from a hive. The drum beat a roundelay that set our blood hopping. There were trumpet-calls back and forth from our ship to the Ste. Anne. Then, to a whacking of cables through blocks, the gig-boats touched water, and all hands were racing for the shore. Godefroy waved a monster flag—lilies of France, gold-wrought on cloth of silk—and Allemand kept beating—and beating—and beating the drum, rumbling out a "Vive le Roi!" to every stroke. Before the keel gravelled on the beach, M. Radisson's foot was on the gunwale, and he leaped ashore. Godefroy followed, flourishing the French flag and yelling at the top of his voice for the King of France. Behind, wading and floundering through the water, came the rest. Godefroy planted the flagstaff. The two crews sent up a shout that startled those strange, primeval silences. Then, M. Radisson stepped forward, hat in hand, whipped out his sword, and held it aloft.

"In the name of Louis the Great, King of France," he shouted, "in the name of His Most Christian Majesty, the King of France, I take possession of all these regions!"

At that, Chouart Groseillers shivered a bottle of wine against the flag-pole. Drums beat, fifes shrieked as for battle, and lusty cheers for the king and Sieur Radisson rang and echoed and re-echoed from our crews. Three times did Allemand beat his drum and three times did we cheer. Then Pierre Radisson raised his sword. Every man dropped to knee. Catholics and Protestants, Calvinists and infidels, and riff-raff adventurers who had no religion but what they swore by, bowed their heads to the solemn thanks which Pierre Radisson uttered for safe deliverance from perilous voyage.*

That was my first experience of the fusion which the New World makes of Old World divisions. We thought we had taken possession of

* Reference to M. Radisson's journal corroborates Mr. Stanhope in this observance, which was never neglected by M. Radisson after season of peril. It is to be noted that he made his prayers *after* not *at* the season of peril.

the land. No, no, 'twas the land had taken possession of us, as the New World ever does, fusing ancient hates and rearing a new race, of which —I wot—no prophet may dare too much!

"He who twiddles his thumbs may gnaw his gums," M. Radisson was wont to say; and I assure you there was no twiddling of thumbs that morning. Bare had M. Radisson finished prayers, when he gave sharp command for Groseillers, his brother-in-law, to look to the building of the Habitation—as the French called their forts—while he himself would go up-stream to seek the Indians for trade. Jean and Godefroy and I were sent to the ship for a birch canoe, which M. Radisson had brought from Quebec.

Our leader took the bow; Godefroy, the stern; Jean and I, the middle. A poise of the steel-shod steering pole, we grasped our paddles, a downward dip, quick followed by Godefroy at the stern, and out shot the canoe, swift, light, lithe, alert, like a racer to the bit, with a gurgling of waters below the gunwales, the keel athrob to the swirl of a turbulent current and a trail of eddies dimpling away on each side. A sharp breeze sprang up abeam, and M. Radisson ordered a blanket sail hoisted on the steersman's fishing-pole. But if you think that he permitted idle paddles because a wind would do the work, you know not the ways of the great explorer. He bade us ply the faster, till the canoe sped between earth and sky like an arrow shot on the level. The shore-line became a blur. Clumps of juniper and pine marched abreast, halted the length of time an eye could rest, and wheeled away. The swift current raced to meet us. The canoe jumped to mount the glossy waves raised by the beam wind. An upward tilt of her prow, and we had skimmed the swell like a winged thing. And all the while M. Radisson's eyes were everywhere. Chips whirled past. There were beaver, he said. Was the water suddenly muddied? Deer had flitted at our approach. Did a fish rise? M. Radisson predicted otter; and where there were otter and beaver and deer, there should be Indians.

As for the rest of us, it had gone to our heads.

We were intoxicated with the wine of the rugged, new, free life. Sky above; wild woods where never foot had trod; air that drew through the nostrils in thirst-quenching draughts; blood atingle to the laughing rhythm of the river—what wonder that youth leaped to a fresh life from the mummified existence of little, old peoples in little, old lands?

We laughed aloud from fulness of life.

Jean laid his paddle athwart, ripped off his buckskin, and smiled back.

"Ramsay feels as if he had room to stretch himself," said he.

"Feel! I feel as if I could run a thousand miles and jump off the ends of the earth——"

"And dive to the bottom of the sea and harness whales and play bowling-balls with the spheres, you young rantipoles," added M. Radisson ironically.

"The fever of the adventurer," said Jean quietly. "My uncle knows it."

I laughed again. "I was wondering if Eli Kirke ever felt this way," I explained.

"Pardieu," retorted M. de Radisson, loosening his coat, "if people moved more and moped less, they'd brew small bile! Come, lads! Come, lads! We waste time!"

And we were paddling again, in quick, light strokes, silent from zest, careless of toil, strenuous from love of it.

Once we came to a bend in the river where the current was so strong that we had dipped our paddles full five minutes against the mill race without gaining an inch. The canoe squirmed like a hunter balking a hedge, and Jean's blade splintered off to the handle. But M. de Radisson braced back to lighten the bow;

the prow rose, a sweep of the paddles, and on we sped!

"Hard luck to pull and not gain a boat length," observed Jean.

"Harder luck not to pull, and to be swept back," corrected M. de Radisson.

We left the main river to thread a labyrinthine chain of waterways, where were portages over brambly shores and slippery rocks, with the pace set at a run by M. de Radisson. Jean and I followed with the pack straps across our foreheads and the provisions on our backs. Godefroy brought up the rear with the bark canoe above his head.

At one place, where we disembarked, M. de Radisson traced the sand with the muzzle of his musket.

"A boot-mark," said he, drawing the faint outlines of a footprint, "and egad, it's not a man's foot either!"

"Impossible!" cried Jean. "We are a thousand miles from any white-man."

"There's nothing impossible on this earth," retorted Radisson impatiently. "But pardieu, there are neither white women in this wilderness, nor ghosts wearing women's boots! I'd give my right hand to know what left that mark!"

After that his haste grew feverish. We

snatched our meals by turns between paddles. He seemed to grudge the waste of each night, camping late and launching early; and it was Godefroy's complaint that each portage was made so swiftly there was no time for that solace of the common voyageur—the boatman's pipe. For eight days we travelled without seeing a sign of human presence but that one vague footmark in the sand.

"If there are no Indians, how much farther do we go, sir?" asked Godefroy sulkily on the eighth day.

"Till we find them," answered M. Radisson.

And we found them that night.

A deer broke from the woods edging the sand where we camped and had almost bounded across our fire when an Indian darted out a hundred yards behind. Mistaking us for his own people, he whistled the hunter's signal to head the game back. Then he saw that we were strangers. Pulling up of a sudden, he threw back his arms, uttered a cry of surprise, and ran to the hiding of the bush.

M. Radisson was the first to pursue; but where the sand joined the thicket he paused and began tracing the point of his rapier round the outlines of a mark.

" What do you make of it, Godefroy? " he demanded of the trader.

The trader looked quizzically at Sieur de Radisson.

" The toes of that man's moccasin turn out," says Godefroy significantly.

" Then that man is no Indian," retorted M. Radisson, " and hang me, if the size is not that of a woman or a boy! "

And he led back to the beach.

" Yon ship was a pirate," began Godefroy, " and if buccaneers be about——"

" Hold your clack, fool," interrupted M. Radisson, as if the fellow's prattle had cut into his mental plannings; and he bade us heap such a fire as could be seen by Indians for a hundred miles. " If once I can find the Indians," meditated he moodily, " I'll drive out a whole regiment of scoundrels with one snap o' my thumb! "

Black clouds rolled in from the distant bay, boding a stormy night; and Godefroy began to complain that black deeds were done in the dark, and we were forty leagues away from the protection of our ships.

" A pretty target that fire will make of us in the dark," whined the fellow.

M. Radisson's eyes glistened sparks.

" I'd as lief be a pirate myself, as be shot

down by pirates," grumbled the trader, giving a hand to hoist the shed of sheet canvas that was to shield us from the rains now aslant against the seaward horizon.

At the words M. Radisson turned sharply; but the heedless fellow gabbled on.

"Where is a man to take cover, an the buccaneers began shooting from the bush behind?" demanded Godefroy belligerently.

M. Radisson reached one arm across the fire. "I'll show you," said he. Taking Godefroy by the ear, with a prick of the sword he led the lazy knave quick march to the beach, where lay our canoe bottom up.

"Crawl under!" M. Radisson lifted the prow.

From very shame—I think it was—Godefroy balked; but M. Radisson brought a cutting rap across the rascal's heels that made him hop. The canoe clapped down, and Godefroy was safe.

"Pardieu," mutters Radisson, "such cowards would turn the marrow o' men's bones to butter!"

Sitting on a log, with his feet to the fire, he motioned Jean and me to come into the shelter of the slant canvas; for the clouds were rolling overhead black as ink and the wind roared up the river-bed with a wall of pelting rain. M. Radisson gazed absently into the flame. The steel lights were at play in his eyes, and his lips parted.

"Storm and cold—man and beast—powers of darkness and devil—knaves and fools and his own sins—he must fight them all, lads," says M. Radisson slowly.

"Who must fight them all?" asks Jean.

"The victor," answers Radisson, and warm red flashed to the surface of the cold steel in his eyes.

"Jean," he began, looking up quickly towards the gathering darkness of the woods.

"Sir?"

"'Tis cold enough for hunters to want a fire."

"Is the fire not big enough?"

"Now, where are your wits, lad? If hunters were hiding in that bush, one could see this fire a long way off. The wind is loud. One could go close without being heard. Pardieu, I'll wager a good scout could creep up to a log like this"—touching the pine on which we sat—"and hear every word we are saying without a soul being the wiser!"

Jean turned with a start, half-suspecting a spy. Radisson laughed.

"Must I spell it out? Eh, lad, afraid to go?"

The taunt bit home. Without a word Jean and I rose.

"Keep far enough apart so that one of you will escape back with the news," called Radisson, as we plunged into the woods.

Of the one who might not escape Pierre Radisson gave small heed, and so did we. Jean took the river side and I the inland thicket, feeling our way blindly through the blackness of forest and storm and night. Then the rain broke—broke in lashing whip-cords with the crackle of fire. Jean whistled and I signalled back; but there was soon such a pounding of rains it drowned every sound. For all the help one could give the other we might have been a thousand miles apart. I looked back. M. Radisson's fire threw a dull glare into the cavernous upper darkness. That was guide enough. Jean could keep his course by the river.

It was plunging into a black nowhere. The trees thinned. I seemed to be running across the open, the rain driving me forward like a wet sail, a roar of wind in my ears and the words of M. Radisson ringing their battle-cry—"Storm and cold—man and beast—powers of darkness and devil—knaves and fools and his own sins—he must fight them all!"—"Who?"—"The victor!"

Of a sudden the dripping thicket gave back a glint. Had I run in a circle and come again on M. Radisson's fire? Behind, a dim glare still shone against the sky.

Another glint from the rain drip, and I dropped like a deer hit on the run. Not a gun-shot away was a hunter's fire. Against the fire were three figures. One stood with his face towards me, an Indian dressed in buckskin, the man who had pursued the deer. The second was hid by an intervening tree; and as I watched, the third faded into the phaseless dark. Who were these night-watchers? I liked not that business of spying—though you may call it scouting, if you will, but I must either report nothing to M. Radisson, or find out more.

I turned to skirt the group. A pistol-shot rang through the wood. A sword flashed to light. Before I had time to think, but not—thanks to M. Picot's lessons long ago—not before I had my own rapier out, an assassin blade would have taken me unawares.

I was on guard. Steel struck fire in red spots as it clashed against steel. One thrust, I know, touched home; for the pistol went whirling out of my adversary's hand, and his sword came through the dark with the hiss of a serpent. Again I seemed to be in Boston Town; but the hunting room had become a northland forest, M. Picot, a bearded man with his back to the fire and his face in the dark, and our slim foils, naked swords that pressed and parried and thrust in many a foul such as the French doctor had taught me was a trick of the infamous Blood! Indeed, I could have sworn that a woman's voice cried out through the dark; but the rain was in my face and a sword striking red against my own. Thanks, yes, thanks a thousand times to M. Picot's lessons; for again and yet again I foiled that lunge of the unscrupulous swordsman till I heard my adversary swearing between clinched teeth. He retreated. I followed. By a dexterous spring he put himself under cover of the woods, leaving me in the open. My only practice in swordsmanship had been with M. Picot, and it was not till long years after that I minded how those lessons seemed to forestall and counter the moves of that ambushed assassin. But the baffling thing was that my enemy's moves countered mine in the very same way.

He had not seen my face, for my back was turned when he came up, and my face in the shade when I whirled. But I stood between the dark and the fire. Every motion of mine he could forecast, while I could but parry and retreat, striving in vain to lure him out, to get into the dark, to strike what I could not see, pushed back and back till I felt the rush that aims not to disarm but to slay.

Our weapons rang with a glint of green lightnings. A piece of steel flew up. My rapier had snapped short at the hilt. A cold point was at my throat pressing me down and back as the foil had caught me that night in M. Picot's house. To right, to left, I swerved, the last blind rushes of the fugitive man. . . .

"Storm and cold—man and beast—powers of darkness and devil—he must fight them all——"

The memory of those words spurred like a battle-cry. Beaten? Not yet! "Leap to meet it! Leap to meet it!"

I caught the blade at my throat with a naked hand. Hot floods drenched my face. The earth swam. We were both in the light now, a bearded man pushing his sword through my hand, and I falling down. Then my antagonist leaped back with a shivering cry of horror, flung the weapon to the ground and fled into the dark.

And when I sat up my right hand held the hilt of a broken rapier, the left was gashed across the palm, and a sword as like my own as two peas lay at my feet.

The fire was there. But I was alone.

CHAPTER IX

VISITORS

THE fire had every appearance of a night bivouac, but there was remnant of neither camp nor hunt. Somewhere on my left lay the river. By that the way led back to M. Radisson's rendezvous. It was risky enough—that threading of the pathless woods through the pitchy dark; but he who pauses to measure the risk at each tread is ill fitted to pioneer wild lands.

Who the assassin was and why he had so suddenly desisted, I knew no more than you do! That he had attacked was natural enough; for whoever took first possession of no-man's-land in those days either murdered his rivals or sold them to slavery. But why had he flung his sword down at the moment of victory?

The pelting of the rain softened to a leafy patter, the patter to a drip, and a watery moon came glimmering through the clouds. With my enemy's rapier in hand I began cutting a course through the thicket. Radisson's fire no longer shone. Indeed, I became mighty uncertain which direction to take, for the rush of the river merged with the beating of the wind. The ground sloped precipitously; and I was holding back by the underbrush lest the bank led to water when an indistinct sound, a smothery murmur like the gurgle of a subterranean pool, came from below.

The wind fell. The swirl of the flowing river sounded far from the rear. I had become confused and was travelling away from the true course. But what was that sound?

I threw a stick forward. It struck hard stone. At the same instant was a sibilant, human—distinctly human—"Hss-h," and the sound had ceased.

That was no laving of inland pond against pebbles. Make of it what you will—there were voices, smothered but talking. "No—no—no" . . . then the warning . . . "Hush!" . . . then the wind and the river and . . . "No—no!" with words like oaths. . . . "No—I say, no! Having come so far, no!—not if it were my own brother!" . . . then the low "Hush!" . . . and pleadings . . . then—"Send Le Borgne!"

And an Indian had rushed past me in the dark with a pine fagot in his hand.

Rising, I stole after him. 'Twas the fellow who had been at the fire with that unknown assailant. He paused over the smouldering embers, searching the ground, found the hilt of the broken sword, lifted the severed blade, kicked leaves over all traces of conflict, and extinguishing the fire, carried off the broken weapon. An Indian can pick his way over known ground without a torch. What was this fellow doing with a torch? Had he been sent for me? I drew back in shadow to let him pass. Then I ran with all speed to the river.

Gray dawn came over the trees as I reached the swollen waters, and the sun was high in mid-heaven when I came to the gravel patch where M. de Radisson had camped. Round a sharp bend in the river a strange sight unfolded.

A score of crested savages with painted bodies sat on the ground. In the centre, clad like a king, with purple doublet and plumed hat and velvet waistcoat ablaze with medals of honour —was M. Radisson. One hand deftly held his scabbard forward so that the jewelled hilt shone against the velvet, and the other was raised impressively above the savages. How had he made the savages come to him? How are some men born to draw all others as the sea draws the streams?

The poor creatures had piled their robes at his feet as offerings to a god.

" What did he give for the pelts, Godefroy? " I asked.

" Words! " says Godefroy, with a grin, " gab and a drop o' rum diluted in a pot o' water! "

" What is he saying to them now? "

Godefroy shrugged his shoulders. " That the gods have sent him a messenger to them; that the fire he brings "—he was handing a musket to the chief—" will smite the Indians' enemy from the earth; that the bullet is magic to outrace the fleetest runner "—this as M. Radisson fired a shot into mid-air that sent the Indians into ecstasies of childish wonder—" that the bottle in his hands contains death, and if the Indians bring their hunt to the white-man, the white-man will never take the cork out except to let death fly at the Indians' enemy "—he lifted a little phial of poison as he spoke—" that the Indian need never feel cold nor thirst, now that the white-man has brought fire-water! "

At this came a harsh laugh from a taciturn Indian standing on the outer rim of the crowd. It was the fellow who had run through the forest with the torch.

" Who is that, Godefroy? "

"Le Borgne."

"Le Borgne need not laugh," retorted M. de Radisson sharply. "Le Borgne knows the taste of fire-water! Le Borgne has been with the white-man at the south, and knows what the white-man says is true."

But Le Borgne only laughed the harder, deep, guttural, contemptuous "huh—huh's!" —a fitting rebuke, methought, for the ignoble deception implied in M. Radisson's words.

Indeed, I would fain suppress this part of M. Radisson's record, for he juggled with truth so oft, when he thought the end justified the means, he finally got a knack of juggling so much with truth that the means would never justify any end. I would fain repress the ignoble faults of a noble leader, but I must even set down the facts as they are, so you may see why a man who was the greatest leader and trader and explorer of his times reaped only an aftermath of universal distrust. He lied his way through thick and thin—as we traders used to say—till that lying habit of his sewed him up in a net of his own weaving like a grub in a cocoon.

Godefroy was giving a hand to bind up my gashed palm when something grunted a "huff-huff" beside us. Le Borgne was there with a queer look on his inscrutable face.

" Le Borgne, you rascal, you know who gave me this," I began, taking careful scrutiny of the Indian.

One eye was glazed and sightless, the other yellow like a fox's; but the fellow was straight, supple, and clean-timbered as a fresh-hewn mast. With a " huh-huh," he gabbled back some answer.

" What does he say, Godefroy? "

" He says he doesn't understand the white-man's tongue—which is a lie," added Godefroy of his own account. " Le Borgne was interpreter for the Fur Company at the south of the bay the year that M. Radisson left the English."

Were my assailants, then, Hudson's Bay Company men come up from the south end of James Bay? Certainly, the voice had spoken English. I would have drawn Godefroy aside to inform him of my adventure, but Le Borgne stuck to us like a burr. Jean was busy helping M. de Radisson at the trade, or what was called " trade," when white men gave an awl for forty beaver-skins.

" Godefroy," I said, " keep an eye on this Indian till I speak to M. de Radisson." And I turned to the group. 'Twas as pretty a bit of colour as I have ever seen. The sea, like silver, on one side; the autumn-tinted woods, brown and yellow and gold, on the other; M. de Radisson in his gay dress surrounded by a score of savages with their faces and naked chests painted a gaudy red, headgear of swans' down, eagle quills depending from their backs, and buckskin trousers fringed with the scalp-locks of the slain.

Drawing M. de Radisson aside, I gave him hurried account of the night's adventures.

"Ha!" says he. "Not Hudson's Bay Company men, or you would be in irons, lad! Not French, for they spoke English. Pardieu! Poachers and thieves—we shall see! Where is that vagabond Cree? These people are southern Indians and know nothing of him.—Godefroy," he called.

Godefroy came running up. "Le Borgne's gone," said Godefroy breathlessly.

"Gone?" repeated Radisson.

"He left word for Master Stanhope from one who wishes him well——"

"One who wishes him well," repeated M. Radisson, looking askance at me.

"For Master Stanhope not to be bitten twice by the same dog!"

Our amazement you may guess: M. de Radisson, suspicious of treachery and private trade and piracy on my part; I as surprised to learn that I had a well-wisher as I had been to discover an unknown foe; and Godefroy, all cock-a-whoop with his news, as is the way of the vulgar.

"Ramsay," said M. Radisson, speaking very low and tense, "as you hope to live and without a lie, what—does—this—mean?"

"Sir, as I hope to live—I—do—not—know!"

He continued to search me with doubting looks. I raised my wounded hand.

"Will you do me the honour to satisfy yourself that wound is genuine?"

"Pish!" says he.

He studied the ground. "There's nothing impossible on this earth. Facts are hard dogs to down.—Jean," he called, "gather up the pelts! It takes a man to trade well, but any fool can make fools drink! Godefroy—give the knaves the rum—but mind yourselves," he warned, "three parts rain-water!" Then facing me, "Take me to that bank!"

He followed without comment.

At the place of the camp-fire were marks of the struggle.

"The same boot-prints as on the sand! A small man," observed Radisson.

But when we came to the sloping bank,

where the land fell sheer away to a dry, pebbly reach, M. Radisson pulled a puzzled brow.

"They must have taken shelter from the rain. They must have been under your feet."

"But where are their foot-marks?" I asked.

"Washed out by the rain," said he; but that was one of the untruths with which a man who is ever telling untruths sometimes deceives himself; for if the bank sheltered the intruders from the rain, it also sheltered their foot-marks, and there was not a trace.

"All the same," said M. de Radisson, "we shall make these Indians our friends by taking them back to the fort with us."

"Ramsay," he remarked on the way, "there's a game to play."

"So it seems."

"Hold yourself in," said he sententiously.

I walked on listening.

"One plays as your friend, the other as your foe! Show neither friend nor foe your hand! Let the game tell! 'Twas the reined-in horse won King Charles's stakes at Newmarket last year! Hold yourself in, I say!"

"In," I repeated, wondering at this homily.

"And hold yourself up," he continued. "That coxcomb of a marquis always trailing his dignity in the dust of mid-road to worry with a common dog like La Chesnaye—pish! Hold your self-respect in the chest of your jacket, man! 'Tis the slouching nag that loses the race! Hold yourself up!"

His words seemed hard sense plain spoken.

"And let your feet travel on," he added.

"In and up and on!" I repeated.

"In and up and on—there's mettle for you, lad!"

And with that terse text—which, I think, comprehended the whole of M. Radisson's philosophy—we were back at the beach.

The Indians were not in such a state as I have seen after many a trading bout. They were able to accompany us. In embarking, M. Radisson must needs observe all the ceremony of two races. Such a whiffing of pipes among the stately, half-drunk Indian chiefs you never saw, with a pompous proffering of the stem to the four corners of the compass, which they thought would propitiate the spirits. Jean blew a blast on the trumpet. I waved the French flag. Godefroy beat a rattling fusillade on the drum, grabbed up his bobbing tipstaff, led the way; and down we filed to the canoes.

At all this ostentation I could not but smile; but no man ever had greater need of pomp to hold his own against uneven odds than Radisson.

VISITORS

As we were leaving came a noise that set us all by the ears—the dull booming reverberations of heavy cannonading.

The Indians shook as with palsy. Jean Groseillers cried out that his father's ships were in peril. Godefroy implored the saints; but with that lying facility which was his doom, M. de Radisson blandly informed the savages that more of his vessels had arrived from France.

Bidding Jean go on to the Habitation with the Indians, he took the rest of us ashore with one redskin as guide, to spy out the cause of the firing.

" 'Twill be a pretty to-do if the English Fur Company's ships arrive before we have a French fort ready to welcome them," said he.

CHAPTER X

THE CAUSE OF THE FIRING

THE landing was but a part of the labyrinthine trickery in which our leader delighted to play; for while Jean delayed the natives we ran overland through the woods, launched our canoe far ahead of the Indian flotilla, and went racing forward to the throbs of the leaping river.

"If a man would win, he must run fast as the hour-glass," observed M. Radisson, poising his steering-pole. "And now, my brave lads," he began, counting in quick, sharp words that rang with command, "keep time—one—two—three! One—two—three!" And to each word the paddles dipped with the speed of a fly-wheel's spokes.

"One—two—three! In and up and on! An you keep yourselves in hand, men, you can win against the devil's own artillery! Speed to your strokes, Godefroy," he urged.

And the canoe answered as a fine-strung racer to the spur. Shore-lines blurred to a green streak. The frosty air met our faces in wind. Gurgling waters curled from the prow in corrugated runnels. And we were running a swift race with a tumult of waves, mounting the swell, dipping, rising buoyant, forward in bounds, with a roar of the nearing rapids, and spray dashing athwart in drifts. M. Radisson braced back. The prow lifted, shot into mid-air, touched water again, and went whirling through the mill-race that boiled below a waterfall. Once the canoe aimed straight as an arrow for rocks in mid-current. M. Radisson's steel-shod pole flashed in the sun. There was a quick thrust, answered by Godefroy's counter-stroke at the stern; and the canoe grazed past the rocks not a hair's-breadth off.

"Sainte Anne ha' mercy!" mumbled Godefroy, baling water from the canoe as we breasted a turn in the river to calmer currents, "Sainte Anne ha' mercy! But the master'd run us over Niagara, if he had a mind."

"Or the River Styx, if 'twould gain his end," sharply added Radisson.

But he ordered our paddles athwart for snatched rest, while he himself kept alert at the bow. With the rash presumption of youth, I offered to take the bow that he might rest; but he threw his head back with a loud laugh, more of scorn than mirth, and bade me nurse a wounded hand. On the evening of the third day we came to the Habitation. Without disembarking, M. de Radisson sent the soldiers on sentinel duty at the river front up to the fort with warning to prepare for instant siege.

" 'Twill put speed in the lazy rascals to finish the fort," he remarked; and the canoe glided out to mid-current again for the far expanse of the bay.

By this we were all so used to M. Radisson's doings, 'twould not have surprised us when the craft shot out from river-mouth to open sea if he had ordered us to circumnavigate the ocean on a chip.

He did what was nigh as venturesome.

A quick, unwarned swerve of his pole, which bare gave Godefroy time to take the cue, and our prow went scouring across the scud of whipping currents where two rivers and an ocean-tide met. The seething waves lashed to foam with the long, low moan of the world-devouring serpent which, legend says, is ever an-hungering to devour voyageurs on life's sea. And for all the world that reef of combing breakers was not unlike a serpent type of malignant elements bent on man's destruction!

Then, to the amaze of us all, we had left the lower river. The canoe was cutting up-stream against a new current; and the moan of the pounding surf receded to the rear. Clouds blew inland, muffling the moon; and M. Radisson ordered us ashore for the night. Feet at a smouldering fire too dull for an enemy to see and heads pillowed on logs, we bivouacked with the frosty ground for bed.

"Bad beds make good risers," was all M. Radisson's comfort, when Godefroy grumbled out some complaint.

A *hard* master, you say? A wise one, say I, for the forces he fought in that desolate land were as adamant. Only the man dauntless as adamant could conquer. And you must remember, while the diamond and the charcoal are of the same family, 'tis the diamond has lustre, because it is *hard*. Faults, M. Radisson had, which were almost crimes; but look you who judge him—his faults were not the faults of nearly all other men, the faults which *are* a crime—*the crime of being weak!*

The first thing our eyes lighted on when the sun rose in flaming darts through the gray haze of dawn was a half-built fort on an island in mid-river. At the water side lay a queer-rigged brigantine, rocking to the swell of the tide. Here, then, was cause of that firing heard across the marsh on the lower river.

"'Tis the pirate ship we saw on the high sea," muttered Godefroy, rubbing his eyes.

"She flies no flag! She has no license to trade! She's a poacher! She will make a prize worth the taking," added M. Radisson sharply. Then, as if to justify that intent—"As *we* have no license, we must either take or be taken!"

The river mist gradually lifted, and there emerged from the fog a stockaded fort with two bastions facing the river and guns protruding from loopholes.

"Not so easy to take that fort," growled Godefroy, who was ever a hanger-back.

"All the better," retorted M. de Radisson. "Easy taking makes soft men! 'Twill test your mettle!"

"Test our mettle!" sulked the trader, a key higher in his obstinacy. "All very well to talk, sir, but how can we take a fort mounted with twenty cannon——"

"I'll tell you *the how* when it's done," interrupted M. de Radisson.

But Godefroy was one of those obstinates who would be silent only when stunned.

"I'd like to know, sir, what we're to do," he began.

"Godefroy, 'twould be waste time to knock sense in your pate! There is only one thing to do always—only one, *the right thing!* Do it, fool! An I hear more clack from you till its done, I'll have your tongue out with the nippers!"

Godefroy cowered sulkily back, and M. de Radisson laughed.

"That will quell him," said he. "When Godefroy's tongue is out he can't grumble, and grumbling is his bread of life!"

Stripping off his bright doublet, M. Radisson hung it from a tree to attract the fort's notice. Then he posted us in ambuscade with orders to capture whatever came.

But nothing came.

And when the fort guns boomed out the noon hour M. Radisson sprang up all impatience.

"I'll wait no man's time," he vowed. "Losing time is losing the game! Launch out!"

Chittering something about our throats being cut, Godefroy shrank back. With a quick stride M. Radisson was towering above him. Catching Godefroy by the scruff of the neck, he threw him face down into the canoe, muttering out it would be small loss if all the cowards in the world had their throats cut.

"The pirates come to trade," he explained. "They will not fire at Indians. Bind your hair back like that Indian there!"

No sooner were we in the range of the fort than M. Radisson uttered the shrill call of a native, bade our Indian stand up, and himself enacted the pantomime of a savage, waving his arms, whistling, and hallooing. With cries of welcome, the fort people ran to the shore and left their guns unmanned. Reading from a syllable book, they shouted out Indian words. It was safe to approach. Before they could arm we could escape. But we were two men, one lad, and a neutral Indian against an armed garrison in a land where killing was no murder.

M. de Radisson stood up and called in the Indian tongue. They did not understand.

"New to it," commented Radisson, "not the Hudson's Bay Company!"

All the while he was imperceptibly approaching nearer. He shouted in French. They shook their heads.

"English highwaymen, blundered in here by chance," said he.

Tearing off the Indian head-band of disguise, he demanded in mighty peremptory tones who they were.

" English," they called back doubtfully.

" What have you come for? " insisted Radisson, with a great swelling of his chest.

" The beaver trade," came a faint voice.

Where had I heard it before? Did it rise from the ground in the woods, or from a far memory of children throwing a bully into the sea?

" I demand to see your license," boldly challenged Radisson.

At that the fellows ashore put their heads together.

" In the name of the king, I demand to see your license instantly," repeated Sieur de Radisson, with louder authority.

" We have no license," explained one of the men, who was dressed with slashed boots, red doublet, and cocked hat.

M. Radisson smiled and poled a length closer.

" A ship without a license! A prize—for the taking! If the rascals complain—the galleys for life! " and he laughed softly.

" This coast is possessed by the King of France," he shouted. " We have a strong garrison! We mistook your firing for more French ships! " Shaping his hands trumpet fashion to his mouth, he called this out again, adding that our Indian was of a nation in league with the French.

The pirates were dumb as if he had tossed a hand grenade among them.

"The ship is ours now, lads," said Radisson softly, poling nearer. "See, lads, the bottom has tumbled from their courage! We'll not waste a pound o' powder in capturing that prize!" He turned suddenly to me—"As I live by bread, 'tis that bragging young dandy-prat —hop-o'-my-thumb—Ben Gillam of Boston Town!"

"Ben Gillam!"

I was thinking of my assailant in the woods. "Ben was tall. The pirate, who came carving at me, was small."

But Ben Gillam it was, turned pirate or privateer—as you choose to call it—grown to a well-timbered rapscallion with head high in air, jack-boots half-way to his waist, a clanking sword at heel, and a nose too red from rum.

As we landed, he sent his men scattering to the fort, and stood twirling his mustaches till the recognition struck him.

"By Jericho—Radisson!" he gasped.

Then he tossed his chin defiantly in air like an unbroken colt disposed to try odds with a master.

"Don't be afraid to land," he called down out of sheer impudence.

"Don't be afraid to have us land," Radisson shouted up to him. "We'll not harm you!"

Ben swore a big oath, fleered a laugh, and kicked the sand with his heels. Raising a hand, he signalled the watchers on the ship.

"Sorry to welcome you in this warlike fashion," said he.

"Glad to welcome you to the domain of His Most Christian Majesty, the King of France," retorted Radisson, leaping ashore.

Ben blinked to catch the drift of that.

"Devil take their majesties!" he ejaculated. "He's king who conquers!"

"No need to talk of conquering when one is master already," corrected M. de Radisson.

"Shiver my soul," blurts out Ben, "I haven't a tongue like an eel, but that's what I mean; and I'm king here, and welcome to you, Radisson!"

"And that's what I mean," laughed M. Radisson, with a bow, quietly motioning us to follow ashore. "No need to conquer where one is master, and welcome to you, Captain Gillam!"

And they embraced each other like spider and fly, each with a free hand to his sword-hilt, and a questioning look on the other's face.

Says M. Radisson: "I've seen that ship before!"

Ben laughs awkwardly. "We captured her from a Dutchman," he begins.

"Oh!" says Sieur Radisson. "I meant outside the straits after the storm!"

Gillam's eyes widen. "Were those your ships?" he asks. Then both men laugh.

"Not much to boast in the way of a fleet," taunts Ben.

"Those are the two smallest we have," quickly explains Radisson.

Gillam's face went blank, and M. Radisson's eyes closed to the watchful slit of a cat mouse-hunting.

"Come! Come!" exclaims Ben, with a sudden flare of friendliness, "I am no baby-eater! Put a peg in that! Shiver my soul if this is a way to welcome friends! Come aboard all of you and test the Canary we got in the hold of a fine Spanish galleon last week! Such a top-heavy ship, with sails like a tinker's tatters, you never saw! And her hold running over with Canary and Madeira — oh! Come aboard! Come aboard!" he urged.

It was Pierre Radisson's turn to blink.

"And drink to the success of the beaver trade," importunes Ben.

'Twas as pretty a piece of play as you could see: Ben, scheming to get the Frenchman captive; M. Radisson, with the lightnings under his brows and that dare-devil rashness of his blood tempting him to spy out the lad's strength.

"Ben was the body of the venture! Where was the brain? It was that took me aboard his ship," M. Radisson afterward confessed to us.

"Come! Come!" pressed Gillam. "I know young Stanhope there"—his mighty air brought the laugh to my face—"young Stanhope there has a taste for fine Canary——"

"But, lad," protested Radisson, with a condescension that was vinegar to Ben's vanity, "we cannot be debtors altogether. Let two of your men stay here and whiff pipes with my fellows, while I go aboard!"

Ben's teeth ground out an assent that sounded precious like an oath; for he knew that he was being asked for hostages of safe-conduct while M. Radisson spied out the ship. He signalled, as we thought, for two hostages to come down from the fort; but scarce had he dropped his hand when fort and ship let out such a roar of cannonading as would have lifted the hair from any other head than Pierre Radisson's.

Godefroy cut a caper. The Indian's eyes bulged with terror, and my own pulse went a-hop; but M. Radisson never changed countenance.

"Pardieu," says he softly, with a pleased smile as the last shot went skipping over the water, "you're devilish fond o' fireworks, to waste good powder so far from home!"

Ben mumbled out that he had plenty of powder, and that some fools didn't know fireworks from war.

M. Radisson said he was glad there was plenty of powder, there would doubtless be use found for it, and he knew fools oft mistook fireworks for war.

With that a cannon-shot sent the sand spattering to our boots and filled the air with powder-dust; but when the smoke cleared, M. Radisson had quietly put himself between Ben and the fort.

Drawing out his sword, the Frenchman ran his finger up the edge.

"Sharp as the next," said he.

Lowering the point, he scratched a line on the sand between the mark of the last shot and us.

"How close can your gunners hit, Ben?" asked Radisson. "Now I'll wager you a bottle of Madeira they can't hit that line without hitting you!"

Ben's hand went up quick enough. The gunners ceased firing and M. Radisson sheathed his sword with a laugh.

" You'll not take the odds? Take advice instead! Take a *man's* advice, and never waste powder! You'll need it all if he's king who conquers! Besides," he added, turning suddenly serious, " if my forces learn you are here I'll not promise I've strength to restrain them! "

" How many have you? " blurted Ben.

" Plenty to spare! Now, if you are afraid of the Hudson's Bay Company ships attacking you, I'd be glad to loan you enough young fire-eaters to garrison the fort here! "

" Thanks," says Ben, twirling his mustaches till they were nigh jerked out, " but how long would they stay? "

" Till you sent them away," says M. de Radisson, with the lights at play under his brows.

" Hang me if I know how long that would be," laughed Gillam, half-puzzled, half-pleased with the Frenchman's darting wits.

" Ben," begins M. Radisson, tapping the lace ruffle of Gillam's sleeve, " you must not fire those guns! "

" No? " questions Gillam.

" My officers are swashing young blades!

What with the marines and the common soldiers and my own guard, 'tis all I can manage to keep the rascals in hand! They must not know you are here!"

Gillam muttered something of a treaty of truce for the winter.

M. Radisson shook his head.

"I have scarce the support to do as I will," he protests.

Young Gillam swore such coolness was scurvy treatment for an old friend.

"Old friend," laughed Radisson afterward. "Did the cub's hangdog of a father not offer a thousand pounds for my head on the end of a pikestaff?"

But with Ben he played the game out.

"The season is too far advanced for you to *escape*," says he with soft emphasis.

"'Tis why I want a treaty," answers the sailor.

"Come, then," laughs the Frenchman, "now—as to terms——"

"Name them," says Gillam.

"If you don't wish to be discovered——"

"I don't wish to be discovered!"

"If you don't wish to be discovered don't run up a flag!"

"One," says Gillam.

" If you don't wish to be discovered, don't let your people leave the island! "

" They haven't," says Gillam.

" What? " asks M. Radisson, glancing sharply at me; for we were both thinking of that night attack.

" They haven't left the island," repeats Gillam.

" Ten lies are as cheap as two," says Radisson to us. Then to Gillam, " Don't let your people leave the island, or they'll meet my forces."

" Two," says Gillam.

" If you don't wish the Fur Company to discover you, don't fire guns! "

" Three," says Gillam.

" That is to keep 'em from connecting with those inlanders," whispered Godefroy, who knew the plays of his master's game better than I. " We can beat 'em single; but if Ben joins the inlanders and the Fur Company against us—" Godefroy completed his prophecy with an ominous shake of the head.

" My men shall not know you are here," M. Radisson was promising.

" One," counts Gillam.

" I'll join with you against the English ships! "

Young Gillam laughed derisively.

"My father commands the Hudson's Bay ship," says he.

"Egad, yes!" retorts M. Radisson nonchalantly, "but your father doesn't command the governor of the Fur Company, who sailed out in his ship."

"The governor does not know that I am here," flouts Ben.

"But he would know if I told him," adds M. de Radisson, "and if I told him the Company's captain owned half the ship poaching on the Company's preserve, the Company's captain and the captain's son might go hang for all the furs they'd get! By the Lord, youngster, I rather suspect both the captain and the captain's son would be whipped and hanged for the theft!"

Ben gave a start and looked hard at Radisson. 'Twas the first time, I think, the cub realized that the pawn in so soft-spoken a game was his own neck.

"Go on," he said, with haste and fear in his look. "I promised three terms. You will keep your people from knowing I am here and join me against the English—go on! What next?"

"I'll defend you against the Indians," coolly capped M. Radisson.

Godefroy whispered in my ear that he would not give a pin's purchase for all the furs the New

Englander would get; and Ben Gillam looked like a man whose shoe pinches. He hung his head hesitating.

" But if you run up a flag, or fire a gun, or let your people leave the island," warned M. Radisson, " I may let my men come, or tell the English, or join the Indians against you."

Gillam put out his hand.

" It's a treaty," said he.

There and then he would have been glad to see the last of us; but M. Radisson was not the man to miss the chance of seeing a rival's ship.

" How about that Canary taken from the foreign ship? A galleon, did you say, tall and slim? Did you sink her or sell her? Send down your men to my fellows! Let us go aboard for the story."

CHAPTER XI

MORE OF M. RADISSON'S RIVALS

So Ben Gillam must take M. Radisson aboard the Susan, or Garçon, as she was called when she sailed different colours, the young fellow with a wry face, the Frenchman, all gaiety. As the two leaders mounted the companion-ladder, hostages came towards the beach to join us. I had scarce noticed them when one tugged at my sleeve, and I turned to look full in the faithful shy face of little Jack Battle.

"Jack!" I shouted, but he only wrung and wrung and wrung at my hand, emitting little gurgling laughs.

Then we linked arms and walked along the beach, where others could not hear.

"Where did you come from?" I demanded.

"Master Ben fished me up on the Grand Banks. I was with the fleet. It was after he met you off the straits; and here I be, Ramsay."

"After he met us off the straits." I was trying to piece some connection between Gillam's ship and the inland assailants. "Jack, tell me! How many days have you been here?"

"Three," says Jack. "Split me fore and aft if we've been a day more!"

It was four since that night in the bush.

"You could not build a fort in three days!"

"'Twas half-built when we came."

"Who did that? Is Captain Gillam stealing the Company's furs for Ben?"

"No-o-o," drawled Jack thoughtfully, "it aren't that. It are something else, I can't make out. Master Ben keeps firing and firing and firing his guns expecting some one to answer."

"The Indians with the pelts," I suggested.

"No-o-o," answered Jack. "Split me fore and aft if it's Indians he wants! He could send up river for them. It's some one as came from his father's ship outside Boston when Master Ben sailed for the north and Captain Gillam was agoing home to England with Mistress Hortense in his ship. When no answer comes to our firing, Master Ben takes to climbing the masthead and yelling like a fog-horn and dropping curses like hail and swearing he'll shoot him as fails to keep appointment as he'd shoot a dog, if he has to track him inland a thousand leagues. Split me fore and aft if he don't!"

"Who shoot what?" I demanded, trying to extract some meaning from the jumbled narrative.

"That's what I don't know," says Jack.

I fetched a sigh of despair.

"What's the matter with your hand? Does it hurt?" he asked quickly.

Poor Jack! I looked into his faithful blue eyes. There was not a shadow of deception there—only the affection that gives without wishing to comprehend. Should I tell him of the adventure? But a loud halloo from Godefroy notified me that M. de Radisson was on the beach ready to launch.

"Almost waste work to go on fortifying," he was warning Ben.

"You forget the danger from your own crews," pleaded young Gillam.

"Pardieu! We can easily arrange that. I promise you never to approach with more than thirty of a guard." (We were twenty-nine all told.) "But remember, don't hoist a flag, don't fire, don't let your people leave the island."

Then we launched out, and I heard Ben muttering under his breath that he was cursed if he had ever known such impudence. In mid-current our leader laid his pole crosswise and laughed long.

"'Tis a pretty prize. 'Twill fetch the price of a thousand beaver-skins! Captain Gillam reckoned short when he furnished young Ben to defraud the Company. He would give a thousand pounds for my head—would he? Pardieu! He shall give five thousand pounds and leave my head where it is! And egad, if he behaves too badly, he shall pay hush-money, or the governor shall know! When we've taken him, lads, who—think you—dare complain?" And he laughed again; but at a bend in the river he turned suddenly with his eyes snapping—"Who a' deuce could that have been playing pranks in the woods the other night? Mark my words, Stanhope, whoever 'twas will prove the brains and the mainspring and the driving-wheel and the rudder of this cub's venture!"

And he began to dip in quick vigorous strokes like the thoughts ferreting through his brain. We had made bare a dozen miles when paddles clapped athwart as if petrified.

Up the wide river, like a great white bird, came a stately ship. It was the Prince Rupert of the Hudson's Bay Company, which claimed sole right to trade in all that north land.

Young Gillam, with guns mounted, to the

rear! A hostile ship, with fighting men and ordnance, to the fore! An unknown enemy inland! And for our leader a man on whose head England and New England set a price!

Do you wonder that our hearts stopped almost as suddenly as the paddles? But it was not fear that gave pause to M. Radisson.

"If those ships get together, the game is lost," says he hurriedly. "May the devil fly away with us, if we haven't wit to stop that ship!"

Act jumping with thought, he shot the canoe under cover of the wooded shore. In a twinkling we had such a fire roaring as the natives use for signals. Between the fire and the river he stationed our Indian, as hunters place a decoy.

The ruse succeeded.

Lowering sail, the Prince Rupert cast anchor opposite our fire; but darkness had gathered, and the English sent no boat ashore till morning.

Posting us against the woods, M. Radisson went forward alone to meet the company of soldiers rowing ashore. The man standing amidships, Godefroy said, was Captain Gillam, Ben's father; but the gentleman with gold-laced doublet and ruffled sleeves sitting back in the sheets was Governor Brigdar, of the Hudson's Bay

Fur Company, a courtier of Prince Rupert's choice.

The clumsy boat grounded in the shallows, and a soldier got both feet in the water to wade. Instantly M. Radisson roared out such a stentorian " Halt! " you would have thought that he had an army at his back. Indeed, that is what the party thought, for the fellow got his feet back in the boat monstrous quick. And there was a vast bandying of words, each asking other who they were, and bidding each other in no very polite terms to mind their own affairs.

Of a sudden M. Radisson wheeled to us standing guard.

" Officers," he shouted, " first brigade!—forward! "

From the manner of him we might have had an army under cover behind that bush.

All at once Governor Brigdar's lace handkerchief was aflutter at the end of a sword, and the representative of King Charles begged leave to land and salute the representative of His Most Christian Majesty, the King of France.

And land they did, pompously peaceful, though their swords clanked so oft every man must have had a hand ready at his baldrick, Pierre Radisson receiving them with the lofty air of a gracious monarch, the others bowing and unhatting and bending and crooking their spines supple as courtiers with a king.

Presently came the soldiers back to us as hostages, while Radisson stepped into the boat to go aboard the Prince Rupert with the captain and governor. Godefroy called out against such rashness, and Pierre Radisson shouted back that threat about the nippers pulling the end off the fellow's tongue.

Serving under the French flag, I was not supposed to know English; but when one soldier said he had seen " Mr. What-d'y-call-'im before," pointing at me, I recognised the mate from whom I had hired passage to England for M. Picot on Captain Gillam's ship.

" Like enough," says the other, " 'tis a land where no man brings his back history."

" See here, fellow," said I, whipping out a crown, " here's for you to tell me of the New Amsterdam gentleman who sailed from Boston last spring! "

" No New Amsterdam gentleman sailed from Boston," answered both in one breath.

" I am not paying for lies," and I returned the crown to my pocket.

Then Radisson came back, urging Captain Gillam against proceeding up the river.

"The Prince Rupert might ground on the shallows," he warned.

"That will keep them apart till we trap one or both," he told us, as we set off in our canoe.

But we had not gone out of range before we were ordered ashore. Picking our way back overland, we spied through the bush for two days, till we saw that Governor Brigdar was taking Radisson's advice, going no farther upstream, but erecting a fort on the shore where he had anchored.

"And now," said Radisson, "we must act."

While we were spying through the woods, watching the English build their fort, I thought that I saw a figure flitting through the bush to the rear. I dared not fire. One shot would have betrayed us to the English. But I pointed my gun. The thing came gliding noiselessly nearer. I clicked the gun-butt without firing. The thing paused. Then I called M. Radisson, who said it was Le Borgne, the wall-eyed Indian. Godefroy vowed 'twas a spy from Ben Gillam's fort. The Indian mumbled some superstition of a manitou. To me it seemed like a caribou; for it faded to nothing the way those fleet creatures have of skimming into distance.

CHAPTER XII

M. RADISSON BEGINS THE GAME

M. RADISSON had reckoned well. His warning to prepare for instant siege set all the young fire-eaters of our Habitation working like beavers to complete the French fort. The marquis took a hand at squaring timbers shoulder to shoulder with Allemand, the pilot; and La Chesnaye, the merchant prince, forgot to strut while digging up earthworks for a parapet. The leaven of the New World was working. Honour was for him only whose brawn won the place; and our young fellows of the birth and the pride were keenest to gird for the task.

On our return from the upper river to the fort, the palisaded walls were finished, guns were mounted on all bastions, the two ships beached under shelter of cannon, sentinels on parade at the main gate, and a long barracks built midway across the courtyard.

Here we passed many a merry hour of a long winter night, the green timbers cracking like pistol-shots to the tightening frost-grip, and the hearth logs at each end of the long, low-raftered hall sending up a roar that set the red shadows dancing among ceiling joists. After ward-room mess, with fare that kings might have envied—teal and partridge and venison and a steak of beaver's tail, and moose nose as an *entrée,* with a tidbit of buffalo hump that melted in your mouth like flakes—the commonalty, as La Chesnaye designated those who sat below the salt, would draw off to the far hearth. Here the sailors gathered close, spinning yarns, cracking jokes, popping corn, and toasting wits, a-merrier far that your kitchen cuddies of older lands. At the other hearth sat M. de Radisson, feet spread to the fire, a long pipe between his lips, and an audience of young blades eager for his tales.

"D'ye mind how we got away from the Iroquois, Chouart?" Radisson asks Groseillers, who sits in a chair rough-hewn from a stump on the other side of the fire.

Chouart Groseillers smiles quietly and strokes his black beard. Jean stretches across a bear-skin on the floor and shouts out, "Tell us! Tell us!"

"We had been captives six months. The Iroquois were beginning to let us wander about alone. Chouart there had sewed his thumb up, where an old squaw had hacked at it with a dull shell. The padre's nails, which the Indians tore off in torture, had grown well enough for him to handle a gun. One day we were allowed out to hunt. Chouart brought down three deer, the padre two moose, and I a couple of bear. That night the warriors came back from a raid on Orange with not a thing to eat but one miserable, little, thin, squealing pig. Pardieu! men, 'twas our chance; and the chance is always hiding round a corner for the man who goes ahead."

Radisson paused to whiff his pipe, all the lights in his eyes laughing and his mouth expressionless as steel.

" 'Tis an insult among Iroquois to leave food at a feast. There were we with food enough to stuff the tribe torpid as winter toads. The padre was sent round to the lodges with a tom-tom to beat every soul to the feast. Chouart and a Dutch prisoner and I cooked like kings' scullions for four mortal hours!——"

"We wanted to delay the feast till midnight," explains Groseillers.

"And at midnight in trooped every man, woman, and brat of the encampment. The padre takes a tom-tom and stands at one end of the lodge beating a very knave of a rub-a-dub and shouting at the top of his voice: 'Eat, brothers, eat! Bulge the eye, swell the coat, loose the belt! Eat, brothers, eat!' Chouart stands at the boiler ladling out joints faster than an army could gobble. Within an hour every brat lay stretched and the women were snoring asleep where they crouched. From the warriors, here a grunt, there a groan! But Chouart keeps ladling out the meat. Then the Dutchman grabs up a drum at the other end of the lodge, and begins to beat and yell: 'Stuff, brudders, stuff! Vat de gut zperets zend, gast not out! Eat, braves, eat!' And the padre cuts the capers of a fiend on coals. Still the warriors eat! Still the drums beat! Still the meat is heaped! Then, one brave bowls over asleep with his head on his knees! Another warrior tumbles back! Guards sit bolt upright sound asleep as a stone!"

"What did you put in the meat, Pierre?" asked Groseillers absently.

Radisson laughed.

"Do you mind, Chouart," he asked, "how the padre wanted to put poison in the meat, and the Dutchman wouldn't let him? Then the Dutchman wanted to murder them all in their sleep, and the padre wouldn't let him?"

Both men laughed.

"And the end?" asked Jean.

"We tied the squealing pig at the door for sentinel, broke ice with our muskets, launched the canoe, and never stopped paddling till we reached Three Rivers." *

At that comes a loud sally of laughter from the sailors at the far end of the hall. Godefroy, the English trader, is singing a rhyme of All Souls' Day, and Allemand, the French pilot, protests.

> "Soul! Soul! For a soul-cake!
> One for Peter, two for Paul,
> Three for ——."

But La Chesnaye shouts out for the knaves to hold quiet. Godefroy bobs his tipstaff, and bawls on:

> "Soul! Soul! For an apple or two!
> If you've got no apples, nuts will do!
> Out with your raisins, down with your gin!
> Give me plenty and I'll begin."

M. Radisson looks down the hall and laughs. "By the saints," says he softly, "a man loses the Christian calendar in this land! 'Tis All Souls' Night! Give the men a treat, La Chesnaye."

---

* See Radisson's own account.

But La Chesnaye, being governor, must needs show his authority, and vows to flog the knave for impudence. Turning over benches in his haste, the merchant falls on Godefroy with such largesse of cuffs that the fellow is glad to keep peace.

The door blows open, and with a gust of wind a silent figure blows in. 'Tis Le Borgne, the one-eyed, who has taken to joining our men of a merry night, which M. de Radisson encourages; for he would have all the Indians come freely.

"Ha!" says Radisson, "I thought 'twas the men I sent to spy if the marsh were safe crossing. Give Le Borgne tobacco, La Chesnaye. If once the fellow gets drunk," he adds to me in an undertone, "that silent tongue of his may wag on the interlopers. We must be stirring, stirring, Ramsay! Ten days past! Egad, a man might as well be a fish-worm burrowing underground as such a snail! We must stir—stir! See here"—drawing me to the table apart from the others—"here we are on the lower river," and he marked the letter X on a line indicating the flow of our river to the bay. "Here is the upper river," and he drew another river meeting ours at a sharp angle. "Here is Governor Brigdar of the Hudson's Bay Company," marking another X on the upper river. "Here is Ben Gillam! We are half-way between them on the south. I sent two men to see if the marsh between the rivers is fit crossing."

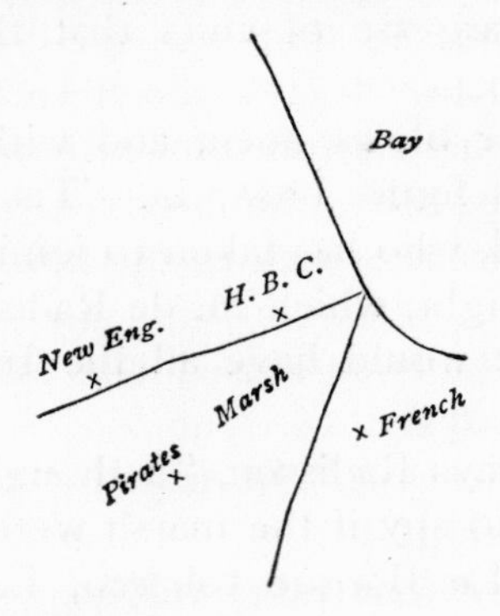

"Fit crossing?"

"When 'tis safe, we might plan a surprise. The only doubt is how many of those pirates are there who attacked you in the woods?"

And he sat back whiffing his pipe and gazing in space. By this, La Chesnaye had distributed so generous a treat that half the sailors were roaring out hilarious mirth. Godefroy astride a bench played big drum on the wrong-end-up of the cook's dish-pan. Allemand attempted to fiddle a poker across the tongs. Voyageurs tried to shoot the big canoe over a waterfall; for when Jean tilted one end of the long bench, they landed as cleanly on the floor as if their craft had plunged. But the copper-faced Le Borgne remained taciturn and tongue-tied.

"Be curse to that wall-eyed knave," muttered Radisson. "He's too deep a man to let go! We must capture him or win him!"

"Perhaps when he becomes more friendly we may track him back to the inlanders," I suggested.

M. de Radisson closed one eye and looked at me attentively.

"La Chesnaye," he called, "treat that fellow like a king!"

And the rafters rang so loud with the merriment that we none of us noticed the door flung open, nor saw two figures stamping off the snow till they had thrown a third man bound at M. de Radisson's feet. The messengers sent to spy out the marsh had returned with a half-frozen prisoner.

"We found him where the ice is soft. He was half dead," explained one scout.

Silence fell. Through the half-dark the Indian glided towards the door. The unconscious prisoner lay face down.

"Turn him over," ordered Radisson.

As our men rolled him roughly over, the

captive uttered a heavy groan. His arms fell away from his face revealing little Jack Battle, the castaway, in a haven as strange as of old.

"Search him before he wakes," commanded Radisson roughly.

"Let me," I asked.

In the pouches of the caribou coat was only pemmican; but my hand crushed against a softness in the inner waistcoat. I pulled it out—a little, old glove, the colour Hortense had dangled the day that Ben Gillam fell into the sea.

"Pish!" says Radisson. "Anything else?"

There crumpled out a yellow paper. M. Radisson snatched it up.

"Pish!" says he, "nothing—put it back!"

It was a page of my copy-book, when I used to take lessons with Rebecca. Replacing paper and glove, I closed up the sailor lad's coat.

"Search his cap and moccasins!"

I was mighty thankful, as you may guess, that other hands than mine found the tell-tale missive—a badly writ letter addressed to "Captain Zechariah Gillium."

Tearing it open, M. Radisson read with stormy lights agleam in his eyes.

"Sir, this sailor lad is an old comrade," I pleaded.

"Then'a God's name take care of him," he flashed out.

But long before I had Jack Battle thawed back to consciousness in my own quarters, Jean came running with orders for me to report to M. Radisson.

"I'll take care of the sailor for you," proffered Jean.

And I hastened to the main hall.

"Get ready," ordered Radisson. "We must stir! That young hop-o'-my-thumb suspects his father has arrived. He has sent this fellow with word of me. Things will be doing. We must stir—we must stir. Read those for news," and he handed me the letter.

The letter was addressed to Ben's father, of the Hudson's Bay ship, Prince Rupert. In writing which was scarcely legible, it ran:

> I take Up my Pen to lett You knowe that cutt-throte french viper Who deserted You at ye fort of ye bay 10 Years ago hath come here for France Threatening us.
>
> he Must Be Stopped. Will i Do It?
>
> have Bin Here Come Six weekes All Souls' day and Not Heard a Word of Him that went inland to Catch ye Furs from ye Savages before they Mett Governor B——. If He Proves False——

There the crushed missive was torn, but the purport was plain. Ben Gillam and his father were in collusion with the inland pirates to get peltries from the Indians before Governor Brigdar came; and the inlanders, whoever they were, had concealed both themselves and the furs. I handed the paper back to M. Radisson.

"We must stir, lad—we must stir," he repeated.

"But the marsh is soft yet. It is unsafe to cross."

"The river is not frozen in mid-current," retorted M. Radisson impatiently. "Get ready! I am taking different men to impress the young spark with our numbers—you and La Chesnaye and the marquis and Allemand. But where a' devil is that Indian?"

Le Borgne had slipped away.

"Is he a spy?" I asked.

"Get ready! Why do you ask questions? The thing is—to do!—do!!—do—!!!"

But Allemand, who had been hauling out the big canoe, came up sullenly.

"Sir," he complained, "the river's running ice the size of a raft, and the wind's a-blowing a gale."

"Man," retorted M. de Radisson with the quiet precision of steel, "if the river were running live fire and the gale blew from the inferno, I—would—go! Stay home and go to bed, Allemand." And he chose one of the common sailors instead.

And when we walked out to the thick edge of the shore-ice and launched the canoe among a whirling drift of ice-pans, we had small hope of ever seeing Fort Bourbon again. The ice had not the thickness of the spring jam, but it was sharp enough to cut our canoe, and we poled our way far oftener than we paddled. Where the currents of the two rivers joined, the wind had whipped the waters to a maelstrom. The night was moonless. It was well we did not see the white turmoil, else M. Radisson had had a mutiny on his hands. When the canoe leaped to the throb of the sucking currents like a cataract to the plunge, La Chesnaye clapped his pole athwart and called out a curse on such rashness. M. Radisson did not hear or did not heed. An ice-pan pitched against La Chesnaye's place, and the merchant must needs thrust out to save himself.

The only light was the white glare of ice. The only guide across that heaving traverse, the unerring instinct of that tall figure at the bow, now plunging forward, now bracing back, now shouting out a "Steady!" that the wind carried to our ears, thrusting his pole to right, to left in lightning strokes, till the canoe suddenly darted up the roaring current of the north river.

Here we could no longer stem both wind and tide. M. Radisson ordered us ashore for rest. Fourteen days were we paddling, portaging, struggling up the north river before we came in range of the Hudson's Bay fort built by Governor Brigdar.

Our proximity was heralded by a low laugh from M. de Radisson. "Look," said he, "their ship aground in mud a mile from the fort. In case of attack, their forces will be divided. It is well," said M. Radisson.

The Prince Rupert lay high on the shallows, fast bound in the freezing sands. Hiding our canoe in the woods, we came within hail and called. There was no answer.

"Drunk or scurvy," commented M. Radisson. "An faith, Ramsay, 'twould be an easy capture if we had big enough fort to hold them all!"

Shaping his hands to a trumpet, he shouted, "How are you, there?"

As we were turning away a fellow came scrambling up the fo'castle and called back: "A little better, but all asleep."

"A good time for us to examine the fort," said M. de Radisson.

Aloud, he answered that he would not disturb the crew, and he wheeled us off through the woods.

"See!" he observed, as we emerged in full view of the stockaded fur post, "palisades nailed on from the inside—easily pushed loose from the outside. Pish!—low enough for a dog to jump."

Posting us in ambush, he advanced to the main edifice behind the wide-open gate. I saw him shaking hands with the Governor of the Hudson's Bay Company, who seemed on the point of sallying out to hunt.

Then he signalled for us to come. I had almost concluded he meant to capture Governor Brigdar on the spot; but Pierre Radisson ever took friends and foes unawares.

"Your Excellency," says he, with the bow of a courtier, "this is Captain Gingras of our new ship."

Before I had gathered my wits, Governor Brigdar was shaking hands.

"And this," continued Radisson, motioning forward the common sailor too quick for surprise to betray us, "this, Your Excellency, is Colonel Bienville of our marines."

Colonel Bienville, being but a lubberly fellow, nigh choked with amazement at the English governor's warmth; but before we knew our leader's drift, the marquis and La Chesnaye were each in turn presented as commanders of our different land forces.

" 'Tis the misfortune of my staff not to speak English," explains Pierre Radisson suavely with another bow, which effectually shut any of our mouths that might have betrayed him.

" Doubtless your officers know Canary better than English," returns Governor Brigdar; and he would have us all in to drink healths.

" Keep your foot in the open door," Pierre Radisson whispered as we passed into the house.

Then we drank the health of the King of England, firing our muskets into the roof; and drank to His Most Christian Majesty of France with another volley; and drank to the confusion of our common enemies, with a clanking of gun-butts that might have alarmed the dead. Upon which Pierre Radisson protested that he would not keep Governor Brigdar from the hunt; and we took our departure.

" And now," said he, hastening through the bush, " as no one took fright at all that firing, what's to hinder examining the ship? "

" Pardieu, Ramsay," he remarked, placing us in ambush again, " an we had a big enough fort, with food to keep them alive, we might have bagged them all."

From which I hold that M. Radisson was not so black a man as he has been painted; for he could have captured the English as they lay weak of the scurvy and done to them, for the saving of fort rations, what rivals did to all foes—shot them in a land which tells no secrets.

From our place on the shore we saw him scramble to the deck. A man in red nightcap rushed forward with an oath.

"And what might you want, stealing up like a thief in the night?" roared the man.

"To offer my services, Captain Gillam," retorted Radisson with a hand to his sword-hilt and both feet planted firm on the deck.

"Services?" bawled Gillam.

"Services for your crew, captain," interrupted Radisson softly.

"Hm!" retorted Captain Gillam, pulling fiercely at his grizzled beard. "Then you might send a dozen brace o' partridges, some oil, and candles."

With that they fell to talking in lower tones; and M. Radisson came away with quiet, unspoken mirth in his eyes, leaving Captain Gillam in better mood.

"Curse me if he doesn't make those partridges an excuse to go back soon," exclaimed La Chesnaye. "The ship would be of some value; but why take the men prisoners? Much better shoot them down as they would us, an they had the chance!"

"La Chesnaye!" uttered a sharp voice. Radisson had heard. "There are two things I don't excuse a fool for—not minding his own business and not holding his tongue."

And though La Chesnaye's money paid for the enterprise, he held his tongue mighty still. Indeed, I think if any tongue had wagged twice in Radisson's hearing he would have torn the offending member out. Doing as we were bid without question, we all filed down to the canoe. Less ice cumbered the upper current, and by the next day we were opposite Ben Gillam's New England fort.

"La Chesnaye and Forêt will shoot partridges," commanded M. de Radisson. Leaving them on the far side of the river, he bade the sailor and me paddle him across to young Gillam's island.

What was our surprise to see every bastion mounted with heavy guns and the walls full manned. We took the precaution of landing under shelter of the ship and fired a musket to call out sentinels. Down ran Ben Gillam and a second officer, armed cap-a-pie, with swaggering insolence that they took no pains to conceal.

"Congratulate you on coming in the nick of time," cried Ben.

"Now what in the Old Nick does he mean by that?" said Radisson. "Does the cub think to cower me with his threats?"

"I trust your welcome includes my four officers," he responded. "Two are with me and two have gone for partridges."

Ben bellowed a jeering laugh, and his second man took the cue.

"Your four officers may be forty devils," yelled the lieutenant; "we've finished our fort. Come in, Monsieur Radisson! Two can play at the game of big talk! You're welcome in if you leave your forty officers out!"

For the space of a second M. Radisson's eyes swept the cannon pointing from the bastion embrasures. We were safe enough. The full hull of their own ship was between the guns and us.

"Young man," said M. Radisson, addressing Ben, "you may speak less haughtily, as I come in friendship."

"Friendship!" flouted Ben, twirling his mustache and showing both rows of teeth.

" Pooh, pooh, M. Radisson! You are not talking to a stripling! "

" I had thought I was—and a very fool of a booby, too," answered M. Radisson coolly.

" Sir! " roared young Gillam with a rumbling of oaths, and he fumbled his sword.

But his sword had not left the scabbard before M. de Radisson sent it spinning through mid-air into the sea.

" I must ask your forgiveness for that, boy," said the Frenchman to Ben, " but a gentleman fights only his equals."

Ben Gillam went white and red by turns, his nose flushing and paling like the wattle of an angry turkey; and he stammered out that he hoped M. de Radisson did not take umbrage at the building of a fort.

" We must protect ourselves from the English," pleaded Ben.

" Pardieu, yes," agreed M. de Radisson, proffering his own sword with a gesture in place of the one that had gone into the sea, " and I had come to offer you twenty men *to hold* the fort! "

Ben glanced questioningly to his second officer.

" Bid that fellow draw off! " ordered M. Radisson.

Dazed like a man struck between the eyes, Ben did as he was commanded.

"I told you that I came in friendship," began Radisson.

Gillam waited.

"Have you lost a man, Ben?"

"No," boldly lied Gillam.

"Has one run away from the island against orders?"

"No, devil take me, if I've lost a hand but the supercargo that I killed."

"I had thought that was yours," said Radisson, with contempt for the ruffian's boast; and he handed out the paper taken from Jack.

Ben staggered back with a great oath, vowing he would have the scalp of the traitor who lost that letter. Both stood silent, each contemplating the other. Then M. Radisson spoke.

"Ben," said he, never taking his glance from the young fellow's face, "what will you give me if I guide you to your father this afternoon? I have just come from Captain Gillam. He and his crew are ill of the scurvy. Dress as a coureur and I pass you for a Frenchman."

"My father!" cried Ben with his jaws agape and his wits at sea.

"Pardieu—yes, I said your father!"

"What do you want in return?" stammered Ben.

Radisson uttered a laugh that had the sound of sword-play.

"Egad, 'tis a hot supper I'd like better than anything else just now! If you feed us well and disguise yourself as a coureur, I'll take you at sundown!"

And in spite of his second officer's signals, Ben Gillam hailed us forthwith to the fort, where M. Radisson's keen eyes took in every feature of door and gate and sally-port and gun. While the cook was preparing our supper and Ben disguising as a French wood-runner, we wandered at will, M. Radisson all the while uttering low laughs and words as of thoughts.

It was—"Caught—neat as a mouse in a trap! Don't let him spill the canoe when we're running the traverse, Ramsay! May the fiends blast La Chesnaye if he opens his foolish mouth in Gillam's hearing! Where, think you, may we best secure him? Are the timbers of your room sound?"

Or else—"Faith, a stout timber would hold those main gates open! Egad, now, an a man were standing in this doorway, he might jam a musket in the hinge so the thing would keep open! Those guns in the bastions though—

think you those cannon are not pushed too far through the windows to be slued round quickly?"

And much more to the same purpose, which told why M. Radisson stooped to beg supper from rivals.

At sundown all was ready for departure. La Chesnaye and the marquis had come back with the partridges that were to make pretence for our quick return to the Prince Rupert. Ben Gillam had disguised as a bush-runner, and the canoe lay ready to launch. Fools and children unconsciously do wise things by mistake, as you know; and 'twas such an unwitting act sprung M. Radisson's plans and let the prize out of the trap.

"Sink me an you didn't promise the loan of twenty men to hold the fort!" exclaimed Ben, stepping down.

"Twenty—and more—and welcome," cried Radisson eagerly.

"Then send Ramsay and Monsieur La Chesnaye back," put in Ben quickly. "I like not the fort without one head while I'm away."

"Willingly," and M. Radisson's eyes glinted triumph.

"Hold a minute!" cried Ben before sitting down. "The river is rough. Let two of my men take their places in the canoe!"

M. Radisson's breath drew sharp through his teeth. But the trap was sprung, and he yielded gracefully enough to hide design.

"A curse on the blundering cub!" he muttered, drawing apart to give me instructions. "Pardieu—you must profit on this, Ramsay! Keep your eyes open. Spoil a door-lock or two! Plug the cannon if you can! Mix sand with their powder! Shift the sentinels! Get the devils insubordinate——"

"M. Radisson!" shouted Gillam.

"Coming!" says Radisson; and he went off with his teeth gritting sand.

CHAPTER XIII

THE WHITE DARKNESS

How much of those instructions we carried out I leave untold. Certainly we could not have been less grateful as guests than Ben Gillam's men were inhospitable as hosts. A more sottish crew of rakes you never saw. 'Twas gin in the morning and rum in the afternoon and vile potions of mixed poisons half the night, with a cracking of the cook's head for withholding fresh kegs and a continual scuffle of fighters over cheating at cards. No marvel the second officer flogged and carved at the knaves like an African slaver. The first night the whole crew set on us with drawn swords because we refused to gamble the doublets from our backs. La Chesnaye laid about with his sword and I with my rapier, till the cook rushed to our rescue with a kettle of lye. After that we escaped to the deck of the ship and locked ourselves inside Ben Gillam's cabin. Here we heard the weather-vanes of the fort bastions creaking for three days to the shift of fickle winds. Shore-ice grew thicker and stretched farther to mid-current. Mock suns, or sun-dogs, as we called them, oft hung on each side of the sun. La Chesnaye said these boded ill weather.

Sea-birds caught the first breath of storm and wheeled landward with shrill calls, and once La Chesnaye and I made out through the ship's glass a vast herd of caribou running to sniff the gale from the crest of an inland hill.

" If Radisson comes not back soon we are storm-bound here for the winter. As you live, we are," grumbled the merchant.

But prompt as the ring of a bell to the clapper came Pierre Radisson on the third day, well pleased with what he had done and alert to keep two of us outside the fort in spite of Ben's urgings to bring the French in for refreshments.

The wind was shifting in a way that portended a nor'easter, and the weather would presently be too inclement for us to remain outside. That hastened M. Radisson's departure, though sun-dogs and the long, shrill whistling of contrary winds foretold what was brewing.

" Sink me, after such kindness, I'll see you part way home! By the Lord Harry, I will!" swore Ben.

M. Radisson screwed his eyes nigh shut and

protested he could not permit young Captain Gillam to take such trouble.

"The young villain," mutters La Chesnaye, "he wants to spy which way we go."

"Come! Come!" cries Ben. "If you say another word I go all the way with you!"

"To spy on our fort," whispers La Chesnaye.

M. Radisson responds that nothing would give greater pleasure.

"I've half a mind to do it," hesitates Ben, looking doubtfully at us.

"To be sure," urges M. Radisson, "come along and have a Christmas with our merry blades!"

"Why, then, by the Lord, I will!" decides Gillam. "That is," he added, "if you'll send the marquis and his man, there, back to my fort as hostages."

M. Radisson twirled his mustaches thoughtfully, gave the marquis the same instructions in French as he had given us when we were left in the New Englander's fort, and turning with a calm face to Ben, bade him get into our canoe.

But when we launched out M. Radisson headed the craft up-stream in the wrong direction, whither we paddled till nightfall. It was cold enough in all conscience to afford Ben Gillam excuse for tipping a flask from his jacket-pouch to his teeth every minute or two; but when we were rested and ready to launch again, the young captain's brain was so befuddled that he scarce knew whether he were in Boston or on Hudson Bay.

This time we headed straight down-stream, Ben nodding and dozing from his place in the middle, M. Radisson, La Chesnaye, and I poling hard to keep the drift-ice off. We avoided the New Englander's fort by going on the other side of the island, and when we shot past Governor Brigdar's stockades with the lights of the Prince Rupert blinking through the dark, Ben was fast asleep.

And all the while the winds were piping overhead with a roar as from the wings of the great storm bird which broods over all that northland. Then the blore of the trumpeting wind was answered by a counter fugue from the sea, with a roll and pound of breakers across the sand of the traverse. Carried by the swift current, we had shot into the bay. It was morning, but the black of night had given place to the white darkness of northern storm. Ben Gillam jerked up sober and grasped an idle pole to lend a hand. Through the whirl of spray M. Radisson's figure loomed black at the bow, and above the boom of tumbling waves came the grinding as of an earthquake.

"We are lost! We are lost!" shrieked Gillam in panic, cowering back to the stern. "The storm's drifted down polar ice from the north and we're caught! We're caught!" he cried.

He sprang to his feet as if to leap into that white waste of seething ice foam. 'Twas the frenzy of terror, which oft seizes men adrift on ice. In another moment he would have swamped us under the pitching crest of a mountain sea. But M. Radisson turned. One blow of his pole and the foolish youth fell senseless to the bottom of the canoe.

"Look, sir, look!" screamed La Chesnaye, "the canoe's getting ice-logged! She's sunk to the gun'ales!"

But at the moment when M. Radisson turned to save young Gillam, the unguided canoe had darted between two rolling seas. Walls of ice rose on either side. A white whirl—a mighty rush—a tumult of roaring waters—the ice walls pitched down—the canoe was caught—tossed up—nipped—crushed like a card-box—and we four flung on the drenching ice-pans to a roll of the seas like to sweep us under, with a footing slippery as glass.

"Keep hold of Gillam! Lock hands!" came

a clarion voice through the storm. "Don't fear, men! There is no danger! The gale will drive us ashore! Don't fear! Hold tight! Hold tight! There's no danger if you have no fear!"

The ice heaved and flung to the roll of the drift.

"Hold fast and your wet sleeves will freeze you to the ice! Steady!" he called, as the thing fell and rose again.

Then, with the hiss of the world serpent that pursues man to his doom, we were scudding before a mountain swell. There was the splintering report of a cannon-shot. The ice split. We clung the closer. The rush of waves swept under us, around us, above us. There came a crash. The thing gave from below. The powers of darkness seemed to close over us, the jaws of the world serpent shut upon their prey, the spirit of evil shrieked its triumph.

Our feet touched bottom. The waves fell back, and we were ashore on the sand-bar of the traverse.

"Run! Run for your lives!" shouted Radisson, jerking up Gillam, whom the shock had brought to his senses. "Lock hands and run!"

And run we did, like those spirits in the twilight of the lost, with never a hope of rescue and never a respite from fear, hand gripping hand, the tide and the gale and the driving sleet yelping wolfishly at our heels! 'Twas the old, old story of Man leaping undaunted as a warrior to conquer his foes—turned back!—beaten!—pursued by serpent and wolf, spirit of darkness and power of destruction, with the light of life flickering low and the endless frosts creeping close to a heart beating faint!

Oh, those were giants that we set forth to conquer in that harsh northland—the giants of the warring elements! And giants were needed for the task.

Think you of that when you hear the slighting scorn of the rough pioneer, because he minceth not his speech, nor weareth ruffs at his wrists, nor bendeth so low at the knee as your Old-World hero!

The earth fell away from our feet. We all four tumbled forward. The storm whistled past overhead. And we lay at the bottom of a cliff that seemed to shelter a multitude of shadowy forms. We had fallen to a ravine where the vast caribou herds had wandered from the storm.

Says M. Radisson, with a depth of reverence which words cannot tell, "Men," says he, "thank God for this deliverance!"

. . . . . .

So unused to man's presence were the caribou, or perhaps so stupefied by the storm, they let us wander to the centre of the herd, round which the great bucks had formed a cordon with their backs to the wind to protect the does and the young. The heat from the multitude of bodies warmed us back to life, and I make no doubt the finding of that herd was God Almighty's provision for our safety.

For three days we wandered with nothing to eat but wild birds done to death by the gale.* On the third day the storm abated; but it was still snowing too heavily for us to see a man's length away. Two or three times the caribou tossed up their heads sniffing the air suspiciously, and La Chesnaye fell to cursing lest the wolf-pack should stampede the herd. At this Gillam, whose hulking body had wasted from lack of bulky rations, began to whimper—

"If the wolf-pack come we are lost!"

"Man," says Radisson sternly, "say thy prayers and thank God we are alive!"

The caribou began to rove aimlessly for a time, then they were off with a rush that bare gave us chance to escape the army of clicking hoofs. We were left unprotected in the falling snow.

---

* See Radisson's account—Prince Society (1885), Boston—Bodleian Library.—Canadian Archives, 1895-'96.

The primal instincts come uppermost at such times, and like the wild creatures of the woods facing a foe, instantaneously we wheeled back to back, alert for the enemy that had frightened the caribou.

"Hist!" whispers Radisson. "Look!"

Ben Gillam leaped into the air as if he had been shot, shrieking out: "It's him! It's him! Shoot him! The thief! The traitor! It's him!"

He dashed forward, followed by the rest of us, hardly sure whether Ben were sane.

Three figures loomed through the snowy darkness, white and silent as the snow itself—vague as phantoms in mist—pointing at us like wraiths of death—spirit hunters incarnate of that vast wilderness riding the riotous storm over land and sea. One swung a weapon aloft. There was the scream as of a woman's cry—and the shrieking wind had swept the snow-clouds about us in a blind fury that blotted all sight. And when the combing billows of drift passed, the apparition had faded. We four stood alone staring in space with strange questionings.

"Egad!" gasped Radisson, "I don't mind when the wind howls like a wolf, but when it takes to the death-scream, with snow like the skirts of a shroud——"

"May the Lord have mercy on us!" muttered La Chesnaye, crossing himself. "It is sign of death! That was a woman's figure. It is sign of death!"

"Sign of death!" raged Ben, stamping his impotent fury, "'tis him—'tis him! The Judas Iscariot, and he's left us to die so that he may steal the furs!"

"Hold quiet!" ordered M. Radisson. "Look, you rantipole—who is that?"

'Twas Le Borgne, the one-eyed, emerging from the gloom of the snow like a ghost. By signs and Indian words the fellow offered to guide us back to our Habitation.

We reached the fort that night, Le Borgne flitting away like a shadow, as he had come.

And the first thing we did was to hold a service of thanks to God Almighty for our deliverance.

CHAPTER XIV

A CHALLENGE

FILLING the air with ghost-shadows, silencing earth, muffling the sea, day after day fell the snow. Shore-ice barred out the pounding surf. The river had frozen to adamant. Brushwood sank in the deepening drifts like a foundered ship, and all that remained visible of evergreens was an occasional spar or snow mushroom on the crest of a branch.

No east, no west, no day, no night; nothing but a white darkness, billowing snow, and a silence as of death. It was the cold, silent, mystic, white world of northern winter.

At one moment the fort door flings wide with a rush of frost like smoke clouds, and in stamps Godefroy, shaking snow off with boisterous noise and vowing by the saints that the drifts are as high as the St. Pierre's deck. M. Groseillers orders the rascal to shut the door; but bare has the latch clicked when young Jean whisks in, tossing snow from cap and gauntlets like a clipper shaking a reef to the spray, and declares that the snow is already level with the fort walls.

"Eh, nephew," exclaims Radisson sharply, "how are the cannon?"

Ben Gillam, who has lugged himself from bed to the hearth for the first time since his freezing, blurts out a taunting laugh. We had done better to build on the sheltered side of an island, he informs us.

"Now, the shivers take me!" cries Ben, "but where a deuce are all your land forces and marines and jack-tars and forty thousand officers?"

He cast a scornful look down our long, low-roofed barracks, counting the men gathered round the hearth and laughing as he counted. M. Radisson affected not to hear, telling Jean to hoist the cannon and puncture embrasures high to the bastion-roofs like Italian towers.

"Monsieur Radisson," impudently mouths Ben, who had taken more rum for his health than was good for his head, "I asked you to inform me where your land forces are?"

"Outside the fort constructing a breast-work of snow."

"Good!" sneers Ben. "And the marines?"

"On the ships, where they ought to be."

"Good!" laughs Gillam again. "And the officers?"

"Superintending the raising of the cannon. And I would have you to know, young man," adds Radisson, "that when a guest asks too many questions, a host may not answer."

But Ben goes on unheeding.

"Now I'll wager that dog of a runaway slave o' mine, that Jack Battle who's hiding hereabouts, I'll wager the hangdog slave and pawn my head you haven't a corporal's guard o' marines and land forces all told!"

M. Radisson never allowed an enemy's taunt to hasten speech or act. He looked at Ben with a measuring glance which sized that fellow very small indeed.

"Then I must decline your wager, Ben," says he. "In the first place, Jack Battle is mine already. In the second, you would lose ten times over. In the third, you have few enough men already. And in the fourth, your head isn't worth pawn for a wager; though I may take you, body and boots, all the same," adds he.

With that he goes off, leaving Ben blowing curses into the fire like a bellows. The young rake bawled out for more gin, and with head sunk on his chest began muttering to himself—

"That black-eyed, false-hearted, slippery French eel!" he mumbles, rapping out an oath.

"Now the devil fly off with me, an I don't slit him like a Dutch herring for a traitor and a knave and a thief and a cheat! By Judas, if he doesn't turn up with the furs, I'll do to him as I did to the supercargo last week, and bury him deep in the bastion! Very fine, him that was to get the furs hiding inland! Him, that didn't add a cent to what Kirke and Stocking paid; they to supply the money, my father to keep the company from knowing, and me to sail the ship—him, that might 'a' hung in Boston but for my father towing him out o' port—him the first to turn knave and steal all the pelts!"

"Who?" quietly puts in M. Groseillers, who had been listening with wide eyes.

But Ben's head rolled drunkenly and he slid down in sodden sleep.

Again the fort door opened with the rush of frost clouds, and in the midst of the white vapour hesitated three men. The door softly closed, and Le Borgne stole forward.

"White-man — promise — no—hurt—good Indian?" he asked.

"The white-man is Le Borgne's friend," assured Groseillers, "but who are these?"

He pointed to two figures, more dead than alive, chittering with cold.

Le Borgne's foxy eye took on a stolid look.

" White-men — lost — in the snow," said he, " white-man from the big white canoe—come walkee — walkee — one — two — three sleep— watchee good Indian—friend—fort! "

M. Groseillers sprang to his feet muttering of treachery from Governor Brigdar of the Hudson's Bay Company, and put himself in front of the intruders so that Ben could not see. But the poor fellows were so frozen that they could only mumble out something about the Prince Rupert having foundered, carrying half the crew to the river bottom. Hurrying the two Englishmen to another part of the fort, M. Groseillers bade me run for Radisson.

I wish that you could have seen the triumphant glint laughing in Pierre Radisson's eyes when I told him.

" Fate deals the cards! 'Tis we must play them! This time the jade hath trumped her partner's ace! Ha, ha, Ramsay! We could 'a' captured both father and son with a flip o' the finger! Now there's only need to hold the son! Governor Brigdar must beg passage from us to leave the bay; but who a deuce are those inlanders that Ben Gillam keeps raving against for hiding the furs? "

And he flung the mess-room door open so forcibly that Ben Gillam waked with a jump. At sight of Le Borgne the young New Englander sprang over the benches with his teeth agleam and murder on his face. But the liquor had gone to his knees. He keeled head over like a top-heavy brig, and when we dragged him up Le Borgne had bolted.

All that night Ben swore deliriously that he would do worse to Le Borgne's master than he had done to the supercargo; but he never by any chance let slip who Le Borgne's master might be, though M. Radisson, Chouart Groseillers, young Jean, and I kept watch by turns lest the drunken knave should run amuck of our Frenchmen. I mind once, when M. Radisson and I were sitting quiet by the bunk where Ben was berthed, the young rake sat up with a fog-horn of a yell and swore he would slice that pirate of a Radisson and all his cursed Frenchies into meat for the dogs.

M. Radisson looked through the candle-light and smiled. "If you want to know your character, Ramsay," says he, "get your enemy talking in his cups!"

"Shiver my soul, if I'd ever come to his fort but to find out how strong the liar is!" cries Ben.

"Hm! I thought so," says M. de Radisson, pushing the young fellow back to his pillow and fastening the fur robes close lest frost steamed through the ill-chinked logs.

By Christmas Ben Gillam and Jack Battle of the New Englanders' fort and the two spies of the Hudson's Bay Company had all recovered enough from their freezing to go about. What with keeping the English and New Englanders from knowing of each other's presence, we had as twisted a piece of by-play as you could want. Ben Gillam and Jack we dressed as bushrangers; the Hudson's Bay spies as French marines. Neither suspected the others were English, nor ever crossed words while with us. And whatever enemies say of Pierre Radisson, I would have you remember that he treated his captives so well that chains would not have dragged them back to their own masters.

"How can I handle all the English of both forts unless I win some of them for friends?" he would ask, never laying unction to his soul for the kindness that he practised.

By Christmas, too, the snow had ceased falling and the frost turned the land to a silent, white, paleocrystic world. Sap-frozen timbers cracked with the loud, sharp snapping of pistol-shots—then the white silence! The river ice splintered to the tightening grip of winter with the grinding of an earthquake, and again the white silence! Or the heavy night air, lying thick with frost smoke like a pall over earth, would reverberate to the deep bayings of the wolf-pack, and over all would close the white silence!

As if to defy the powers of that deathly realm, M. de Radisson had the more logs heaped on our hearth and doubled the men's rations. On Christmas morning he had us all out to fire a salute, Ben Gillam and Jack and the two Fur Company spies disguised as usual, and the rest of us muffled to our eyes. Jackets and tompions were torn from the cannon. Unfrosted priming was distributed. Flags were run up on boats and bastions. Then the word was given to fire and cheer at the top of our voices.

Ben Gillam was sober enough that morning but in the mood of a ruffian stale from overnight brawls. Hardly had the rocking echoes of cannonading died away when the rascal strode boldly forward in front of us all, up with his musket, took quick aim at the main flagstaff and fired. The pole splintered off at the top and the French flag fluttered to the ground.

"There's for you — you Frenchies!" he shouted. "See the old rag tumble!"

'Twas the only time M. Radisson gave vent to wrath.

"Dog!" he ground out, wrenching the gun from Gillam's hands.

"Avast! Avast!" cries Ben. "He who lives in glass-houses needs not to throw stones! Mind that, ye pirate!"

"Dog!" repeats M. Radisson, "dare to show disrespect to the Most Christian of Kings!"

"Most Christian of Kings!" flouts Ben. "I'll return to my fort! Then I'll show you what I'll give the Most Christian of Kings!"

La Chesnaye rushed up with rash threat; but M. de Radisson pushed the merchant aside and stood very still, looking at Ben.

"Young man," he began, as quietly as if he were wishing Ben the season's compliments, "I brought you to this fort for the purpose of keeping you in this fort, and it is for me to say when you may leave this fort!"

Ben rumbled out a string of oaths, and M. Radisson motioned the soldiers to encircle him. Then all Ben's pot-valiant bravery ebbed.

"Am I a prisoner?" he demanded savagely.

"Prisoner or guest, according to your conduct," answered Radisson lightly. Then to the men—"Form line—march!"

At the word we filed into the guard-room,

where the soldiers relieved Gillam of pistol and sword.

"Am I to be shot? Am I to be shot?" cried Gillam, white with terror at M. Radisson's order to load muskets. "Am I to be shot?" he whimpered.

"Not unless you do it yourself, and 'twould be the most graceful act of your life, Ben! And now," said M. Radisson, dismissing all the men but one sentinel for the door, "and now, Ben, a Merry Christmas to you, and may it be your last in Hudson Bay!"

With that he left Ben Gillam prisoner; but he ordered special watch to be kept on the fort bastions lest Ben's bravado portended attack. The next morning he asked Ben to breakfast with our staff.

"The compliments of the morning to you. And I trust you rested well!" M. Radisson called out.

Ben wished that he might be cursed if any man could rest well on bare boards rimed with frost like curdled milk.

"Cheer up, man! Cheer up!" encourages Radisson. "There's to be a capture to-day!"

"A capture!" reiterates Ben, glowering black across the table and doffing his cap with bad grace.

"Aye, I said a capture! Egad, lad, one fort and one ship are prize enough for one day!"

"Sink my soul," flouts Gillam, looking insolently down the table to the rows of ragged sailors sitting beyond our officers, "if every man o' your rough-scuff had the nine lives of a cat, their nine lives would be shot down before they reached our palisades!"

"Is it a wager?" demands M. Radisson.

"A wager—ship and fort and myself to boot if you win!"

"Done!" cries La Chesnaye.

"Ah, well," calculates M. Radisson, "the ship and the fort are worth something! When we've taken them, Ben can go. Nine lives for each man, did you say?"

"A hundred, if you like," boasts the New Englander, letting fly a broadside of oaths at the Frenchman's slur. "A hundred men with nine lives, if you like! We've powder for all!"

"Ben!" M. Radisson rose. "Two men are in the fort now! Pick me out seven more! That will make nine! With those nine I own your fort by nightfall or I set you free!"

"Done!" shouts Ben. "Every man here a witness!"

"Choose!" insists M. Radisson.

Sailors and soldiers were all on their feet gesticulating and laughing; for Godefroy was translating into French as fast as the leaders talked.

"Choose!" urges M. Radisson, leaning over to snuff out the great breakfast candle with bare fingers as if his hand were iron.

"Shiver my soul, then," laughs Ben, in high feather, "let the first be that little Jack Sprat of a half-frozen Battle! He's loyal to me!"

"Good!" smiles M. Radisson. "Come over here, Jack Battle."

Jack Battle jumped over the table and stood behind M. Radisson as second lieutenant, Ben's eyes gaping to see Jack's disguise of bushranger like himself.

"Go on," orders M. Radisson, "choose whom you will!"

The soldiers broke into ringing cheers.

"Devil take you, Radisson," ejaculates Ben familiarly, "such cool impudence would chill the Nick!"

"That is as it may be," retorts Radisson. "Choose! We must be off!"

Again the soldiers cheered.

"Well, there's that turncoat of a Stanhope with his fine airs. I'd rather see him shot next than any one else!"

"Thank you, Ben," said I.

"Come over here, Ramsay," orders Radisson. "That's two. Go on! Five more!"

The soldiers fell to laughing and Ben to pulling at his mustache.

"That money-bag of a La Chesnaye next," mutters Ben. "He's lady enough to faint at first shot."

"There'll be no first shot. Come, La Chesnaye! Three. Go on! Go on, Ben! Your wits work slow!"

"Allemand, the pilot! He is drunk most of the time."

"Four," counts M. Radisson. "Come over here, Allemand! You're drunk most of the time, like Ben. Go on!"

"Godefroy, the English trader—he sulks—he's English—he'll do!"

"Five," laughs M. Radisson.

And for the remaining two, Ben Gillam chose a scullion lad and a wretched little stowaway, who had kept hidden under hatches till we were too far out to send him back. At the last choice our men shouted and clapped and stamped and broke into snatches of song about conquerors.

CHAPTER XV

THE BATTLE NOT TO THE STRONG

M. Radisson turned the sand-glass up to time our preparations. Before the last grain fell we seven were out, led by M. Radisson, speeding over the snow-drifted marsh through the thick frosty darkness that lies like a blanket over that northland at dawn. The air hung heavy, gray, gritty to the touch with ice-frost. The hard-packed drifts crisped to our tread with little noises which I can call by no other name than frost-shots. Frost pricked the taste to each breath. Endless reaches of frost were all that met the sight. Frost-crackling the only sound. Frost in one's throat like a drink of water, and the tingle of the frost in the blood with a leap that was fulness of life.

Up drifts with the help of our muskets! Down hills with a rush of snow-shoes that set the powdery snow flying! Skimming the levels with the silent speed of wings! Past the snow mushrooms topping underbrush and the snow cones of the evergreens and the snow billows of under rocks and the snow-wreathed antlers of the naked forest in a world of snow!

The morning stars paled to steel pin-pricks through a gray sky. Shadows took form in the frost. The slant rays of a southern sun struck through the frost clouds in spears. Then the frost smoke rose like mist, and the white glare shone as a sea. In another hour it would be high noon of the short shadow. Every coat—beaver and bear and otter and raccoon—hung open, every capote flung back, every runner hot as in midsummer, though frost-rime edged the hair like snow. When the sun lay like a fiery shield half-way across the southern horizon, M. Radisson called a halt for nooning.

"Now, remember, my brave lads," said he, after he had outlined his plans, drawing figures of fort and ship and army of seven on the snow, "now, remember, if you do what I've told you, not a shot will be fired, not a drop of blood spilled, not a grain of powder used, and to every man free tobacco for the winter——"

"If we succeed," interjects Godefroy sullenly.

"*If*," repeats M. Radisson; "an I hear that word again there will be a carving!"

Long before we came to the north river near

the Hudson's Bay Company's fort, the sun had wheeled across the horizon and sunk in a sea of snow, but now that the Prince Rupert had foundered, the capture of these helpless Englishmen was no object to us. Unless a ship from the south end of the bay came to rescue them they were at our mercy. Hastening up the river course we met Governor Brigdar sledding the ice with a dog-team of huskies.

"The compliments of the season to Your Excellency!" shouted Radisson across the snow.

"The same to the representative of France," returned Governor Brigdar, trying to get away before questions could be asked.

"I don't see your ship," called Radisson.

"Four leagues down the river," explained the governor.

"*Under* the river," retorted Radisson, affecting not to hear.

"No—down the river," and the governor whisked round a bluff out of call.

The gray night shadows gathered against the woods. Stars seeded the sky overhead till the whole heavens were aglow. And the northern lights shot their arrowy jets of fire above the pole, rippled in billows of flame, scintillated with the faint rustling of a flag in a gale, or swung midway between heaven and earth like censers to the invisible God of that cold, far, northern world.

Then the bastions of Ben Gillam's fort loomed above the wastes like the peak of a ship at sea, and M. Radisson issued his last commands. Godefroy and I were to approach the main gate. M. Radisson and his five men would make a detour to attack from the rear.

A black flag waved above the ship to signal those inland pirates whom Ben Gillam was ever cursing, and the main gates stood wide ajar. Half a mile away Godefroy hallooed aloud. A dozen New Englanders, led by the lieutenant, ran to meet us.

"Where is Master Ben?" demanded the leader.

"Le capitaine," answered Godefroy, affecting broken English, "le capitaine, he is fatigue. He is back—voilá—how you for speak it?—avec, monsieur! Le capitaine, he has need, he has want for you to go with food."

At that, with a deal of unguarded gabbling, they must hail us inside for refreshments, while half a dozen men ran in the direction Godefroy pointed with the food for their master. No sooner were their backs turned than Godefroy whispers instructions to the marquis and his man, who had been left as hostages. Forêt strolled casually across to the guard-room, where the powder was stored. Here he posted himself in the doorway with his sword jammed above the hinge. His man made a precipitate rush to heap fires for our refreshment, dropping three logs across the fort gates and two more athwart the door of the house. Godefroy and I, on pretext of scanning out the returning travellers, ran one to the nigh bastion, the other to the fore-deck of the ship, where was a swivel cannon that might have done damage.

Then Godefroy whistled.

Like wolves out of the earth rose M. Radisson and his five men from the shore near the gates. They were in possession before the lieutenant and his men had returned. On the instant when the surprised New Englanders ran up, Radisson bolted the gates.

"Where is my master?" thundered the lieutenant, beating for admission.

"Come in." M. Radisson cautiously opened the gate, admitting the lieutenant alone.

"It is not a question of where your master is, but of mustering your men and calling the roll," said the Frenchman to the astounded lieutenant. "You see that my people are in control of your powder-house, your cannon, and your ship. Your master is a prisoner in my fort. Now summon your men, and be glad Ben Gillam is not here to kill more of you as he killed your supercargo!"

Half an hour from the time we had entered the fort, keys, arms, and ammunition were in M. de Radisson's hands without the firing of a shot, and the unarmed New Englanders assigned to the main building, where we could lock them if they mutinied. To sound of trumpet and drum, with Godefroy bobbing his tipstaff, M. Radisson must needs run up the French flag in place of the pirate ensign. Then, with the lieutenant and two New Englanders to witness capitulation, he marched from the gates to do the same with the ship. Allemand and Godefroy kept sentinel duty at the gates. La Chesnaye, Forêt, and Jack Battle held the bastions, and the rest stood guard in front of the main building.

From my place I saw how it happened.

The lieutenant stepped back to let M. de Radisson pass up the ship's ladder first. The New Englanders followed, the lieutenant still waiting at the bottom step; and when M. Radisson's back was turned the lieutenant darted down the river bank in the direction of Governor Brigdar's fort.

The flag went up and M. Radisson looked back to witness the salute. Then he discovered the lieutenant's flight. The New Englanders' purpose was easily guessed—to lock forces with Governor Brigdar, and while our strength was divided attack us here or at the Habitation.

"One fight at a time," says Radisson, summoning to council in the powder-house all hands but our guard at the gate. "You, Allemand and Godefroy, will cross the marsh to-night, bidding Chouart be ready for attack and send back re-enforcements here! You two lads"—pointing to the stowaway and scullion—"will boil down bears' grease and porpoise fat for a half a hundred cressets! Cut up all the brooms in the fort! Use pine-boughs! Split the green wood and slip in oiled rags! Have a hundred lights ready by ten of the clock! Go—make haste, or I throw you both into the pot!

"You, Forêt and La Chesnaye, transfer all the New Englanders to the hold of the ship and batten them under! If there's to be fighting, let the enemies be outside the walls. And you, Ramsay, will keep guard at the river bastion all night! And you, Jack Battle, will gather all the hats and helmets and caps in the fort, and divide them equally between the two front bastions——"

"Hats and helmets?" interrupts La Chesnaye.

"La Chesnaye," says M. Radisson, whirling, "an any one would question me this night he had best pull his tongue out with the tongs! Go, all of you!"

But Godefroy, ever a dour-headed knave, must test the steel of M. de Radisson's mood.

"D'ye mean me an' the pilot to risk crossing the marsh by night——"

But he got no farther. M. de Radisson was upon him with a cudgel like a flail on wheat.

"An you think it risk to go, I'll make it greater risk to stay! An you fear to obey, I'll make you fear more to disobey! An you shirk the pain of toeing the scratch, I'll make it a deal more painful to lag behind!"

"But at night—at night," roared Godefroy between blows.

"The night—knave," hissed out Radisson, "the night is lighter than morning with the north light. The night"—this with a last drive —"the night is same as day to man of spirit! 'Tis the sort of encouragement half the world needs to succeed," said M. Radisson, throwing down the cudgel.

And Godefroy, the skulker, was glad to run for the marsh. The rest of us waited no urgings, but were to our posts on the run.

I saw M. Radisson passing fife, piccolo, trumpet, and drum to the two tatterdemalion lads of our army.

"Now blow like fiends when I give the word," said he.

Across the courtyard, single file, marched the New Englanders from barracks to boat, La Chesnaye leading with drawn sword, the marquis following with pointed musket.

Forêt and La Chesnaye then mounted guard at the gate. The sailor of our company was heaping cannon-balls ready for use. Jack Battle scoured the fort for odd headgear. M. de Radisson was everywhere, seizing papers, burying ammunition, making fast loose stockades, putting extra rivets in hinges, and issuing quick orders that sent Jack Battle skipping to the word. Then Jack was set to planting double rows of sticks inside on a level with the wall. The purpose of these I could not guess till M. Radisson ordered hat, helmet, or cap clapped atop of each pole.

Oh, we were a formidable army, I warrant you, seen by any one mounting the drift to spy across our walls!

But 'twas no burlesque that night, as you may know when I tell you that Governor Brigdar's forces played us such a trick they were under shelter of the ship before we had discovered them.

Forêt and La Chesnaye were watching from loopholes at the gates, and I was all alert from my place in the bastion. The northern lights waved overhead in a restless ocean of rose-tinted fire. Against the blue, stars were aglint with the twinkle of a million harbour lights. Below, lay the frost mist, white as foam, diaphanous as a veil, every floating icy particle aglimmer with star rays like spray in sunlight. Through the night air came the far howlings of the running wolf-pack. The little ermine, darting across the level with its black tail-tip marking the snow in dots and dashes, would sit up quickly, listen and dive under, to wriggle forward like a snake; or the black-eyed hare would scurry off to cover of brushwood.

Of a sudden sounded such a yelling from the New Englanders imprisoned in the ship, with a beating of guns on the keel, that I gave quick alarm. Forêt and La Chesnaye sallied from the gate. Pistol-shots rang out as they rounded the ship's prow into shadow. At the same instant, a man flung forward out of the frost cloud beating for admittance. M. de Radisson opened.

"The Indians! The Indians! Where are

the New Englanders?" cried the man, pitching headlong in.

And when he regained his feet, Governor Brigdar, of the Hudson's Bay Company, stood face to face with M. de Radisson.

"A right warm welcome, Your Excellency," bowed M. de Radisson, bolting the gate. "The New Englanders are in safe keeping, sir, and so are you!"

The bewildered governor gasped at M. Radisson's words. Then he lost all command of himself.

"Radisson, man," he stormed, "this is no feint—this is no time for acting! Six o' my men shot on the way—four hiding by the ship and the Indians not a hundred yards behind! Take my sword and pistol," he proffered, M. de Radisson still hesitating, "but as you hope for eternal mercy, call in my four men!"

After that, all was confusion.

Forêt and the marquis rushed pell-mell for the fort with four terrified Englishmen disarmed. The gates were clapped to. Myriad figures darted from the frost mist—figures with war-paint on their faces and bodies clothed in white to disguise approach. English and French, enemies all, crouched to the palisades against the common foe, with sword-thrust for the hands catching at pickets to scale the wall and volleying shots that scattered assailants back. The redskins were now plainly visible through the frost. When they swerved away from shelter of the ship, every bastion let go the roar of a cannon discharge. There was the sudden silence of a drawing off, then the shrill "Ah—o-o-o-oh! Ah—o-o-o-oh! Ah—o-o-o-oh!" of Indian war-cry!

And M. Radisson gave the signal.

Instantaneously half a hundred lights were aflare. Red tongues of fire darted from the loopholes. Two lads were obeying our leader's call to run—run—run, blowing fife, beating drum like an army's band, while streams of boiling grease poured down from bastions and lookout. Helmets, hats, and caps sticking round on the poles were lighted up like the heads of a battalion; and oft as any of us showed himself he displayed fresh cap. One Indian, I mind, got a stockade off and an arm inside the wall. That arm was never withdrawn, for M. Radisson's broadsword came down, and the Indian reeled back with a yelping scream. Then the smoke cleared, and I saw what will stay with me as long as memory lasts—M. Radisson, target for arrows or shot, long hair flying and red doublet alight in the flare of the torches, was standing on top of the pickets with his right arm waving a sword.

"Whom do you make them out to be, Ramsay?" he called. "Is not yon Le Borgne?"

I looked to the Indians. Le Borgne it was, thin and straight, like a mast-pole through mist, in conference with another man—a man with a beard, a man who was no Indian.

"Sir!" I shouted back. "Those are the inland pirates. They are leading the Indians against Ben Gillam, and not against us at all."

At that M. Radisson extends a handkerchief on the end of his sword as flag of truce, and the bearded man waves back. Down from the wall jumps M. Radisson, running forward fearlessly where Indians lay wounded, and waving for the enemy to come. But the two only waved back in friendly fashion, wheeled their forces off, and disappeared through the frost.

"Those were Ben Gillam's cut-throats trying to do for him! When they saw us on the walls, they knew their mistake," says M. de Radisson as he re-entered the gate. "There's only one way to find those pirates out, Ramsay. Nurse these wounded Indians back to life, visit the tribe, and watch! After Chouart's re-enforcements come, I'll send you and Jack Battle, with Godefroy for interpreter!"

To Governor Brigdar and his four refugees M. de Radisson was all courtesy.

"And how comes Your Excellency to be out so late with ten men?" he asked, as we supped that night.

"We heard that you were here. We were coming to visit you," stammered Governor Brigdar, growing red.

"Then let us make you so welcome that you will not hasten away! Here, Jack Battle, here, fellow, stack these gentlemen's swords and pistols where they'll come to no harm! Ah! No? But I must relieve you, gentlemen! Your coming was a miracle. I thank you for it. It has saved us much trouble. A pledge to the pleasure—and the length—of your stay, gentlemen," and they stand to the toast, M. de Radisson smiling at the lights in his wine.

But we all knew very well what such welcome meant. 'Twas Radisson's humour to play the host that night, but the runaway lieutenant was a prisoner in our guard-house.

CHAPTER XVI

WE SEEK THE INLANDERS

In the matter of fighting, I find small difference between white-men and red. Let the lust of conquest but burn, the justice of the quarrel receives small thought. Your fire-eating prophet cares little for the right of the cause, provided the fighter come out conqueror; and many a poet praises only that right which is might over-trampling weakness. I have heard the withered hag of an Indian camp chant as spirited war-song as your minstrels of butchery; but the strange thing of it is, that the people, who have taken the sword in a wantonness of conquest, are the races that have been swept from the face of the earth like dead leaves before the winter blast; but the people, who have held immutably by the power of right, which our Lord Christ set up, the meek and the peacemakers and the children of God, these are they that inherit the earth.

Where are the tribes with whom Godefroy and Jack Battle and I wandered in nomadic life over the northern wastes? Buried in oblivion black as night, but for the lurid memories flashed down to you of later generations. Where are the Puritan folk, with their cast-iron, narrow creeds damning all creation but themselves, with their foibles of snivelling to attest sanctity, with such a wolfish zeal to hound down devils that they hounded innocents for witchcraft? Spreading over the face of the New World, making the desert to bloom and the waste places fruitful gardens? And the reason for it all is simply this: Your butchering Indian, like your swashing cavalier, founded his *right* upon *might*; your Puritan, grim but faithful, to the outermost bounds of his tragic errors, founded his *might* upon *right*.

We learn our hardest lessons from unlikeliest masters. This one came to me from the Indians of the blood-dyed northern snows.

. . . . . .

"Don't show your faces till you have something to report about those pirates, who led the Indians," was M. Radisson's last command, as we sallied from the New Englanders' fort with a firing of cannon and beating of drums.

Godefroy, the trader, muttered under his breath that M. Radisson need never fear eternal torment.

"Why?" I asked.

"Because, if he goes *there*," answered Godefroy, "he'll get the better o' the Nick."

I think the fellow was smarting from recent punishment. He and Allemand, the drunken pilot, had been draining gin kegs on the sly and replacing what they took with snow water. That last morning at prayers Godefroy, who was half-seas over, must yelp out a loud "Amen" in the wrong place. Without rising from his knees, or as much as changing his tone, M. de Radisson brought the drunken knave such a cuff it flattened him to the floor.

Then prayers went on as before.

The Indians, whom we had nursed of their wounds, were to lead us to the tribe, one only being held by M. Radisson as hostage for safe conduct. In my mind, that trust to the Indians' honour was the single mistake M. Radisson made in the winter's campaign. In the first place, the Indian has no honour. Why should he have, when his only standard of right is conquest? In the second place, kindness is regarded as weakness by the Indian. Why should it not be, when his only god is victory? In the third place, the lust of blood, to kill, to butcher, to mutilate, still surged as hot in their veins as on the night when they had attempted to scale our walls. And again I ask why not, when the law of their life was to kill or to be killed? These questions I put to you because life put them to me. At the time my father died, the gentlemen of King Charles's court were already affecting that refinement of philosophy which justifies despotism. From justifying despotism, 'twas but a step to justifying the wicked acts of tyranny; and from that, but another step to thrusting God's laws aside as too obsolete for our clever courtiers. "Give your unbroken colt tether enough to pull itself up with one sharp fall," M. Radisson used to say, "and it will never run to the end of its line again."

The mind of Europe spun the tissue of foolish philosophy. The savage of the wilderness went the full tether; and I leave you to judge whether the *might* that is *right* or the *right* that is *might* be the better creed for a people.

But I do not mean to imply that M. Radisson did not understand the savages better than any man of us in the fort. He risked three men as pawns in the game he was playing for mastery of the fur trade. Gamester of the wilderness as he was, Pierre Radisson was not the man to court a certain loss.

The Indians led us to the lodges of the hostiles safely enough; and their return gave us entrance if not welcome to the tepee village. We had entered a ravine and came on a cluster of wigwams to the lee side of a bluff. Dusk hid our approach; and the absence of the dogs that usually infest Indian camps told us that these fellows were marauders. Smoke curled up from the poles crisscrossed at the tepee forks, but we could descry no figures against the tent-walls as in summer, for heavy skins of the chase overlaid the parchment. All was silence but in one wigwam. This was an enormous structure, built on poles long as a mast, with moose-hides scattered so thickly upon it that not a glint of firelight came through except the red glow of smoke at the peak. There was a low hum of suppressed voices, then one voice alone in solemn tones, then guttural grunts of applause.

"In council," whispered Godefroy, steering straight for the bearskin that hung flapping across the entrance.

Bidding Jack Battle stand guard outside, we followed the Indians who had led us from the fort. Lifting the tent-flap, we found ourselves inside. A withered creature with snaky, tangled hair, toothless gums, eyes that burned like embers, and a haunched, shrivelled figure, stood gesticulating and crooning over a low monotone in the centre of the lodge.

As we entered, the draught from the door sent a tongue of flame darting to mid-air from the central fire, and scores of tawny faces with glance intent on the speaker were etched against the dark. These were no camp families, but braves, deep in war council. The elder men sat with crossed feet to the fore of the circle. The young braves were behind, kneeling, standing, and stretched full length. All were smoking their long-stemmed pipes and listening to the medicine-man, or seer, who was crooning his low-toned chant. The air was black with smoke.

Always audacious, Godefroy, the trader, advanced boldly and sat down in the circle. I kept back in shadow, for directly behind the Indian wizard was a figure lying face downward, chin resting in hand, which somehow reminded me of Le Borgne. The fellow rolled lazily over, got to his knees, and stood up. Pushing the wizard aside, this Indian faced the audience. It *was* Le Borgne, his foxy eye yellow as flame, teeth snapping, and a tongue running at such a pace that we could scarce make out a word of his jargon.

"What does he say, Godefroy?"

"Sit down," whispered the trader, "you are safe."

This was what the Indian was saying as Godefroy muttered it over to me:

"Were the Indians fools and dogs to throw away two fish for the sake of one? The French were friends of the Indians. Let the Indians find out what the French would give them for killing the English. He, Le Borgne, the one-eyed, was brave. He would go to the Frenchman's fort and spy out how strong they were. If the French gave them muskets for killing the English, after the ships left in the spring the Indians could attack the fort and kill the French. The great medicine-man, the white hunter, who lived under the earth, would supply them with muskets——"

"He says the white hunter who lives under the earth is giving them muskets to make war," whispered Godefroy. "That must be the pirate."

"Listen!"

"Let the braves prepare to meet the Indians of the Land of Little White Sticks, who were coming with furs for the white men—" Le Borgne went on.

"Let the braves send their runners over the hills to the Little White Sticks sleeping in the sheltered valley. Let the braves creep through the mist of the morning like the lynx seeking the ermine. And when the Little White Sticks were all asleep, the runners would shoot fire arrows into the air and the braves would slay—slay—slay the men, who might fight, the women, who might run to the whites for aid, and the children, who might live to tell tales."

"The devils!" says Godefroy under his breath.

A log broke on the coals with a flare that painted Le Borgne's evil face fiery red; and the fellow gabbled on, with figure crouching stealthily forward, foxy eye alight with evil, and teeth glistening.

"Let the braves seize the furs of the Little White Sticks, trade the furs to the white-man for muskets, massacre the English, then when the great white chief's big canoes left, kill the Frenchmen of the fort."

"Ha," says Godefroy. "Jack's safe outside! We'll have a care to serve you through the loopholes, and trade you only broken muskets!"

A guttural grunt applauded Le Borgne's advice, and the crafty scoundrel continued:

"The great medicine-man, the white hunter, who lived under the earth, was their friend. Was he not here among them? Let the braves hear what he advised."

The Indians grunted their approbation.

Some one stirred the fire to flame. There was a shuffling movement among the figures in the dark. Involuntarily Godefroy and I had risen to our feet. Emerging from the dusk to the firelight was a white man, gaudily clothed in tunic of scarlet with steel breastplates and gold lace enough for an ambassador. His face was hidden by Le Borgne's form. Godefroy pushed too far forward; for the next thing, a shout of rage rent the tent roof. Le Borgne was stamping out the fire. A red form with averted face raced round the lodge wall to gain the door. Then Godefroy and I were standing weapons in hand, with the band of infuriated braves brandishing tomahawks about our heads. Le Borgne broke through the circle and confronted us with his face agleam.

"Le Borgne, you rascal, is this a way to treat your friends?" I demanded.

"What you—come for?" slowly snarled Le Borgne through set teeth.

"To bring back your wounded and for furs, you fool," cried Godefroy, "and if you don't call your braves off, you can sell no more pelts to the French."

Le Borgne gabbled out something that drove the braves back.

"We have no furs yet," said he.

" But you will have them when you raid the Little White Sticks," raged Godefroy, caring nothing for the harm his words might work if he saved his own scalp.

Le Borgne drew off to confer with the braves. Then he came back and there was a treacherous smile of welcome on his bronze face.

" The Indians thought the white-men spies from the Little White Sticks," he explained in the mellow, rhythmic tones of the redman. " The Indians were in war council. The Indians are friends of the French."

" Look out for him, Godefroy," said I.

" If the French are friends to the Indians, let the white-men come to battle against the Little White Sticks," added Le Borgne.

" Tell him no! We'll wait here till they come back! "

" He says they are not coming back," answered Godefroy, " and hang me, Ramsay, an I'd not face an Indian massacre before I go back empty-handed to M. Radisson. We're in for it," says he, speaking English too quick for Le Borgne's ear. " If we show the white feather now, they'll finish us. They'll not harm us till they've done for the English and got more muskets. And that red pirate is after these same furs! Body o' me, an you hang back, scared o' battle, you'd best not come to the wilderness."

"The white-men will go with the Indians, but the white-men will not fight with the Little Sticks," announced Godefroy to Le Borgne, proffering tobacco enough to pacify the tribe.

'Twas in vain that I expostulated against the risk of going far inland with hostiles, who had attacked the New England fort and were even now planning the slaughter of white-men. Inoffensiveness is the most deadly of offences with savagery, whether the savagery be of white men or red. Le Borgne had the insolence to ask why the tribe could not as easily kill us where we were as farther inland; and we saw that remonstrances were working the evil that we wished to avoid—increasing the Indians' daring. After all, Godefroy was right. The man who fears death should neither go to the wilderness nor launch his canoe above a whirlpool unless he is prepared to run the rapids. This New World had never been won from darkness if men had hung back from fear of spilt blood.

'Twas but a moment's work for the braves to deck out in war-gear. Faces were blackened with red streaks typifying wounds; bodies clad in caribou skins or ermine-pelts white as the snow to be crossed; quivers of barbed and poisonous arrows hanging over their backs in otter and beaver skins; powder in buffalo-horns for those who had muskets; shields of toughened hide on one arm, and such a number of scalp-locks fringing every seam as told their own story of murderous foray. While the land still smoked under morning frost and the stars yet pricked through the gray darkness, the warriors were far afield coasting the snow-billows as on tireless wings. Up the swelling drifts water-waved by wind like a rolling sea, down cliffs crumbling over with snowy cornices, across the icy marshes swept glare by the gales, the braves pressed relentlessly on. Godefroy, Jack Battle, and I would have hung to the rear and slipped away if we could; but the fate of an old man was warning enough. Muttering against the braves for embroiling themselves in war without cause, he fell away from the marauders as if to leave. Le Borgne's foxy eye saw the move. Turning, he rushed at the old man with a hiss of air through his teeth like a whistling arrow. His musket swung up. It clubbed down. There was a groan; and as we rounded a bluff at a pace that brought the air cutting in our faces, I saw the old man's body lying motionless on the snow.

If this was the beginning, what was the end? Godefroy vowed that the man was only an Indian, and his death was no sin.

" The wolves would 'a' picked his bones soon anyway. He wore a score o' scalps at his belt. Pah, an we could get furs without any Indians, I'd see all their skulls go! " snapped the trader.

" If killing's no murder, whose turn comes next? " asked Jack.

And that gave Godefroy pause.

CHAPTER XVII

A BOOTLESS SACRIFICE

For what I now tell I offer no excuse. I would but record what savagery meant. Then may you who are descended from the New World pioneers know that your lineage is from men as heroic as those crusaders who rescued our Saviour's grave from the pagans; for crusaders of Old World and New carried the sword of destruction in one hand, but in the other, a cross that was light in darkness. Then may you, my lady-fingered sentimentalist, who go to bed of a winter night with a warming-pan and champion the rights of the savage from your soft place among cushions, realize what a fine hero your redman was, and realize, too, what were the powers that the white-man crushed!

For what I do not tell I offer no excuse. It is not permitted to relate *all* that savage warfare meant. Once I marvelled that a just God could order his chosen people to exterminate any race. Now I marvel that a just God hath not exterminated many races long ago.

We reached the crest of a swelling upland as the first sun-rays came through the frost mist in shafts of fire. A quick halt was called. One white-garbed scout went crawling stealthily down the snow-slope like a mountain-cat. Then the frost thinned to the rising sun and vague outlines of tepee lodges could be descried in the clouded valley.

An arrow whistled through the air glancing into snow with a soft whirr at our feet. It was the signal. As with one thought, the warriors charged down the hill, leaping from side to side in a frenzy, dancing in a madness of slaughter, shrieking their long, shrill—" Ah—oh!—Ah—oh!"—yelping, howling, screaming their war-cry—" Ah—oh!—Ah—oh!—Ah—oh ! " — like demons incarnate. The medicine - man had stripped himself naked and was tossing his arms with maniacal fury, leaping up and down, yelling the war-cry, beating the tom-tom, rattling the death-gourd. Some of the warriors went down on hands and feet, sidling forward through the mist like the stealthy beasts of prey that they were.

Godefroy, Jack Battle, and I were carried before the charge helpless as leaves in a hurricane.

All slid down the hillside to the bottom of a ravine. With the long bound of a tiger-spring, Le Borgne plunged through the frost cloud.

The lodges of the victims were about us. We had evidently come upon the tribe when all were asleep.

Then that dark under-world of which men dream in wild delirium became reality. Pandemonium broke its bounds.

. . . . .

And had I once thought that Eli Kirke's fanatic faith painted too lurid a hell? God knows if the realm of darkness be half as hideous as the deeds of this life, 'tis blacker than prophet may portray.

Day or night, after fifty years, do I close my eyes to shut the memory out! But the shafts are still hurlting through the gray gloom. Arrows rip against the skin shields. Running fugitives fall pierced. Men rush from their lodges in the daze of sleep and fight barehanded against musket and battle-axe and lance till the snows are red and scalps steaming from the belts of conquerors. Women fall to the feet of the victors, kneeling, crouching, dumbly pleading for mercy; and the mercy is a spear-thrust that pinions the living body to earth. Maimed, helpless and living victims are thrown aside to await slow death. Children are torn from their mothers' arms—but there—memory revolts and the pen fails!

It was in vain for us to flee. Turn where we would, pursued and pursuer were there.

"Don't flinch! Don't flinch!" Godefroy kept shouting. "They'll take it for fear! They'll kill you by torture!"

Almost on the words a bowstring twanged to the fore and a young girl stumbled across Jack Battle's feet with a scream that rings, and rings, and rings in memory like the tocsin of a horrible dream. She was wounded in the shoulder. Getting to her knees she threw her arms round Jack with such a terrified look of helpless pleading in her great eyes as would have moved stone.

"Don't touch her! Don't touch her! Don't touch her!" screamed Godefroy, jerking to pull Jack free. "It will do no good! Don't help her! They'll kill you both——"

"Great God!" sobbed Jack, with shivering horror, "I can't help helping her——"

But there leaped from the mist a figure with uplifted spear.

May God forgive it, but I struck that man dead!

It was a bootless sacrifice at the risk of three

lives. But so was Christ's a bootless sacrifice at the time, if you measure deeds by gain. And so has every sacrifice worthy of the name been a bootless sacrifice, if you stop to weigh life in a goldsmith's scale!

Justice is blind; but praise be to God, so is mercy!

And, indeed, I have but quoted our Lord and Saviour, not as an example, but as a precedent. For the act I merited no credit. Like Jack, I could not have helped helping her. The act was out before the thought.

Then we were back to back fighting a horde of demons.

Godefroy fought cursing our souls to all eternity for embroiling him in peril. Jack Battle fought mumbling feverishly, deliriously, unconscious of how he shot or what he said—"Might as well die here as elsewhere! Might as well die here as elsewhere! Damn that Indian! Give it to him, Ramsay! You shoot while I prime! Might as well die here as elsewhere——"

And all fought resolute to die hard, when, where, or how the dying came!

To that desperate game there was but one possible end. It is only in story-books writ for sentimental maids that the good who are weak defeat the wicked who are strong. We shattered many an assailant before the last stake was dared, but in the end they shattered my sword-arm, which left me helpless as a hull at ebb-tide. Then Godefroy, the craven rascal, must throw up his arms for surrender, which gave Le Borgne opening to bring down the butt of his gun on Jack's crown.

The poor sailor went bundling over the snow like a shot rabbit.

When the frost smoke cleared, there was such a scene as I may not paint; for you must know that your Indian hero is not content to kill. Like the ghoul, he must mutilate. Of all the Indian band attacked by our forces, not one escaped except the girl, whose form I could descry nowhere on the stained snow.

Jack Battle presently regained his senses and staggered up to have his arms thonged behind his back. The thongs on my arms they tightened with a stick through the loop to extort cry of pain as the sinew cut into the shattered wrist. An the smile had cost my last breath, I would have defied their tortures with a laugh. They got no cry from me. Godefroy, the trader, cursed us in one breath and in the next threatened that the Indians would keep us for torture.

"You are the only man who can speak their language," I retorted. "Stop whimpering and warn these brutes what Radisson will do if they harm us! He will neither take their furs nor give them muskets! He will arm their enemies to destroy them! Tell them that!"

But as well talk to tigers. Le Borgne alone listened, his foxy glance fastened on my face with a strange, watchful look, neither hostile nor friendly. To Godefroy's threats the Indian answered that "white-man talk—not true—of all," pointing to Jack Battle, "him no friend great white chief—him captive——"

Then Godefroy burst out with the unworthiest answer that ever passed man's lips.

"Of course he's a captive," screamed the trader, "then take him and torture him and let us go! 'Twas him stopped the Indian getting the girl!"

"Le Borgne," I cut in sharply, "Le Borgne, it was I who stopped the Indian killing the girl! You need not torture the little white-man. He is a good man. He is the friend of the great white chief."

But Le Borgne showed no interest. While the others stripped the dead and wreaked their ghoulish work, Le Borgne gathered up the furs of the Little Sticks and with two or three young men stole away over the crest of the hill.

Then the hostiles left the dead and the half-dead for the wolves.

Prodded forward by lance-thrusts, we began the weary march back to the lodges. The sun sank on the snowy wastes red as a shield of blood; and with the early dusk of the northern night purpling the shadowy fields in mist came a south wind that filled the desolate silence with restless wailings as of lament for eternal wrong, moaning and sighing and rustling past like invisible spirits that find no peace.

Some of the Indians laid hands to thin lips with a low "Hs-s-h," and the whole band quickened pace. Before twilight had deepened to the dark that precedes the silver glow of the moon and stars and northern lights, we were back where Le Borgne had killed the old man. The very snow had been picked clean, and through the purple gloom far back prowled vague forms.

Jack Battle and I looked at each other, but the Indian fellow, who was our guard, emitted a harsh, rasping laugh. As for Godefroy, he was marching abreast of the braves gabbling a mumble-jumble of pleadings and threats, which, I know very well, ignored poor Jack. Godefroy would make a scapegoat of the weak to save his own neck, and small good his cowardice did him!

The moon was high in mid-heaven flooding a white world when we reached the lodges. We three were placed under guards, while the warriors feasted their triumph and danced the scalp-dance to drive away the spirits of the dead. To beat of tom-tom and shriek of gourd-rattles, the whole terrible scene was re-enacted. Stripping himself naked, but for his moccasins, the old wizard pranced up and down like a fiend in the midst of the circling dancers. Flaming torches smoked from poles in front of the lodges, or were waved and tossed by the braves. Flaunting fresh scalps from lance-heads, with tomahawk in the other hand, each warrior went through all the fiendish moves and feints of attack—prowling on knees, uttering the yelping, wolfish yells, crouching for the leap, springing through mid-air, brandishing the battle-axe, stamping upon the imaginary prostrate foe, stooping with a glint of the scalping knife, then up, with a shout of triumph and the scalp waving from the lance, all in time to the dull thum—thum—thum of the tom-tom and the screaming chant of the wizard. Still the south wind moaned about the lodges; and the dancers shouted the louder to drown those ghost-cries of the dead. Faster and faster beat the drum. Swifter and swifter darted the braves, hacking their own flesh in a frenzy of fear till their shrieks out-screamed the wind.

Then the spirits were deemed appeased.

The mad orgy of horrors was over, but the dancers were too exhausted for the torture of prisoners. The older men came to the lodge where we were guarded and Godefroy again began his importunings.

Setting Jack Battle aside, they bade the trader and me come out.

"Better one be tortured than three," heartlessly muttered Godefroy to Jack. "Now they'll set us free for fear of M. Radisson, and we'll come back for you."

But Godefroy had miscalculated the effects of his threats. At the door stood a score of warriors who had not been to the massacre. If we hoped to escape torture the wizard bade us follow these men. They led us away with a sinister silence. When we reached the crest of the hill, half-way between the lodges and the massacre, Godefroy took alarm. This was not the direction of our fort. The trader shouted out that M. Radisson would punish them well if they did us harm. At that one of the taciturn fellows turned. They would take care to do us no harm, he said, with an evil laugh. On the ridge of the hill they paused, as if seeking a mark. Two spindly wind-stripped trees stood straight as mast-poles above the snow. The leader went forward to examine the bark for Indian signal, motioning Godefroy and me closer as he examined the trees.

With the whistle of a whip-lash through air the thongs were about us, round and round ankle, neck, and arms, binding us fast. Godefroy shouted out a blasphemous oath and struggled till the deer sinew cut his buckskin. I had only succeeded in wheeling to face our treacherous tormentors when the strands tightened. In the struggle the trader had somehow got his face to the bark. The coils circled round him. The thongs drew close. The Indians stood back. They had done what they came to do. They would not harm us, they taunted, pointing to the frost-silvered valley, where lay the dead of their morning crime.

Then with harsh gibes, the warriors ran down the hillside, leaving us bound.

CHAPTER XVIII

FACING THE END

BELOW the hill on one side flickered the moving torches of the hostiles. On the other side, where the cliff fell sheer away, lay the red-dyed snows with misty shapes moving through the frosty valley.

A wind of sighs swept across the white wastes. Short, sharp barkings rose from the shadowy depth of the ravine. Then the silence of desolation . . . then the moaning night-wind . . . then the shivering cry of the wolf-pack scouring on nightly hunt.

For a moment neither Godefroy nor I spoke. Then the sinews, cutting deep, wakened consciousness.

"Are they gone?" asked Godefroy hoarsely.

"Yes," said I, glancing to the valley.

"Can't you break through the thongs and get a hand free?"

"My back is to the tree. We'll have to face it, Godefroy—don't break down, man! We must face it!"

"Face what?" he shuddered out. "Is anything there? Face what?" he half screamed.

"The end!"

He strained at the thongs till he had strength to strain no more. Then he broke out in a volley of maledictions at Jack Battle and me for interfering with the massacre, to which I could answer never a word; for the motives that merit greatest applause when they succeed, win bitterest curses when they fail.

The northern lights swung low. Once those lights seemed censers of flame to an invisible God. Now they shot across the steel sky like fiery serpents, and the rustling of their fire was as the hiss when a fang strikes. A shooting star blazed into light against the blue, then dropped into the eternal darkness.

"Godefroy," I asked, "how long will this last?"

"Till the wolves come," said he huskily.

"A man must die some time," I called back; but my voice belied the bravery of the words, for something gray loomed from the ravine and stood stealthily motionless in the dusk behind the trader. Involuntarily a quick "Hist!" went from my lips.

"What's that?" shouted Godefroy. "Is anything there?"

"I am cold," said I.

And on top of that lie I prayed—prayed with wide-staring eyes on the thing whose head had turned towards us—prayed as I have never prayed before or since!

"Are you sure there's nothing?" cried the trader. "Look on both sides! I'm sure I feel something!"

Another crouching form emerged from the gloom—then another and another—silent and still as spectres. With a sidling motion they prowled nearer, sniffing the air, shifting watchful look from Godefroy to me, from me to Godefroy. A green eye gleamed nearer through the mist. Then I knew.

The wolves had come.

Godefroy screamed out that he heard something, and again bade me look on both sides of the hill.

"Keep quiet till I see," said I; but I never took my gaze from the green eyes of a great brute to the fore of the gathering pack.

"But I feel them — but I hear them!" shouted Godefroy, in an agony of terror.

What gain to keep up pretence longer? Still holding the beast back with no other power than the power of the man's eye over the brute, I called out the truth to the trader.

"Don't move! Don't speak! Don't cry out! Perhaps we can stare them back till daylight comes!"

Godefroy held quiet as death. Some subtle power of the man over the brute puzzled the leader of the pack. He shook his great head with angry snarls and slunk from side to side to evade the human eye, every hair of his fur bristling. Then he threw up his jaws and uttered a long howl, answered by the far cry of the coming pack. Sniffing the ground, he began circling—closing in—closing in——

Then there was a shout—a groan, a struggle—a rip as of teeth—from Godefroy's place!

Then with naught but a blazing of comets dropping into an everlasting dark, with naught but a ship of fire billowing away to the flame of the northern lights, with naught but the rush of a sea, blinding, deafening, bearing me to the engulfment of the eternal—I lost knowledge of this life!

CHAPTER XIX

AFTERWARD

A long shudder, and I had awakened in stifling darkness. Was I dreaming, or were there voices, English voices, talking about me?

"It was too late! He will die!"

"Draw back the curtain! Give him plenty of air!"

In the daze of a misty dream, M. Picot was there with the foils in his hands; and Hortense had cried out as she did that night when the button touched home. A sweet, fresh gust blew across my face with a faint odour of the pungent flames that used to flicker under the crucibles of the dispensary. How came I to be lying in Boston Town? Was M. Radisson a myth? Was the northland a dream?

I tried to rise, but whelming shadows pushed me down; and through the dark shifted phantom faces.

Now it was M. Radisson quelling mutiny, tossed on plunging ice-drift, scouring before the hurricane, leaping through red flame over the fort wall, while wind and sea crooned a chorus like the hum of soldiers singing and marching to battle. "Storm and cold, man and beast, powers of darkness and devil—he must fight them all," sang the gale. "Who?" asked a voice. In the dark was a lone figure clinging to the spars of a wreck. "The victor," shrieked the wind. Then the waves washed over the castaway, leaving naught but the screaming gale and the pounding seas and the eternal dark.

Or it was M. Picot, fencing in mid-room. Of a sudden, foils turn to swords, M. Picot to a masked man, and Boston to the northland forest. I fall, and when I awaken M. Picot is standing, candle in hand, tincturing my wounds.

Or the dark is filled with a multitude—men and beasts; and the beasts wear a crown of victory and the men are drunk with the blood of the slain.

Or stealthy, crouching, wolfish forms steal through the frost mist, closer and closer till there comes a shout—a groan—a rip as of teeth—then I am up, struggling with Le Borgne, the one-eyed, who pushes me back to a couch in the dark.

Like the faces that hover above battle in soldiers' dreams was a white face framed in curls with lustrous eyes full of lights. Always when the darkness thickened and I began slipping—slipping into the folds of bottomless deeps—always the face came from the gloom, like a star of hope; and the hope drew me back.

"There is nothing—nothing—nothing at all to fear," says the face.

And I laugh at the absurdity of the dream.

"To think of dreaming that Hortense would be here—would be in the northland—Hortense, the little queen, who never would let me tell her——"

"Tell her what?" asks the face.

"Hah! What a question! There is only one thing in all this world to tell her!"

And I laughed again till I thought there must be some elf scrambling among the rafters of that smothery ceiling. It seemed so absurd to be thrilled with love of Hortense with the breath of the wolves yet hot in one's face!

"The wolves got Godefroy," I would reason, "how didn't they get me? How did I get away? What was that smell of fur——"

Then some one was throwing fur robes from the couch. The phantom Hortense kneeled at the pillow.

"There are no wolves—it was only the robe," she says.

" And I suppose you will be telling me there are no Indians up there among the rafters? "

" Give me the candle. Go away, Le Borgne! Leave me alone with him," says the face in the gloom. " Look," says the shadow, " I am Hortense! "

A torch was in her hand and the light fell on her face. I was as certain that she knelt beside me as I was that I lay helpless to rise. But the trouble was, I was equally certain there were wolves skulking through the dark and Indians skipping among the rafters.

" Ghosts haven't hands," says Hortense, touching mine lightly; and the touch brought the memory of those old mocking airs from the spinet.

Was it flood of memory or a sick man's dream? The presence seemed so real that mustering all strength, I turned—turned to see Le Borgne, the one-eyed, sitting on a log-end with a stolid, watchful, unreadable look on his crafty face.

Bluish shafts of light struck athwart the dark. A fire burned against the far wall. The smoke had the pungent bark smell of the flame that used to burn in M. Picot's dispensary. This, then, had brought the dreams of Hortense, now so far away. Skins hung everywhere; but in places the earth showed through. Like a gleam of sunlight through dark came the thought—this was a cave, the cave of the pirates whose voices I had heard from the ground that night in the forest, one pleading to save me, the other sending Le Borgne to trap me.

Leaning on my elbow, I looked from the Indian to a bearskin partition hiding another apartment. Le Borgne had carried the stolen pelts of the massacred tribe to the inland pirates. The pirates had sent him back for me.

And Hortense was a dream. Ah, well, men in their senses might have done worse than dream of a Hortense!

But the voice and the hand were real.

" Le Borgne," I ask, " was any one here? "

Le Borgne's cheeks corrugate in wrinkles of bronze that leer an evil laugh, and he pretends not to understand.

" Le Borgne, was any one here with you? "

Le Borgne shifts his spread feet, mutters a guttural grunt, and puffs out his torch; but the shafted flame reveals his shadow. I can still hear him beside me in the dark.

" Le Borgne is the great white chief's friend," I say; " and the white-man is the great white chief's friend. Where are we, Le Borgne? "

Le Borgne grunts out a low huff-huff of a laugh.

"Here; white-man is here," says Le Borgne; and he shuffles away to the bearskin partition hiding another apartment.

Ah well as I said, one might do worse than dream of Hortense. But in spite of all your philosophers say about there being no world but the world we spin in our brains, I could not woo my lady back to it. Like the wind that bloweth where it listeth was my love. Try as I might to call up that pretty deceit of a Hortense about me in spirit, my perverse lady came not to the call.

Then, thoughts would race back to the mutiny on the stormy sea, to the roar of the breakers crashing over decks, to M. Radisson leaping up from dripping wreckage, muttering between his teeth—"Blind god o' chance, they may crush, but they shall not conquer; they may kill, but I snap my fingers in their faces to the death!"

Then, uncalled, through the darkness comes her face.

"God is love," says she.

If I lie there like a log, never moving, she seems to stay; but if I feel out through the darkness for the grip of a living hand, for the substance of a reality on which souls anchor, like the shadow of a dream she is gone.

I mind once in the misty region between delirium and consciousness, when the face slipped from me like a fading light, I called out eagerly that love was a phantom; for her God of love had left me to the blind gods that crush, to the storm and the dark and the ravening wolves.

Like a light flaming from dark, the face shone through the gloom.

"Love, a phantom," laughs the mocking voice of the imperious Hortense I knew long ago; and the thrill of her laugh proves love the realest phantom life can know.

Then the child Hortense becomes of a sudden the grown woman, grave and sweet, with eyes in the dark like stars, and strange, broken thoughts I had not dared to hope shining unspoken on her face.

"Life, a phantom—substance, the shadow—love, the all," the dream-face seems to be saying. "Events are God's thoughts—storms and darkness and prey are his puppets, the blind gods, his slaves—God is love; for you are here! . . . You are here! . . . You are here with me!"

When I feel through the dark this time is the grip of a living hand.

Then we lock arms and sweep through space, the northern lights curtaining overhead, the stars for torches, and the blazing comets heralding a way.

"The very stars in their courses fight for us," says Hortense.

And I, with an earthy intellect groping behind the winged love of the woman, think that she refers to some of M. Picot's mystic astrologies.

"No—no," says the dream-face, with the love that divines without speech, "do you not understand? The stars fight for us—because—because——"

"Because God is love," catching the gleam of the thought; and the stars that fight in their courses for mortals sweep to a noonday splendour.

And all the while I was but a crazy dreamer lying captive, wounded and weak in a pirate cave. Oh, yes, I know very well what my fine gentlemen dabblers in the new sciences will say—the fellow was daft and delirious—he had lost grip on reality and his fevered wits mixed a mumble-jumble of ancient symbolism with his own adventures. But before you reduce all this great universe to the dimensions of a chemist's crucible, I pray you to think twice whether the mind that fashioned the crucible be not greater than the crucible; whether the Master-mind that shaped the laws of the universe be not greater than the universe; whether when man's mind loses grip—as you call it—of the little, nagging, insistent realities it may not leap free like the jagged lightnings from peak to peak of a consciousness that overtowers life's commoner levels! Spite of our boastings, each knows neither more nor less than life hath taught him. For me, I know what the dream-voice spoke proved true: life, the shadow of a great reality; love, the all; the blind gods of storm and dark and prey, the puppets of the God of gods, working his will; and the God of gods a God of love, realest when love is near.

Once, I mind, the dark seemed alive with wolfish shades, sniffing, prowling, circling, creeping nearer like that monster wolf of fable set on by the powers of evil to hunt Man to his doom. A nightmare of fear bound me down. The death-frosts settled and tightened and closed—but suddenly, Hortense took cold hands in her palms, calling and calling and calling me back to life and hope and her. Then I waked.

Though I peopled the mist with many shadows, Le Borgne alone stood there.

CHAPTER XX

WHO THE PIRATES WERE

How long I lay in the pirates' cave I could not tell; for day and night were alike with the pale-blue flame quivering against the earth-wall, gusts of cold air sweeping through the door, low-whispered talks from the inner cave.

At last I surprised Le Borgne mightily by sitting bolt upright and bidding him bring me a meal of buffalo-tongue or teal. With the stolid repartee of the Indian he grunted back that I had tongue enough; but he brought the stuff with no ill grace. After that he had much ado to keep me off my feet. Finally, I promised by the soul of his grandfather neither to spy nor listen about the doors of the inner cave, and he let me up for an hour at a time to practise walking with the aid of a lance-pole. As he found that I kept my word, he trusted me alone in the cave, sitting crouched on the log-end with a buckskin sling round my shattered sword-arm, which the wolves had not helped that night at the stake.

In the food Le Borgne brought was always a flavour of simples or drugs. One night—at least I supposed it was night from the chill of the air blowing past the bearskin—just as Le Borgne stooped to serve me, his torch flickered out. Before he could relight, I had poured the broth out and handed back an empty bowl.

Then I lay with eyes tight shut and senses wide awake. The Indian sat on the log-end watching. I did not stir. Neither did I fall asleep as usual. The Indian cautiously passed a candle across my face. I lay motionless as I had been drugged. At that he stalked off. Voices began in the other apartment. Two or three forms went tip-toeing about the cave. Shadows passed athwart the flame. A gust of cold; and with half-closed eyes I saw three men vanish through the outer doorway over fields no longer snow-clad.

Had spring come? How long had I lain in the cave? Before I gained strength to escape, would M. Radisson have left for Quebec? Then came a black wave of memory—thought of Jack Battle, the sailor lad, awaiting our return to rescue him. From the first Jack and I had held together as aliens in Boston Town. Should I lie like a stranded hull while he perished? Risking spies on the watch, I struggled up and staggered across the cave to that blue flame quivering so mysteriously. As I neared, the mystery vanished, for it was nothing more than one of those northern beds of combustibles—gas, tar, or coal—set burning by the ingenious pirates.*

The spirit was willing enough to help Jack, but the flesh was weak. Presently I sank on the heaped pelts all atremble. I had promised not to spy nor eavesdrop, but that did not prohibit escape. But how could one forage for food with a right arm in bands and a left unsteady as aim of a girl? Le Borgne had befriended me twice—once in the storm, again on the hill. Perhaps he might know of Jack. I would wait the Indian's return. Meanwhile I could practise my strength by walking up and down the cave.

The walls were hung with pelts. Where the dry clay crumbled, the roof had been timbered. A rivulet of spring water bubbled in one dark corner. At the same end an archway led to inner recesses. Behind the skin doorway sounded heavy breathing, as of sleepers. I had promised not to spy. Turning, I retraced the way to the outer door. Here another pelt swayed heav-

---

* In confirmation of Mr. Stanhope's record it may be stated that on the western side of the northland in the Mackenzie River region are gas and tar veins that are known to have been burning continuously for nearly two centuries.

ily in the wind. Dank, earthy smells of spring, odours of leaves water-soaked by melting snows, the faint perfume of flowers pushing up through mats of verdure, blew in on the night breeze.

Pushing aside the flap, I looked out. The spur of a steep declivity cut athwart the cave. Now I could guess where I was. This was the hill down which I had stumbled that night the voices had come from the ground. Here the masked man had sprung from the thicket. Not far off M. Radisson had first met the Indians. To reach the French Habitation I had but to follow the river.

That hope set me pacing again for exercise; and the faster I walked the faster raced thoughts over the events of the crowded years. Again the Prince Rupert careened seaward, bearing little Hortense to England. Once more Ben Gillam swaggered on the water-front of Boston Town, boasting all that he would do when he had ship of his own. Then Jack Battle, building his castles of fortune for love of Hortense, and all unconsciously letting slip the secret of good Boston men deep involved in pirate schemes. The scene shifted to the far north, and a masked man had leaped from the forest dark only to throw down his weapon when the firelight shone on my face. Again the white darkness of the storm, the three shadowy figures and Le Borgne sent to guide us back to the fort. Again, to beat of drum and shriek of fife, M. Radisson was holding his own against the swarming savages that assailed the New Englanders' fort. Then I was living over the unspeakable horror of the Indian massacre ending in that awful wait on the crest of the hill.

The memory brought a chill as of winter cold. With my back to both doors I stood shuddering over the blue fire. Whatever logicians may say, we do not reason life's conclusions out. Clouds blacken the heavens till there comes the lightning-flash. So do our intuitions leap unwarned from the dark. 'Twas thus I seemed to fathom the mystery of those interlopers. Ben Gillam had been chosen to bring the pirate ship north because his father, of the Hudson's Bay Company, could screen him from English spies. Mr. Stocking, of Boston, was another partner to the venture, who could shield Ben from punishment in New England. But the third partner was hiding inland to defraud the others of the furs. That was the meaning of Ben's drunken threats. Who was the third partner? Had not Eli Kirke planned trading in the north with Mr. Stocking? Were the pirates some agents of my uncle? Did that explain why my life had been three times spared? One code of morals for the church and another for the trade is the way of many a man; but would the agents of a Puritan deacon murder a rival in the dark of a forest, or lead Indians to massacre the crew of partners, or take furs gotten at the price of a tribe's extermination?

Turning that question over, I heard the inner door-flap lift. There was no time to regain the couch, but a quick swerve took me out of the firelight in the shadow of a great wolfskin against the wall. You will laugh at the old idea of honour, but I had promised not to spy, and I never raised my eyes from the floor. There was no sound but the gurgling of the spring in the dark and the sharp crackle of the flame.

Thinking the wind had blown the flap, I stepped from hiding. Something vague as mist held back in shadow. The lines of a white-clad figure etched themselves against the cave wall. It floated out, paused, moved forward.

Then I remember clutching at the wolfskin like one clinching a death-grip of reality, praying God not to let go a soul's anchor-hold of reason.

For when the figure glided into the slant blue rays of the shafted flame it was Hortense—the Hortense of the dreams, sweet as the child, grave as the grown woman—Hortense with closed eyes and moving lips and hands feeling out in the dark as if playing invisible keys.

She was asleep.

Then came the flash that lighted the clouds of the past.

The interloper, the pirate, the leader of Indian marauders, the defrauder of his partners, was M. Picot, the French doctor, whom Boston had outlawed, and who was now outlawing their outlawry. We do not reason out our conclusions, as I said before. At our supremest moments we do not *think*. Consciousness leaps from summit to summit like the forked lightnings across the mountain-peaks; and the mysteries of life are illumined as a spread-out scroll. In that moment of joy and fear and horror, as I crouched back to the wall, I did not *think*. I *knew*—knew the meaning of all M. Picot's questionings on the fur trade; of that murderous attack in the dark when an antagonist flung down his weapon; of the spying through the frosted woods; of the figures in the white darkness; of the attempt to destroy Ben Gillam's fort; of the rescue from the crest of the hill; and of all those strange delirious dreams.

It was as if the past focused itself to one flaming point, and the flash of that point illumined life, as deity must feel to whom past and present and future are one.

And all the while, with temples pounding like surf on rock and the roar of the sea in my ears, I was not *thinking*, only *knowing* that Hortense was standing in the blue-shafted light with tremulous lips and white face and a radiance on her brow not of this life.

Her hands ran lightly over imaginary keys. The blue flame darted and quivered through the gloom. The hushed purr of the spring broke the stillness in metallic tinklings. A smile flitted across the sleeper's face. Her lips parted. The crackle of the flame seemed loud as tick of clock in death-room.

"To get the memory of it," she said.

And there stole out of the past mocking memories of that last night in the hunting-room, filling the cave with tuneless melodies like thoughts creeping into thoughts or odour of flowers in dark.

But what was she saying in her sleep?

"Blind gods of chance"—the words that had haunted my delirium, then quick-spoken snatches too low for me to hear—"no—no"—then more that was incoherent, and she was gliding back to the cave.

She had lifted the curtain door—she was

whispering—she paused as if for answer—then with face alight, "The stars fight for us—" she said; and she had disappeared.

The flame set the shadows flickering. The rivulet gurgled loud in the dark. And I came from concealment as from a spirit world.

Then Hortense was no dream, and love was no phantom, and God—was what?

There I halted. The powers of darkness yet pressed too close for me to see through to the God that was love. I only knew that He who throned the universe was neither the fool that ignorant bigots painted, nor the blind power, making wanton war of storm and dark and cold. For had not the blind forces brought Hortense to me, and me to Hortense?

Consciousness was leaping from summit to summit like the forked lightnings, and the light that burned was the light that transfigures life for each soul.

The spell of a presence was there.

Then it came home to me what a desperate game the French doctor had played. That sword-thrust in the dark meant death; so did the attack on Ben Gillam's fort; and was it not Le Borgne, M. Picot's Indian ally, who had counselled the massacre of the sleeping tribe? You must not think that M. Picot was worse than other traders of those days! The north is a desolate land, and though blood cry aloud from stones, there is no man to hear.

I easily guessed that M. Picot would try to keep me with him till M. Radisson had sailed. Then I must needs lock hands with piracy.

Hortense and I were pawns in the game.

At one moment I upbraided him for bringing Hortense to this wilderness of murder and pillage. At another I considered that a banished gentleman could not choose his goings. How could I stay with M. Picot and desert M. de Radisson? How could I go to M. de Radisson and abandon Hortense?

"Straight is the narrow way," Eli Kirke oft cried out as he expounded Holy Writ.

Ah, well, if the narrow way is straight, it has a trick of becoming tangled in a most terrible snarl!

Wheeling the log-end right about, I sat down to await M. Picot. There was stirring in the next apartment. An ebon head poked past the door curtain, looked about, and withdrew without detecting me. The face I remembered at once. It was the wife of M. Picot's blackamoor. Only three men had passed from the cave. If the blackamoor were one, M. Picot and Le Borgne *must* be the others.

WHO THE PIRATES WERE

Footsteps grated on the pebbles outside. I rose with beating heart to meet M. Picot, who held my fate in his hands. Then a ringing pistol-shot set my pulse jumping.

I ran to the door. Something plunged heavily against the curtain. The robe ripped from the hangings. In the flood of moonlight a man pitched face forward to the cave floor. He reeled up with a cry of rage, caught blindly at the air, uttered a groan, fell back.

"M. Picot!"

Blanched and faint, the French doctor lay with a crimsoning pool wet under his head.

"I am shot! What will become of her?" he groaned. "I am shot! It was Gillam! It was Gillam!"

Hortense and the negress came running from the inner cave. Le Borgne and the blackamoor dashed from the open with staring horror.

"Lift me up! For God's sake, air!" cried M. Picot.

We laid him on the pelts in the doorway, Le Borgne standing guard outside.

Hortense stooped to stanch the wound, but the doctor motioned her off with a fierce impatience, and bade the negress lead her away. Then he lay with closed eyes, hands clutched to the pelts, and shuddering breath.

The blackamoor had rushed to the inner cave for liquor, when M. Picot opened his eyes with a strange far look fastened upon me.

"Swear it," he commanded.

And I thought his mind wandering.

He groaned heavily. "Don't you understand? It's Hortense. Swear you'll restore her—" and his breath came with a hard metallic rattle that warned the end.

"Doctor Picot," said I, "if you have anything to say, say it quickly and make your peace with God!"

"Swear you'll take her back to her people and treat her as a sister," he cried.

"I swear before God that I shall take Hortense back to her people, and that I shall treat her like a sister," I repeated, raising my right hand.

That seemed to quiet him. He closed his eyes.

"Sir," said I, "have you nothing more to say? Who are her people?"

"Is . . . is . . . any one listening?" he asked in short, hard breaths.

I motioned the others back.

"Listen"—the words came in quick, rasping breaths. "She is not mine . . . it was at night . . . they brought her . . . ward o' the court

. . . lands . . . they wanted me." There was a sharp pause, a shivering whisper. "I didn't poison her"—the dying man caught convulsively at my hands—"I swear I had no thought of harming her. . . . They . . . paid. . . . I fled. . . ."

"Who paid you to poison Hortense? Who is Hortense?" I demanded; for his life was ebbing and the words portended deep wrong.

But his mind was wandering again, for he began talking so fast that I could catch only a few words. "Blood! Blood! Colonel Blood!" Then "Swear it," he cried.

That speech sapped his strength. He sank back with shut eyes and faint breathings.

We forced a potion between his lips.

"Don't let Gillam," he mumbled, "don't let Gillam . . . have the furs."

A tremor ran through his stiffening frame. A little shuddering breath—and M. Picot had staked his last pawn in life's game.

CHAPTER XXI

HOW THE PIRATES CAME

INSIDE our Habitation all was the confusion of preparation for leaving the bay. Outside, the Indians held high carnival; for Allemand, the gin-soaked pilot, was busy passing drink through the loopholes to a pandemonium of savages raving outside the stockades. 'Tis not a pretty picture, that memory of white-men besotting the Indian; but I must even set down the facts as they are, bidding you to remember that the white trader who besotted the Indian was the same white trader who befriended all tribes alike when the hunt failed and the famine came. La Chesnaye, the merchant prince, it was, who managed this low trafficking. Indeed, for the rubbing together of more doubloons in his money-bags I think that La Chesnaye's servile nature would have bargained to send souls in job lots blindfold over the gangplank. But, as La Chesnaye said when Pierre Radisson remonstrated against the knavery, the gin was nine parts rain-water.

"The more cheat, you, to lay such unction to your conscience," says M. de Radisson. "Be an honest knave, La Chesnaye!"

Forêt, the marquis, stalked up and down before the gate with two guards at his heels. All day long birch canoes and log dugouts and tubby pirogues and crazy rafts of loose-lashed pine logs drifted to our water-front with bands of squalid Indians bringing their pelts. Skin tepees rose outside our palisades like an army of mushrooms. Naked brats with wisps of hair coarse as a horse's mane crawled over our mounted cannon, or scudded between our feet like pups, or felt our European clothes with impudent wonder. Young girls having hair plastered flat with bear's grease stood peeping shyly from tent flaps. Old squaws with skin withered to a parchment hung over the campfires, cooking. And at the loopholes pressed the braves and the bucks and the chief men exchanging beaver-skins for old iron, or a silver fox for a drink of gin, or ermine enough to make His Majesty's coronation robe for some flashy trinket to trick out a vain squaw. From dawn to dusk ran the patter of moccasined feet, man after man toiling up from river-front to fort gate with bundles of peltries on his back and a carrying strap across his brow.

Unarmed, among the savages, pacifying drunken hostiles at the water-front, bidding Jean and me look after the carriers, in the gateway, helping Sieur de Groseillers to sort the furs—Pierre Radisson was everywhere. In the guard-house were more English prisoners than we had crews of French; and in the mess-room sat Governor Brigdar of the Hudson's Bay Company, who took his captivity mighty ill and grew prodigious pot-valiant over his cups. Here, too, lolled Ben Gillam, the young New Englander, rumbling out a drunken vengeance against those inland pirates, who had deprived him of the season's furs.

Once, I mind, when M. Radisson came suddenly on these two worthies, their fuddled heads were close together above the table.

"Look you," Ben was saying in a big, rasping whisper, "I shot him—I shot him with a brass button. The black arts are powerless agen brass. Devil sink my soul if I didn't shoot him! The red—spattered over the brush——"

M. Radisson raised a hand to silence my coming.

Ben's nose poked across the table, closer to Governor Brigdar's ear.

"But look you, Mister What's-yer-name," says he.

"Don't you Mister me, you young cub!" interrupts the governor with a pompous show of drunken dignity.

"A fig for Your Excellency," cries the young blackguard. "Who's who when he's drunk? As I was a-telling, look you, though the red spattered the bushes, when I run up he'd vanished into air with a flash o' powder from my musket! 'Twas by the black arts that nigh hanged him in Boston Town——"

At that, Governor Brigdar claps his hand to the table and swears that he cares nothing for black arts if only the furs can be found.

"The furs—aye," husks Ben, "if we can only find the furs! An our men hold together, we're two to one agen the Frenchies——"

"Ha," says M. Radisson. "Give you good-morning, gentlemen, and I hope you find yourselves in health."

The two heads flew apart like the halves of a burst cannon-shell. Thereafter, Radisson kept Ben and Governor Brigdar apart.

Of Godefroy and Jack Battle we could learn naught. Le Borgne would never tell what he and M. Picot had seen that night they rescued me from the hill. Whether Le Borgne and the hostiles of the massacre lied or no, they both told the same story of Jack. While the tribe was still engaged in the scalp-dance, some one had untied Jack's bands. When the braves went to torture their captive, he had escaped. But whither had he gone that he had not come back to us? Like the sea is the northland, full of nameless graves; and after sending scouts far and wide, we gave up all hope of finding the sailor lad.

But in the fort was another whose presence our rough fellows likened to a star flower on the stained ground of some hard-fought battle. After M. Radisson had quieted turbulent spirits by a reading of holy lessons, Mistress Hortense queened it over our table of a Sunday at noon. Waiting upon her at either hand were the blackamoor and the negress. A soldier in red stood guard behind; and every man, officer, and commoner down the long mess-table tuned his manners to the pure grace of her fair face.

What a hushing of voices and cleansing of wits and disusing of oaths was there after my little lady came to our rough Habitation!

I mind the first Sunday M. Radisson led her out like a queen to the mess-room table. When our voyageurs went upstream for M. Picot's hidden furs, her story had got noised about the fort. Officers, soldiers, and sailors had seated themselves at the long benches on either side the table; but M. Radisson's place was empty and a sort of throne chair had been extemporized at the head of the table. An angry question went from group to group to know if M. Radisson designed such place of honour for the two leaders of our prisoners—under lock in the guard-room. M. de Groseillers only laughed and bade the fellows contain their souls and stomachs in patience. A moment later, the door to the quarters where Hortense lived was thrown open by a red-coated soldier, and out stepped M. Radisson leading Hortense by the tips of her dainty fingers, the ebon faces of the two blackamoors grinning delight behind.

You could have heard a pin fall among our fellows. Then there was a noise of armour clanking to the floor. Every man unconsciously took to throwing his pistol under the table, flinging sword-belt down and hiding daggers below benches. Of a sudden, the surprise went to their heads.

"Gentlemen," began M. Radisson.

But the fellows would have none of his grand speeches. With a cheer that set the rafters ringing, they were on their feet; and to Mistress Hortense's face came a look that does more for the making of men than all New England's laws or my uncle's blasphemy boxes or King Charles's dragoons. You ask what that look was? Go to, with your teasings! A lover is not to be asked his whys! I ask you in return why you like the spire of a cathedral pointing up instead of down; or why the muses lift souls heavenward? Indeed, of all the fine arts granted the human race to lead men's thoughts above the sordid brutalities of living, methinks woman is the finest; for God's own hand fashioned her, and she was the last crowning piece of all His week's doings. The finest arts are the easiest spoiled, as you know very well; and if you demand how Mistress Hortense could escape harm amid all the wickedness of that wilderness, I answer it is a thing that your townsfolk cannot know.

It is of the wilderness.

The wilderness is a foster-mother that teacheth hard, strange paradoxes. The first is *the sin of being weak*; and the second is that *death is the least of life's harms.*

Wrapped in those furs for which he had staked his life like many a gamester of the wilderness, M. Picot lay buried in that sandy stretch outside the cave door. Turning to lead Hortense away before Le Borgne and the blackamoor began filling the grave, I found her stonily silent and tearless.

But it was she who led me.

Scrambling up the hillside like a chamois of the mountains, she flitted lightly through the greening to a small open where campers had built night fires. Her quick glance ran from tree to tree. Some wood-runner had blazed a trail by notching the bark. Pausing, she turned with the frank, fearless look of the wilderness woman. She was no longer the elusive Hortense of secluded life. A change had come—the change of the hothouse plant set out to the buffetings of the four winds of heaven to perish from weakness or gather strength from hardship. Your woman of older lands must hood fair eyes, perforce, lest evil masking under other eyes give wrong intent to candour; but in the wilderness each life stands stripped of pretence, honestly good or evil, bare at what it is; and purity clear as the noonday sun needs no trick of custom to make it plainer.

"Is not this the place?" she asked.

Looking closer, from shrub to open, I recognised the ground of that night attack in the woods.

"Hortense, then it was you that I saw at the fire with the others?"

She nodded assent. She had not uttered one word to explain how she came to that wild land; nor had I asked.

"It was you who pleaded for my life in the cave below my feet?"

"I did not know you had heard! I only sent Le Borgne to bring you back!"

"I hid as he passed."

"But I sent a message to the fort——"

"Not to be bitten by the same dog twice—I thought that meant to keep away?"

"What?" asked Hortense, passing her hand over her eyes. "Was that the message he gave you? Then monsieur had bribed him! I sent for you to come to us. Oh, that is the reason you never came——"

"And that is the reason you have hidden from me all the year and never sent me word?"

"I thought — I thought —" She turned away. "Ben Gillam told monsieur you had left Boston on our account——"

"And you thought I wanted to avoid you——"

"I did not blame you," she said. "Indeed, indeed, I was very weak—monsieur must have bribed Le Borgne—I sent word again and again—but you never answered!"

"How could you misunderstand— O Hortense, after that night in the hunting-room, how could you believe so poorly of me!"

She gave a low laugh. "That's what your good angel used to plead," she said.

"Good angel, indeed!" said I, memory of the vows to that miscreant adventurer fading. "That good angel was a lazy baggage! She should have compelled you to believe!"

"Oh—she did," says Hortense quickly. "The poor thing kept telling me and telling me to trust you till I——"

"Till you what, Hortense?"

She did not answer at once.

"Monsieur and the blackamoor and I had gone to the upper river watching for the expected boats——"

"Hortense, were you the white figure behind the bush that night we were spying on the Prince Rupert!"

"Yes," she said, "and you pointed your gun at me!"

I was too dumfounded for words. Then a suspicion flashed to my mind. "Who sent Le Borgne for us in the storm, Hortense?"

"Oh," says Hortense, "that was nothing! Monsieur pretended that he thought you were caribou. He wanted to shoot. Oh," she said, "oh, how I have hated him! To think—to think that he would shoot when you helped us in Boston!"

"Hortense, who sent Le Borgne and M. Picot to save me from the wolves?"

"Oh," says Hortense bravely, with a shudder between the words, "that was—that was nothing—I mean—one would do as much for anybody—for—for—for a poor little stoat, or—or—a caribou if the wolves were after it!"

And we laughed with the tears in our eyes. And all the while that vow to the dying adventurer was ringing like a faint death toll to hope. I remember trying to speak a gratitude too deep for words.

"Can—I ever—ever repay you—Hortense?" I was asking.

"Repay!" she said with a little bitter laugh. "Oh! I hate that word repay! I hate all give-and-take and so-much-given-for-so-much-got!" Then turning to me with her face aflame: "I am—I am—oh—why can't you understand?" she asked.

And then—and then—there was a wordless cry—her arms reached out in mute appeal—there was no need of speech.

The forest shone green and gold in the sunlight. The wind rustled past like a springtime presence, a presence that set all the pines swaying and the aspens aquiver with music of flower legend and new birth and the joy of life. There was a long silence; and in that silence the pulsing of the mighty forces that lift mortals to immortality.

Then a voice which only speaks when love speaks through the voice was saying, "Do you remember your dreams?"

"What?" stooping to cull some violets that had looked well against the green of her hunting-suit.

"'Blind gods of chance—blind gods of chance'—you used to say that over and over!"

"Ah, M. Radisson taught me that! God bless the blind gods of chance—Hortense teaches me that; for"—giving her back her own words —"you are here—you are here—you are here with me! God bless the gods of chance!"

"Oh," she cried, "were you not asleep? Monsieur let me watch after you had taken the sleeping drug."

"The stars fight for us in their courses," said I, handing up the violets.

"Ramsay," she asked with a sudden look straight through my eyes, "what did he make you promise when—when—he was dying?"

The question brought me up like a sail hauled

short. And when I told her, she uttered strange reproaches.

"Why—why did you promise that?" she asked. "It has always been his mad dream. And when I told him I did not want to be restored, that I wanted to be like Rebecca and Jack and you and the rest, he called me a little fool and bade me understand that he had not poisoned me as he was paid to do because it was to his advantage to keep me alive. Courtiers would not assassinate a stray waif, he said; there was wealth for the court's ward somewhere; and when I was restored, I was to remember who had slaved for me. Indeed, indeed, I think that he would have married me, but that he feared it would bar him from any property as a king's ward——"

"Is that all you know?"

"That is all. Why—why—did you promise?"

"What else was there to do, Hortense? You can't stay in this wilderness."

"Oh, yes," says Hortense wearily, and she let the violets fall. "What—what else was there to do?"

She led the way back to the cave.

"You have not asked me how we came here," she began with visible effort.

"Tell me no more than you wish me to know!"

"Perhaps you remember a New Amsterdam gentleman and a page boy leaving Boston on the Prince Rupert?"

"Perhaps," said I.

"Captain Gillam of the Prince Rupert signalled to his son outside the harbour. Monsieur had been bargaining with Ben all winter. Ben took us to the north with Le Borgne for interpreter——"

"Does Ben know you are here?"

"Not as Hortense! I was dressed as a page. Then Le Borgne told us of this cave and monsieur plotted to lead the Indians against Ben, capture the fort and ship, and sail away with all the furs for himself. Oh, how I have hated him!" she exclaimed with a sudden impetuous stamp.

Leaving her with the slaves, I took Le Borgne with me to the Habitation. Here, I told all to M. Radisson. And his quick mind seized this, too, for advantage.

"Precious pearls," he exclaims, "but 'tis a gift of the gods!'

"Sir?"

"Pardieu, Chouart; listen to this," and he tells his kinsman, Groseillers.

" Why not? " asks Groseillers. " You mean to send her to Mary Kirke? "

Mary Kirke was Pierre Radisson's wife, who would not leave the English to go to him when he had deserted England for France.

" Sir John Kirke is director of the English Company now. He hath been knighted by King Charles. Mary and Sir John will present this little maid at the English court. An she be not a nine days' wonder there, my name is not Pierre Radisson. If she's a court ward, some of the crew must take care of her."

Groseillers smiled. " An the French reward us not well for this winter's work, that little maid may open a door back to England; eh, kinsman? "

'Twas the same gamestering spirit carrying them through all hazard that now led them to prepare for fresh partnership, lest France played false. And as history tells, France played very false indeed.

CHAPTER XXII

WE LEAVE THE NORTH SEA

So Sieur Radisson must fit out a royal flotilla to carry Mistress Hortense to the French Habitation. And gracious acts are like the gift horse: you must not look them in the mouth. For the same flotilla that brought Hortense brought all M. Picot's hoard of furs. Coming down the river, lying languidly back among the peltries of the loaded canoe, Hortense, I mind, turned to me with that honest look of hers and asked why Sieur Radisson sent to fetch her in such royal state.

"I am but a poor beggar like your little Jack Battle," she protested.

I told her of M. Radisson's plans for entrance to the English court, and the fire that flashed to her eyes was like his own.

"Must a woman ever be a cat's-paw to man's ambitions?" she asked, with a gleam of the dark lights. "Oh, the wilderness is different," says Hortense with a sigh. "In the wild land, each is for its own! Oh, I love it!" she adds, with a sudden lighting of the depths in her eyes.

"Love—what?"

"The wilderness," says Hortense. "It is hard, but it's free and it's pure and it's true and it's strong!"

And she sat back among the pillows.

When we shot through racing rapids—"sauter les rapides," as our French voyageurs say—she sat up all alert and laughed as the spray splashed athwart. Old Allemand, the pilot, who was steersman on this canoe, forgot the ill-humour of his gin thirst, and proffered her a paddle.

"Here, pretty thing," says he, "try a stroke yourself!"

And to the old curmudgeon's surprise she took it with a joyous laugh, and paddled half that day.

Bethink you who know what warm hearts beat inside rough buckskin whether those voyageurs were her slaves or no! The wind was blowing; Mistress Hortense's hair tossed in a way to make a man swear (vows, not oaths), and Allemand said that I paddled worse than any green hand of a first week. At the Habitation we disembarked after nightfall to conceal our movements from the English. After her arrival, none of us caught a glimpse of Mistress Hortense except of a Sunday at noon, but of her presence there was proof enough. Did voices grow loud in the mess-room? A hand was raised. Some one pointed to the far door, and the voices fell. Did a fellow's tales slip an oath or two? There was a hush. Some one's thumb jerked significantly shoulderwise to the door, and the story-teller leashed his oats for a more convenient season.

" Oh, lordy," taunts an English prisoner out on parole one day, " any angels from kingdom come that you Frenchies keep meek as lambs? "

Allemand, not being able to explain, knocked the fellow flat.

It would scarce have been human nature had not some of the ruffians uttered slurs on the origin of such an one as Hortense found in so strange a case. The mind that feedeth on carrion ever goeth with the large mouth, and for the cleansing of such natures I wot there is no better physic than our crew gave those gossips. What the sailors did I say not. Enough that broken heads were bound by our chirurgeon for the rest of the week.

That same chirurgeon advised a walk outside the fort walls for Mistress Hillary's health. By the goodness of Providence, the duty of escorting her fell to me. Attended by the blackamoor and a soldier, with a musket across my shoulder, I led her out of a rear sally-port and so avoided the scenes of drunkenness among the Indians at the main gate. We got into hiding of a thicket, but boisterous shouting came from the Indian encampment. I glanced at Hortense. She was clad in a green hunting-suit, and by the light of the setting sun her face shone radiant.

"You are not afraid?"

A flush of sheer delight in life flooded her cheeks.

"Afraid?" she laughed.

"Hortense! Hortense! Do you not hear the drunken revel? Do you know what it means? This world is full of what a maid must fear. 'Tis her fear protects her."

"Ah?" asks Hortense.

And she opened the tight-clasped hunting-cloak. A Spanish poniard hung against the inner folds.

"'Tis her courage must protect her. The wilderness teaches that," says Hortense, "the wilderness and men like Picot."

Then we clasped hands and ran like children from thicket to rock and rock to the long stretches of shingly shore. Behind came the blackamoor and the soldier. The salt spray flew in our faces, the wind through our hair; and in our hearts, a joy untold. Where a great obelisk of rock thrust across the way, Hortense halted. She stood on the lee side of the rock fanning herself with her hat.

"Now you are the old Hortense!"

"I *am* older, hundreds of years older," laughed Hortense.

The westering sun and the gold light of the sea and the caress of a spring wind be perilous setting for a fair face. I looked and looked again.

"Hortense, should an oath to the dead bind the living?"

"If it was right to take the oath, yes," said Hortense.

"Hortense, I may never see you alone again. I promised to treat you as I would treat a sister——"

"But—" interrupts Hortense.

Footsteps were approaching along the sand. I thought only of the blackamoor and soldier.

"I promised to treat you as I would a sister—but what—Hortense?"

"But—but I didn't promise to treat you as I would a brother——"

Then a voice from the other side of the rock: "Devil sink my soul to the bottom of the sea if that viper Frenchman hasn't all our furs packed away in his hold!"

Then—"A pox on him for a meddlesome—" the voice fell.

Then Ben Gillam again: "Shiver my soul! Let 'im set sail, I say! Aren't you and me to be shipped on a raft for the English fort at the foot o' the bay?"

"We'll send 'em all to the bottom o' hell first."

"An you give the word, all my men will rise!"

"Capture the fort—risk the ships—butcher the French!"

Hortense raised her hand and pointed along the shore. Our two guards were lumbering up and would presently betray our presence. Stealing forward we motioned their silence. I sent both to listen behind the rock, while Hortense and I struck into cover of the thicket to regain the fort.

"Do not fear," said I. "M. Radisson has kept the prisoners in hand. He will snuff this pretty conspiracy out before Brigdar and Ben get their heads apart."

She gave that flitting look which laughs at fear and hastened on. We could not go back as we had come without exposing ourselves to the two conspirators, and our course lay nearer the Indian revel. About a mile from the fort Hortense stopped short. Through the underbrush crawled two braves with their eyes leering at us.

"Hortense," I urged, "run for the rear gate! I'll deal with these two alone. There may be more! Run, my dear!"

"Give me your musket," she said, never taking her eyes from the savages.

Wondering not a little at the request, I handed her the weapon.

"Now run," I begged, for a sand crane flapped up where the savages had prowled a pace nearer.

Quick as it rose Hortense aimed. There was a puff of smoke. The bird fell shot at the savages' feet, and the miscreants scudded off in terror.

"That was better," said Hortense, "*you* would have killed a man."

In vain I urged her to hasten back. She walked.

"You know it may be the last time," she laughed, mocking my grave air of the beach.

"Hortense—Hortense—how am I to keep a promise?"

But she did not answer a word till we reached the sally-port. There she turned with a brave enough look till her eyes met mine, when all was the confusion that men give their lives to win.

"Yes—yes—keep your promise. If you had not come, I had died; if I had not come, you had died. Let us keep faith with truth, for that's keeping faith with God—and—and—God bless you," she whispered brokenly, and she darted through the gate.

. . . . . .

And the next morning we embarked, young Jean Groseillers remaining with ten Frenchmen to hold the fort; Brigdar and Ben aboard our ship instead of going to the English at the foot of the bay; half the prisoners under hatches in M. Groseillers's ship; the other half sent south on the raft—a plan which effectually stopped that conspiracy of Ben's. Not one glimpse of our fair passenger had we on all that voyage south, for what with Ben's oaths and Governor Brigdar's drinking, the cabin was no place for Hortense.

At Isle Percée, entering the St. Lawrence, lay a messenger from La Chesnaye's father with a missive that bore ill news.

M. de la Barre, the new governor, had ordered our furs confiscated because we had gone north without a license, and La Chesnaye had thriftily rigged up this ship to send half our cargo across to France before the Farmers of the Revenue could get their hands upon it. It was this gave rise to the slander that M. de Radisson ran off with half La Chesnaye's furs—which the records de la marine will disprove, if you search them.

On this ship with her blackamoors sailed Mistress Hortense, bearing letters to Sir John Kirke, director of the Hudson's Bay Company and father of M. Radisson's wife.

"Now praise be Heaven, that little ward will open the way for us in England, Chouart," said M. de Radisson, as he moodily listened to news of the trouble abrewing in Quebec.

And all the way up the St. Lawrence, as the rolling tide lapped our keel, I was dreaming of a far, cold paleocrystic sea, mystic in the frost-clouds that lay over it like smoke. Then a figure emerged from the white darkness. I was snatched up, with the northern lights for chariot, two blazing comets our steeds, and the north star a charioteer.

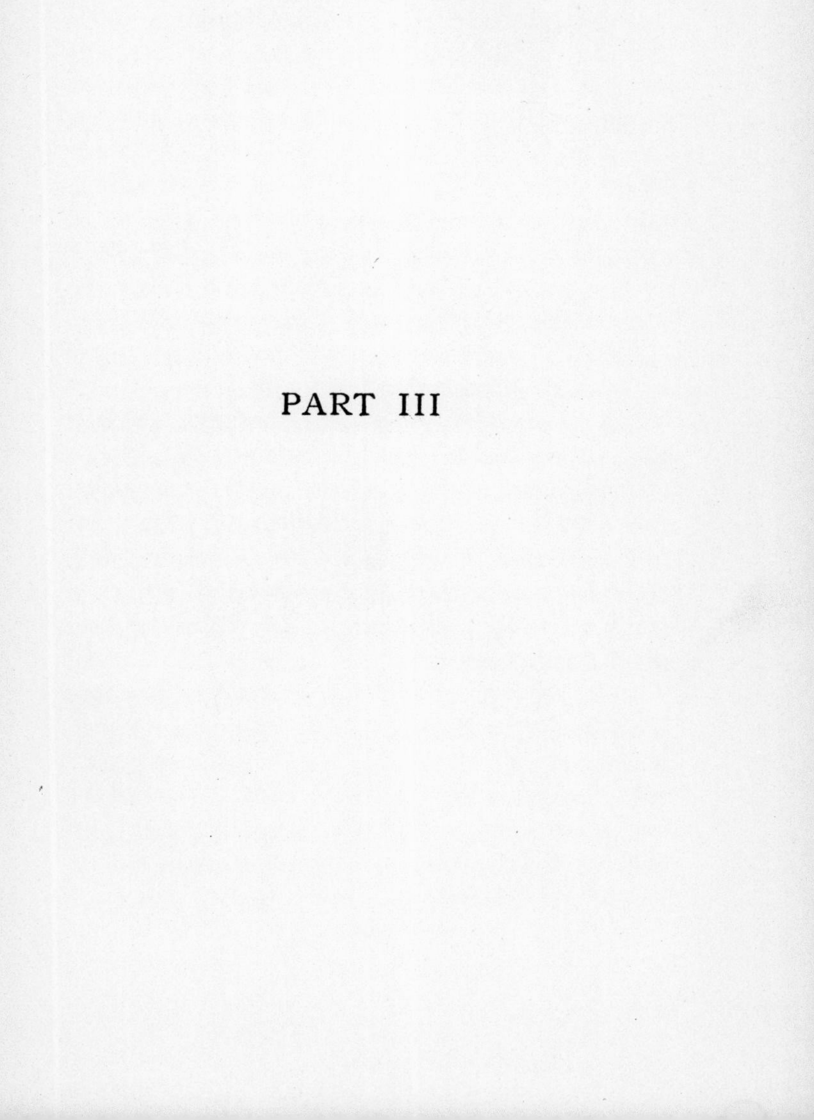

PART III

CHAPTER XXIII

A CHANGE OF PARTNERS

OLD folks are wont to repeat themselves, but that is because they would impress those garnered lessons which age no longer has strength to drive home at one blow.

Royalist and Puritan, each had his lesson to learn, as I said before. Each marked the pendulum swing to a wrong extreme, and the pendulum was beating time for your younger generations to march by. And so I say to you who are wiser by the follies of your fathers, look not back too scornfully; for he who is ever watching to mock at the tripping of other men's feet is like to fall over a very small stumbling-block himself.

Already have I told you of holy men who would gouge a man's eye out for the extraction of one small bean, and counted burnings life's highest joy, and held the body accursed as a necessary evil for the tabernacling of the soul. Now must I tell you of those who wantoned " in the lust of the flesh and the lust of the eye and the pride of life," who burned their lives out at a shrine of folly, and who held that the soul and all things spiritual had gone out of fashion except for the making of vows and pretty conceits in verse by a lover to his lady.

For Pierre Radisson's fears of France playing false proved true. Bare had our keels bumped through that forest of sailing craft, which ever swung to the tide below Quebec fort, when a company of young cadets marches down from the Castle St. Louis to escort us up to M. de la Barre, the new governor.

"Hm," says M. Radisson, looking in his half-savage buckskins a wild enough figure among all those young jacks-in-a-box with their gold lace and steel breastplates. "Hm—let the governor come to us! An you will not go to a man, a man must come to you!"

"I am indisposed," says he to the cadets. "Let the governor come to me."

And come he did, with a company of troops fresh out from France and a roar of cannon from the ramparts that was more for the frightening than welcoming of us.

M. de Radisson bade us answer the salute by a firing of muskets in mid-air. Then we all let go a cheer for the Governor of New France.

"I must thank Your Excellency for the welcome sent down by your cadets," says M. de Radisson, meeting the governor half-way across the gang-plank.

M. de la Barre, an iron-gray man past the prime of life, gave spare smile in answer to that.

"I bade my cadets request you to *report* at the castle," says he, with a hard wrinkling of the lines round his lips.

"I bade your fellows report that I was indisposed!"

"Did the north not agree with Sieur Radisson?" asks the governor dryly.

"Pardieu!—yes—better than the air of Quebec," retorts M. Radisson.

By this the eyes of the listeners were agape, M. Radisson not budging a pace to go ashore, the governor scarce courting rebuff in sight of his soldiers.

"Radisson," says M. de la Barre, motioning his soldiers back and following to our captain's cabin, "a fellow was haltered and whipped for disrespect to the bishop yesterday!"

"Fortunately," says M. Radisson, touching the hilt of his rapier, "gentlemen settle differences in a simpler way!"

They had entered the cabin, where Radisson

bade me stand guard at the door, and at our leader's bravado M. de la Barre saw fit to throw off all disguise.

"Radisson," he said, "those who trade without license are sent to the galleys——"

"And those who go to the galleys get no more furs to divide with the Governor of New France, and the governor who gets no furs goes home a poor man."

M. de la Barre's sallow face wrinkled again in a dry laugh.

"La Chesnaye has told you?"

"La Chesnaye's son——"

"Have the ships a good cargo? They must remain here till our officer examines them."

Which meant till the governor's minions looted both vessels for His Excellency's profit. M. Radisson, who knew that the better part of the furs were already crossing the ocean, nodded his assent.

"But about these English prisoners, of whom La Chesnaye sent word from Isle Percée?" continues the governor.

"The prisoners matter nothing—'tis their ship has value——"

"She must go back," interjects M. de la Barre.

"Back?" exclaims M. Radisson.

"Why didn't you sell her to some Spanish adventurer before you came here?"

"Spanish adventurer—Your Excellency? I am no butcher!"

"Eh—man!" says the governor, tapping the table with a document he pulled from his great-coat pocket and shrugging his shoulders with a deprecating gesture of the hands, "if her crew feared sharks, they should have defended her against capture. Now—your prize must go back to New England and we lose the profit! Here," says he, "are orders from the king and M. Colbert that nothing be done to offend the subjects of King Charles of England——"

"Which means that Barillon, the French ambassador——?"

M. de la Barre laid his finger on his lips. "Walls have ears! If one king be willing to buy and another to sell himself and his country, loyal subjects have no comment, Radisson." *

"Loyal subjects!" sneers M. de Radisson.

"And that reminds me, M. Colbert orders Sieur Radisson to present himself in Paris and

* The reference is evidently to the secret treaty by which King Charles of England received annual payment for compliance with King Louis's schemes for French aggression.

report on the state of the fur-trade to the king!"

"Ramsay," said M. Radisson to me, after Governor la Barre had gone, "this is some new gamestering!"

"Your court players are too deep for me, sir!"

"Pish!" says he impatiently, "plain as day—we must sail on the frigate for France, or they imprison us here—in Paris we shall be kept dangling by promises, hangers-on and do-nothings till the moneys are all used—then——"

"Then—sir?"

"Then, active men are dangerous men, and dangerous men may lie safe and quiet in the sponging-house!"

"Do we sail in that case?"

"Egad, yes! Why not? Keep your colours flying and you may sail into hell, man, and conquer, too! Yes—we sail! Man or devil, don't swerve, lad! Go your gait! Go your gait! Chouart here will look after the ships! Paris is near London, and praise be Providence for that little maid of thine! We shall presently have letters from her — and," he added, "from Sir John Kirke of the Hudson's Bay Company!"

And it was even as he foretold. I find, on

looking over the tattered pages of a handbook, these notes:

Oct. 6.—Ben Gillam and Governor Brigdar this day sent back to New England. There will be great complaints against us in the English court before we can reach London.

Nov. 11.—Sailed for France in the French frigate.

Dec. 18.—Reach Rochelle—hear of M. Colbert's death.

Jan. 30.—Paris—all our furs seized by the French Government in order to keep M. Radisson powerless—Lord Preston, the English ambassador, complaining against us on the one hand, and battering our doors down on the other, with spies offering M. Radisson safe passage from Paris to London.

I would that I had time to tell you of that hard winter in Paris, M. Radisson week by week, like a fort resisting siege, forced to take cheaper and cheaper lodgings, till we were housed between an attic roof and creaking rat-ridden floor in the Faubourg St. Antoine. But not one jot did M. Radisson lose of his kingly bearing, though he went to some fête in Versailles with beaded moccasins and frayed plushes and tattered laces and hair that one of the pretty wits declared the birds would be anesting in for hay-coils. In that Faubourg St. Antoine house, I mind, we took grand apartments on the ground floor, but up and up we went, till M. Radisson vowed we'd presently be under the stars—as the French say when they are homeless—unless my Lord Preston, the English ambassador, came to our terms.

That starving of us for surrender was only another trick of the gamestering in which we were enmeshed. Had Captain Godey, Lord Preston's messenger, succeeded in luring us back to England without terms, what a pretty pickle had ours been! France would have set a price on us. Then must we have accepted any kick-of-toe England chose to offer—and thanked our new masters for the same, else back to France they would have sent us.

But attic dwellers stave off many a woe with empty stomachs and stout courage. When April came, boats for the fur-trade should have been stirring, and my Lord Preston changes his tune. One night, when Pierre Radisson sat spinning his yarns of captivity with Iroquois to our attic neighbours, comes a rap at the door, and in walks Captain Godey of the English Embassy. As soon as our neighbours had gone, he counts out one hundred gold pieces on the table. Then he hands us a letter signed by the Duke of

York, King Charles's brother, who was Governor of the Hudson's Bay Company, granting us all that we asked.

Thereupon, Pierre Radisson asks leave of the French court to seek change of air; but the country air we sought was that of England in May, not France, as the court inferred.

CHAPTER XXIV

UNDER THE ÆGIS OF THE COURT

THE roar of London was about us.

Sign-boards creaked and swung to every puff of wind. Great hackney-coaches, sunk at the waist like those old gallipot boats of ours, went ploughing past through the mud of mid-road, with bepowdered footmen clinging behind and saucy coachmen perched in front. These flunkeys thought it fine sport to splash us passers-by, or beguiled the time when there was stoppage across the narrow street by lashing rival drivers with their long whips and knocking cock-hats to the gutter. 'Prentices stood ringing their bells and shouting their wares at every shop-door. "What d'ye lack? What d'ye lack? What d'ye please to lack, good sirs? Walk this way for kerseys, sayes, and perpetuanoes! Bands and ruffs and piccadillies! Walk this way! Walk this way!"

"Pardieu, lad!" says M. Radisson, elbowing a saucy spark from the wall for the tenth time in as many paces. "Pardieu, you can't hear yourself think! Shut up to you!" he called to a bawling 'prentice dressed in white velvet waistcoat like a showman's dummy to exhibit the fashion. "Shut up to you!"

And I heard the fellow telling his comrades my strange companion with the tangled hair was a pirate from the Barbary States. Another saucy vender caught at the chance.

"Perukes! Perukes! Newest French periwigs!" he shouts, jangling his bell and putting himself across M. Radisson's course. "You'd please to lack a periwig, sir! Walk this way! Walk this way——"

"Out of my way!" orders Radisson with a hiss of his rapier round the fellow's fat calves. "'Tis a milliner's doll the town makes of a man! Out of my way!"

And the 'prentice went skipping. We were to meet the directors of the Hudson's Bay Company that night, and we had come out to refurbish our scant, wild attire. But bare had we turned the corner for the linen-draper's shops of Fleet Street when M. Radisson's troubles began. Idlers eyed us with strange looks. Hucksters read our necessitous state and ran at heel shouting their wares. Shopmen saw needy customers in us and sent their 'prentices running. Chairmen splashed us as they passed; and impudent dandies powdered and patched and laced and bewigged like any fizgig of a girl would have elbowed us from the wall to the gutter for the sport of seeing M. Radisson's moccasins slimed.

"Egad," says M. Radisson, "an I spill not some sawdust out o' these dolls, or cut their stay-strings, may the gutter take us for good and all! Pardieu! An your wig's the latest fashion, the wits under 't don't matter——"

"Have a care, sir," I warned, "here comes a fellow!"

'Twas a dandy in pink of fashion with a three-cornered hat coming over his face like a waterspout, red-cheeked from carminative and with the high look in his eyes of one who saw common folk from the top of church steeple. His lips were parted enough to show his teeth; and I warrant you my fine spark had posed an hour at the looking-glass ere he got his neck at the angle that brought out the swell of his chest. He was dressed in red plush with silk hose of the same colour and a square-cut, tailed coat out of whose pockets stuck a roll of paper missives.

"Verse ready writ by some penny-a-liner for any wench with cheap smiles," says M. Radisson aloud.

But the fellow came on like a strutting peacock with his head in air. Behind followed his page with cloak and rapier. In one hand our dandy carried his white gloves, in the other a lace gewgaw heavy with musk, which he fluttered in the face of every shopkeeper's daughter.

"Give the wall! Give the wall!" cries the page. "Give the wall to Lieutenant Blood o' the Tower!"

"S'blood," says M. Radisson insolently, "let us send that snipe sprawling!"

At that was a mighty awakening on the part of my fine gentleman.

"Blood is my name," says he. "Step aside!"

"An Blood is its name," retorts M. Radisson, "'tis bad blood; and I've a mind to let some of it, unless the thing gets out of my way!"

With which M. Radisson whips out his sword, and my grand beau condescends to look at us.

"Boy," he commands, "call an officer!"

"Boy," shouts M. Radisson, "call a chirurgeon to mend its toes!" and his blade cut a swath across the dandy's shining pumps.

At that was a jump!

Whatever the beaux of King Charles's court

may have been, they were not cowards! Grasping his sword from the page, the fellow made at us. What with the lashing of the coachmen riding post-haste to see the fray, the jostling chairmen calling out "A fight! A fight!" and the 'prentices yelling at the top of their voices for "A watch! A watch!" we had had it hot enough then and there for M. Radisson's sport; but above the mêlée sounded another shrill alarm, the "Gardez l'eau! Gardy loo!" of some French kitchen wench throwing her breakfast slops to mid-road from the dwelling overhead.*

Only on the instant had I jerked M. Radisson back; and down they came—dish-water—and coffee leavings—and porridge scraps full on the crown of my fine young gentleman, drenching his gay attire as it had been soaked in soapsuds of a week old. Something burst from his lips a deal stronger than the modish French oaths then in vogue. There was a shout from the rabble. I dragged rather than led M. Radisson pell-mell into a shop from front to rear, over a score of garden walls, and out again from rear to front, so that we gave the slip to all those officers now running for the scene of the broil.

"Egad's life," cried M. de Radisson, laugh-

* The old expression which the law compelled before throwing slops in mid-street.

ing and laughing, " 'tis the narrowest escape I've ever had! Pardieu—to escape the north sea and drown in dish-water! Lord—to beat devils and be snuffed out by a wench in petticoats! 'Tis the martyrdom of heroes! What a tale for the court!"

And he laughed and laughed again till I must needs call a chair to get him away from onlookers. In the shop of a draper a thought struck him.

" Egad, lad, that young blade was Blood!"

" So he told you."

" Did he? Son of the Blood who stole the crown ten years ago, and got your own Stanhope lands in reward from the king!"

What memories were his words bringing back?—M. Picot in the hunting-room telling me of Blood, the freebooter and swordsman. And that brings me to the real reason for our plundering the linen-drapers' shops before presenting ourselves at Sir John Kirke's mansion in Drury Lane, where gentlemen with one eye cocked on the doings of the nobility in the west and the other keen for city trade were wont to live in those days.

For six years M. Radisson had not seen Mistress Mary Kirke—as his wife styled herself after he broke from the English—and I had not heard one word of Hortense for nigh as many months. Say what you will of the dandified dolls who wasted half a day before the looking-glass in the reign of Charles Stuart, there are times when the bravest of men had best look twice in the glass ere he set himself to the task of conquering fair eyes. We did not drag our linen through a scent bath nor loll all morning in the hands of a man milliner charged with the duty of turning us into showmen's dummies—as was the way of young sparks in that age.

But that was how I came to buy yon monstrous wig costing forty guineas and weighing ten pounds and coming half-way to a man's waist. And you may set it down to M. Radisson's credit that he went with his wiry hair flying wild as a lion's mane. Nothing I could say would make him exchange his Indian moccasins for the high-heeled pumps with a buckle at the instep.

"I suppose," he had conceded grudgingly, "we must have a brat to carry swords and cloaks for us, or we'll be taken for some o' your cheap-jack hucksters parading latest fashions," and he bade our host of the Star and Garter have some lad searched out for us by the time we should be coming home from Sir John Kirke's that night.

UNDER THE ÆGIS OF THE COURT

A mighty personage with fat chops and ruddy cheeks and rounded waistcoat and padded calves received us at the door of Sir John Kirke's house in Drury Lane. Sir John was not yet back from the Exchange, this grand fellow loftily informed us at the entrance to the house. A glance told him that we had neither page-boy nor private carriage; and he half-shut the door in our faces.

"Now the devil take *this thing* for a half-baked, back-stairs, second-hand kitchen gentleman," hissed M. Radisson, pushing in. "Here, my fine fellow," says he with a largesse of vails his purse could ill afford, "here, you saucepans, go tell Madame Radisson her husband is here!"

I have always held that the vulgar like insolence nigh as well as silver; and Sieur Radisson's air sent the feet of the kitchen steward pattering. "Confound him!" muttered Radisson, as we both went stumbling over footstools into the dark of Sir John's great drawing-room, "Confound him! An a man treats a man as a man in these stuffed match-boxes o' towns, looking man as a man on the level square in the eye, he only gets himself slapped in the face for it! An there's to be any slapping in the face, be the first to do it, boy! A man's a man by the measure of his stature in the wilderness. Here, 'tis by the measure of his clothes——"

But a great rustling of flounced petticoats down the hallway broke in on his speech, and a little lady had jumped at me with a cry of "Pierre, Pierre!" when M. Radisson's long arms caught her from her feet.

"You don't even remember what your own husband looked like," said he. "Ah, Mary, Mary—don't *dear* me! I'm only dear when the court takes me up! But, egad," says he, setting her down on her feet, "you may wager these pretty ringlets of yours, I'm mighty dear for the gilded crew this time!"

Madame Radisson said she was glad of it; for when Pierre was rich they could take a fine house in the West End like my Lord So-and-So; but in the next breath she begged him not to call the Royalists a gilded crew.

"And who is this?" she asked, turning to me as the servants brought in candles.

"Egad, and you might have asked that before you tried to kiss him! You always did have a pretty choice, Mary! I knew it when you took me! That," says he, pointing to me, "that is the kite's tail!"

"But for convenience' sake, perhaps the kite's tail may have a name," retorts Madame Radisson.

"To be sure—to be sure—Stanhope, a young Royalist kinsman of yours."

"Royalist?" reiterates Mary Kirke with a world of meaning to the high-keyed question, "then my welcome was no mistake! Welcome waits Royalists here," and she gave me her hand to kiss just as an elderly woman with monster white ringlets all about her face and bejewelled fingers and bare shoulders and flowing draperies swept into the room, followed by a serving-maid and a page-boy. With the aid of two men, her daughter, a serving-maid. and the page, it took her all of five minutes by the clock to get herself seated. But when her slippered feet were on a Persian rug and the displaced ringlets of her monster wig adjusted by the waiting abigail and smelling-salts put on a marquetry table nearby and the folds of the gown righted by the page-boy, Lady Kirke extended a hand to receive our compliments. I mind she called Radisson her "dear, sweet savage," and bade him have a care not to squeeze the stones of her rings into the flesh of her fingers.

"As if any man would want to squeeze such a ragbag o' tawdry finery and milliners' tinsel," said Radisson afterward to me.

I, being younger, was "a dear, bold fellow," with a tap of her fan to the words and a look over the top of it like to have come from some saucy jade of sixteen.

After which the serving-maid must hand the smelling-salts and the page-boy haste to stroke out her train.

"Egad," says Radisson when my lady had informed us that Sir John would await Sieur Radisson's coming at the Fur Company's offices, "egad, there'll be no getting Ramsay away till he sees some one else!"

"And who is that?" simpers Lady Kirke, languishing behind her fan.

"Who, indeed, but the little maid we sent from the north sea."

"La," cries Lady Kirke with a sudden livening, "an you always do as well for us all, we can forgive you, Pierre! The courtiers have cried her up and cried her up, till your pretty savage of the north sea is like to become the first lady of the land! Sir John comes home with your letter to me—boy, the smelling-salts!—so!—and I say to him, 'Sir John, take the story to His Royal Highness!' Good lack, Pierre, no sooner hath the Duke of York heard the tale than off he goes with it to King Charles! His Majesty hath an eye for a pretty baggage. Oh, I promise you, Pierre, you have done finely for us all!"

And the lady must simper and smirk and tap Pierre Radisson with her fan, with a glimmer of ill-meaning through her winks and nods that might have brought the blush to a woman's cheeks in Commonwealth days.

"Madame," cried Pierre Radisson with his eyes ablaze, "that sweet child came to no harm or wrong among our wilderness of savages! An she come to harm in a Christian court, by Heaven, somebody'll answer me for't!"

"Lackaday! Hoighty-toighty, Pierre! How you stamp! The black-eyed monkey hath been named maid of honour to Queen Catherine! How much better could we have done for her?"

"Maid of honour to the lonely queen?" says Radisson. "That is well!"

"She is ward of the court till a husband be found for her," continues Lady Kirke.

"There will be plenty willing to be found," says Pierre Radisson, looking me wondrous straight in the eye.

"Not so sure—not so sure, Pierre! We catch no glimpse of her nowadays; but they say young Lieutenant Blood o' the Tower shadows the court wherever she is——"

"A well-dressed young man?" adds Radisson, winking at me.

"And carries himself with a grand air," amplifies my lady, puffing out her chest, " but then, Pierre, when it comes to the point, your pretty wench hath no dower—no property——"

" Heaven be praised for that!" burst from my lips.

At which there was a sudden silence, followed by sudden laughter to my confusion.

" And so Master Stanhope came seeking the bird that had flown," twitted Radisson's mother-in-law. " Faugh—faugh—to have had the bird in his hand and to let it go! But—ta-ta!" she laughed, tapping my arm with her fan, " some one else is here who keeps asking and asking for Master Stanhope. Boy," she ordered, " tell thy master's guest to come down!"

Two seconds later entered little Rebecca of Boston Town. Blushing pink as apple-blossoms, dressed demurely as of old, with her glances playing a shy hide-and-seek under the downcast lids, she seemed as alien to the artificial grandeur about her as meadow violets to the tawdry splendour of a flower-dyer's shop.

" Fie, fie, sly ladybird," called out Sir John's wife, " here are friends of yours!"

At sight of us, she uttered a little gasp of pleasure.

" So—so—so joysome to see Boston folk," she stammered.

"Fie, fie!" laughed Lady Kirke. "Doth Boston air bring red so quick to all faces?"

"If they be not painted too deep," said Pierre Radisson loud and distinct. And I doubt not the coquettish old dame blushed red, though the depth of paint hid it from our eyes; for she held her tongue long enough for me to lead Rebecca to an alcove window.

Some men are born to jump in sudden-made gaps. Such an one was Pierre Radisson; for he set himself between his wife and Lady Kirke, where he kept them achattering so fast they had no time to note little Rebecca's unmasked confusion.

"This is an unexpected pleasure, Rebecca!"

She glanced up as if to question me.

"Your fine gallants have so many fine speeches——"

"Have you been here long?"

"A month. My father came to see about the furs that Ben Gillam lost in the bay," explains Rebecca.

"Oh!" said I, vouching no more.

"The ship was sent back," continues Rebecca, all innocent of the nature of her father's venture, "and my father hopes that King Charles may get the French to return the value of the furs."

"Oh!"

There was a little silence. The other tongues prattled louder. Rebecca leaned towards me.

"Have you seen her?" she asked.

"Who?"

She gave an impetuous little shake of her head. "You know," she said.

"Well?" I asked.

"She hath taken me through all the grand places, Ramsay; through Whitehall and Hampton Court and the Tower! She hath come to see me every week!"

I said nothing.

"To-morrow she goes to Oxford with the queen. She is not happy, Ramsay. She says she feels like a caged bird. Ramsay, why did she love that north land where the wicked Frenchman took her?"

"I don't know, Rebecca. She once said it was strong and pure and free."

"Did you see her oft, Ramsay?"

"No, Rebecca; only at dinner on Sundays."

"And—and—all the officers were there on the Sabbath?"

"All the officers were there!"

She sat silent, eyes downcast, thinking.

"Ramsay?"

"Well?"

"Hortense will be marrying some grand courtier."

"May he be worthy of her."

"I think many ask her."

"And what does Mistress Hortense say?"

"I think," answers Rebecca meditatively, "from the quantity of love-verse writ, she must keep saying—No."

Then Lady Kirke turns to bid us all go to the Duke's Theatre, where the king's suite would appear that night. Rebecca, of course, would not go. Her father would be expecting her when he came home, she said. So Pierre Radisson and I escorted Lady Kirke and her daughter to the play, riding in one of those ponderous coaches, with four belaced footmen clinging behind and postillions before. At the entrance to the playhouse was a great concourse of crowding people, masked ladies, courtiers with pages carrying torches for the return after dark, merchants with linkmen, work folk with lanterns, noblemen elbowing tradesmen from the wall, tradesmen elbowing mechanics; all pushing and jostling and cracking their jokes with a freedom of speech that would have cost dear in Boston Town. The beaux, I mind, had ready-writ love-verses sticking out of pockets thick as bailiffs' yellow papers; so that a gallant could have stocked his own munitions by picking up the missives dropped at the feet of disdainfuls. Of the play, I recall nothing but that some favourite of the king, Mary Davies, or the famous Nell, or some such an one, danced a monstrous bold jig. Indeed, our grand people, taking their cue from the courtiers' boxes, affected a mighty contempt for the play, except when a naughty jade on the boards stepped high, or blew a kiss to some dandy among the noted folk. For aught I could make out, they did not come to hear, but to be heard; the ladies chattering and ogling; the gallants stalking from box to box and pit to gallery, waving their scented handkerchiefs, striking a pose where the greater part of the audience could see the flash of beringed fingers, or taking a pinch of snuff with a snap of the lid to call attention to its gold-work and naked goddesses.

"Drat these tradespeople, kinsman!" says Lady Kirke, as a fat townsman and his wife pushed past us, "drat these tradespeople!" says she as we were taking our place in one of the boxes, "'tis monstrous gracious of the king to come among them at all!"

Methought her memory of Sir John's career had been suddenly clipped short; but Pierre Radisson only smiled solemnly. Some jokes, like dessert, are best taken cold, not hot.

Then there was a craning of necks; and the king's party came in, His Majesty grown sallow with years but gay and nonchalant as ever, with Barillon, the French ambassador, on one side and Her Grace of Portsmouth on the other. Behind came the whole court; the Duchess of Cleveland, whom our wits were beginning to call "a perennial," because she held her power with the king and her lovers increased with age; statesmen hanging upon her for a look or a smile that might lead the way to the king's ear; Sir George Jeffreys, the judge, whose name was to become England's infamy; Queen Catherine of Braganza, keeping up hollow mirth with those whose presence was insult; the Duke of York, soberer than his royal brother, the king, since Monmouth's menace to the succession; and a host of hangers-on ready to swear away England's liberties for a licking of the crumbs that fell from royal lips.

Then the hum of the playhouse seemed as the beating of the north sea; for Lady Kirke was whispering, "There! There! There she is!" and Hortense was entering one of the royal boxes accompanied by a foreign-looking, elderly woman, and that young Lieutenant Blood, whom we had encountered earlier in the day.

"The countess from Portugal—Her Majesty's friend," murmurs Lady Kirke. "Ah, Pierre, you have done finely for us all!"

And there oozed over my Lady Kirke's countenance as fine a satisfaction as ever radiated from the face of a sweating cook.

"How?" asks Pierre Radisson, pursing his lips.

"Sir John hath dined twice with His Royal Highness——"

"The Duke is Governor of the Company, and Sir John is a director."

"Ta-ta, now there you go, Pierre!" smirks my lady. "An your pretty baggage had not such a saucy way with the men—why—who can tell——"

"Madame," interrupted Pierre Radisson, "God forbid! There be many lords amaking in strange ways, but we of the wilderness only count honour worth when it's won honourably."

But Lady Kirke bare heard the rebuke. She was all eyes for the royal box. "La, now, Pierre," she cries, "see! The king hath recognised you!" She lurched forward into fuller view of onlookers as she spoke. "Wella-day! Good lack! Pierre Radisson, I do believe!

—Yes!—See!—His Majesty is sending for you!"

And a page in royal colours appeared to say that the king commanded Pierre Radisson to present himself in the royal box. With his wiry hair wild as it had ever been on the north sea, off he went, all unconscious of the contemptuous looks from courtier and dandy at his strange, half-savage dress. And presently Pierre Radisson is seated in the king's presence, chatting unabashed, the cynosure of all eyes. At the stir, Hortense had turned towards us. For a moment the listless hauteur gave place to a scarce hidden start. Then the pallid face had looked indifferently away.

"The huzzy!" mutters Lady Kirke. "She might 'a' bowed in sight of the whole house! Hoighty-toighty! We shall see, an the little moth so easily blinded by court glare is not singed for its vanity! Ungrateful baggage! See how she sits, not deigning to listen one word of all the young lieutenant is saying! Mary?"

"Yes——"

"You mind I told her—I warned the saucy miss to give more heed to the men—to remember what it might mean to us——"

"Yes," adds Madame Radisson, "and she said she hated the court——"

"Faugh!" laughs Lady Kirke, fussing and fuming and shifting her place like a peacock with ruffled plumage, "pride before the fall—I'll warrant, you men spoiled her in the north! Very fine, forsooth, when a pauper wench from no one knows where may slight the first ladies of the land!"

"Madame," said I, "you are missing the play!"

"Master Stanhope," said she, "the play must be marvellous moving! Where is your colour of a moment ago?"

I had no response to her railing. It was as if that look of Hortense had come from across the chasm that separated the old order from the new. In the wilderness she was in distress, I her helper. Here she was of the court and I—a common trader. Such fools does pride make of us, and so prone are we to doubt another's faith!

"One slight was enough," Lady Kirke was vowing with a toss of her head; and we none of us gave another look to the royal boxes that night, though all about the wits were cracking their jokes against M. Radisson's "Medusa locks," or "the king's idol, with feet of clay and face of brass," thereby meaning M. Radisson's moccasins and swarth skin. At the door we were awaiting M. Radisson's return when the royal company came out. I turned suddenly and met Hortense's eyes blazing with a hauteur that forbade recognition. Beside her in lover-like pose lolled that milliners' dummy whom we had seen humbled in the morning.

Then, promising to rejoin Pierre Radisson at the Fur Company's offices, I made my adieux to the Kirkes and flung out among those wild revellers who scoured London streets of a dark night.

CHAPTER XXV

JACK BATTLE AGAIN

THE higher one's hopes mount the farther they have to fall; and I, who had mounted to stars with Hortense, was pushed to the gutter by the king's dragoons making way for the royal equipage. There was a crackling of whips among the king's postillions. A yeoman thrust the crowd back with his pike. The carriages rolled past. The flash of a linkman's torch revealed Hortense sitting languid and scornful between the foreign countess and that milliner's dummy of a lieutenant. Then the royal carriages were lost in the darkness, and the streets thronged by a rabble of singing, shouting, hilarious revellers.

Different generations have different ways of taking their pleasure, and the youth of King Charles's day were alternately bullies on the street and dandies at the feet of my lady disdainful. At the approach of the shouting, night-watchmen threw down their lanterns and took to their heels. Street-sweeps tossed their brooms in mid-road with cries of "The Scowerers! The Scowerers!" Hucksters fled into the dark of side lanes. Shopkeepers shot their door-bolts. Householders blew out lights. Fruit-venders made off without their baskets, and small urchins shrieked the alarm of "Baby-eaters! Baby-eaters!"

One sturdy watch, I mind, stood his guard, laying about with a stout pike in a way that broke our fine revellers' heads like soft pumpkins; but him they stood upon his crown in some goodwife's rain-barrel with his lantern tied to his heels. At the rush of the rabble for shelves of cakes and pies, one shopman levelled his blunderbuss. That brought shouts of "A sweat! A sweat!" In a twinkling the rascals were about him. A sword pricked from behind. The fellow jumped. Another prick, and yet another, till the good man was dancing such a jig the sweat rolled from his fat jowls and he roared out promise to feast the whole rout. A peddler of small images had lingered to see the sport, and enough of it he had, I promise you; for they dumped him into his wicker basket and trundled it through the gutter till the peddler and his little white saints were black as chimney-sweeps. Nor did our merry blades play their pranks on poor folk alone. At Will's Coffee House, where sat Dryden and other mighty quidnuncs spinning their poetry and politics over full cups, before mine host got his doors barred our fellows had charged in, seized one of the great wits and set him singing Gammer Gurton's Needle, till the gentlemen were glad to put down pennies for the company to drink healths.

By this I had enough of your gentleman bully's brawling, and I gave the fellows the slip to meet Pierre Radisson at the General Council of Hudson's Bay Adventurers to be held in John Horth's offices in Broad Street. Our gentlemen adventurers were mighty jealous of their secrets in those days. I think they imagined their great game-preserve a kind of Spanish gold-mine safer hidden from public ken, and they held their meetings with an air of mystery that pirates might have worn. For my part, I do not believe there were French spies hanging round Horth's office for knowledge of the Fur Company's doings, though the doorkeeper, who gave me a chair in the anteroom, reported that a strange-looking fellow with a wife as from foreign parts had been asking for me all that day, and refused to leave till he had learned the address of my lodgings.

"'Ave ye taken the hoath of hallegiance, sir?" asked the porter.

"I was born in England," said I dryly.

"Your renegade of a French savage is atakin' the hoath now," confided the porter, jerking his thumb towards the inner door. "They do say as 'ow it is for love of Mary Kirke and not the English——"

"Your renegade of a French—who?" I asked sharply, thinking it ill omen to hear a flunkey of the English Company speaking lightly of our leader.

But at the question the fellow went glum with a tipping and bowing and begging of pardon. Then the councillors began to come: Arlington and Ashley of the court, one of those Carterets, who had been on the Boston Commission long ago and first induced M. Radisson to go to England, and at last His Royal Highness the Duke of York, deep in conversation with my kinsman, Sir John Kirke.

"It can do no harm to employ him for one trip," Sir John was saying.

"He hath taken the oath?" asks His Royal Highness.

"He is taking it to-night; but," laughs Sir John, "we thought he was a good Englishman once before."

"Your company used him ill. You must keep him from going over to the French again."

"Till he undo the evil he has done—till he capture back all that he took from us—then," says Sir John cautiously, "then we must consider whether it be politic to keep a gamester in the company."

"Anyway," adds His Highness, "France will not take him back."

And the door closed on the councillors while I awaited Radisson in the anteroom. A moment later Pierre Radisson came out with eyes alight and face elate.

"I've signed to sail in three days," he announced. "Do you go with me or no?"

Two memories came back: one of a face between a westering sun and a golden sea, and I hesitated; the other, of a cold, pallid, disdainful look from the royal box.

"I go."

And entering the council chamber, I signed the papers without one glance at the terms. Gentlemen sat all about the long table, and at the head was the governor of the company—the Duke of York, talking freely with M. de Radisson.

My Lord Ashley would know if anything but furs grew in that wild New World.

"Furs?" says M. Radisson. "Sir, mark my words, 'tis a world that grows empires—also men," with an emphasis which those court dandies could not understand.

But the wise gentlemen only smiled at M. Radisson's warmth.

"If it grew good soldiers for our wars—" begins one military gentleman.

"Aye," flashes back M. Radisson ironically, "if it grows men for your wars and your butchery and your shambles! Mark my words: it is a land that grows men good for more than killing," and he smiles half in bitterness.

"'Tis a prodigious expensive land in diplomacy when men like you are let loose in it," remarks Arlington.

His Royal Highness rose to take his leave.

"You will present a full report to His Majesty at Oxford," he orders M. Radisson in parting.

Then the council dispersed.

"Oxford," says M. Radisson, as we picked our way home through the dark streets; "an I go to meet the king at Oxford, you will see a hornets' nest of jealousy about my ears."

I did not tell him of the double work implied in Sir John's words with the prince, for Sir John Kirke was Pierre Radisson's father-in-law. At the door of the Star and Garter mine host calls out that a strange-looking fellow wearing a grizzled beard and with a wife as from foreign parts had been waiting all afternoon for me in my rooms.

"From foreign parts!" repeats M. Radisson, getting into a chair to go to Sir John's house in Drury Lane. "If they're French spies, send them right about, Ramsay! We've stopped gamestering!"

"We have; but perhaps the others haven't."

"Let them game," laughs M. Radisson scornfully, as the chair moved off.

Not knowing what to expect I ran up-stairs to my room. At the door I paused. That morning I had gone from the house light-hearted. Now interest had died from life. I had but one wish, to reach that wilderness of swift conflict, where thought has no time for regret. The door was ajar. A coal fire burned on the hearth. Sitting on the floor were two figures with backs towards me, a ragged, bearded man and a woman with a shawl over her head. What fools does hope make of us! I had almost called out Hortense's name when the noise of the closing door caught their hearing. I was in the north again; an Indian girl was on her knees clinging to my feet, sobbing out incoherent gratitude; a pair of arms were belabouring my shoulders; and a voice was saying with broken gurgles of joy:

"Ship ahoy, there! Ease your helm! Don't heave all your ballast overboard!"—a clapping of hands on my back—"Port your helm! Ease her up! All sheets in the wind and the storms'l aflutter! Ha—ha!" with a wringing and a wringing like to wrench my hands off—"Anchor out! Haul away! Home with her . . . !"

"Jack Battle!"

It was all I could say.

There he was, grizzled and bronzed and weather-worn, laughing with joy and thrashing his arms about as if to belabour me again.

"But who is this, Jack?"

I lifted the Indian woman from her knees. It was the girl my blow had saved that morning long ago.

"Who—what is this?"

"My wife," says Jack, swinging his arms afresh and proud as a prince.

"Your wife? . . . Where . . . who married you?"

"There warn't no parson," says Jack, "that is, there warn't no parson nearer nor three thousand leagues and more. And say," adds Jack, "I s'pose there was marryin' afore there *could* be parsons! She saved my life. She hain't no folks. I hain't no folks. She got away that morning o' the massacre—she see them take us captive—she gets a white pelt to hide her agen the snow—she come, she do all them cold miles and lets me loose when the braves ain't watching . . . she risks her life to save my life—she don't belong to nobody. I don't belong to nobody. There waren't no parson, but we're married tight . . . and—and—let not man put asunder," says Jack.

For full five minutes there was not a word.

The east was trying to understand the west!

"Amen, Jack," said I. "God bless you—you are a man!"

"We mean to get a parson and have it done straight yet," explained Jack, "but I wanted you to stand by me——"

"Faith, Jack, you've done it pretty thorough without any help——"

"Yes, but folks won't understand," pleaded Jack, "and—and—I'd do as much for you—I wanted you to stand by me and tell me where to say 'yes' when the parson reads the words——"

"All right—I shall," I promised, laughing.

If only Hortense could know all this! That is the sorrow of rifted lives—the dark between, on each side the thoughts that yearn.

"And—and," Jack was stammering on, "I thought, perhaps, Mistress Rebecca 'd be willing to stand by Mizza," nodding to the young squaw, " that is, if you asked Rebecca," pleaded Jack.

" We'll see," said I.

For the New England conscience was something to reckon with!

" How did you come here? " I asked.

" Mizza snared rabbits and I stole back my musket when we ran away and did some shooting long as powder lasted——"

" And then? "

" And then we used bow and arrow. We hid in the bush till the hostiles quit cruisin'; but the spring storms caught us when we started for the coast. I s'pose I'm a better sailor on water than land, for split me for a herring if my eyes didn't go blind from snow! We hove to in the woods again, Mizza snaring rabbit and building a lodge and keepin' fire agoin' and carin' for me as if I deserved it. There I lay water-logged, odd's man—blind as a mole till the spring thaws came. Then Mizza an' me built a raft; for sez I to Miz, though she didn't understand : ' Miz,' sez I, ' water don't flow uphill! If we rig up a craft, that river'll carry us to the bay! ' But she only gets down on the ground the way she did with you and puts my foot on her neck. Lordy," laughs Jack, " s'pose I don't know what a foot on a neck feels like? I sez: ' Miz, if you ever do that again, I'll throw you overboard!' Then the backwash came so strong from the bay, we had to wait till the floods settled. While we swung at anchor, man, what d'y' think happened? I taught Miz English. Soon as ever she knew words enough I told her if I was a captain I'd want a mate! She didn't catch the wind o' that, lad, till we were navigating our raft downstream agen the ice-jam. Ship ahoy, you know, the ice was like to nip us, and lackin' a life-belt I put me arm round her waist! Ease your helm! Port—a little! Haul away! But she understood—when she saw me save her from the jam before I saved myself."

And Jack Battle stood away arm's length from his Indian wife and laughed his pride.

"And by the time we'd got to the bay you'd gone, but Jean Groseillers sent us to the English ship that came out expecting to find Governor Brigdar at Nelson. We shipped with the company boat, and here we be."

"And what are you going to do?"

"Oh, I get work enough on the docks to pay for Mizza's lessons——"

"Lessons?"

"Yes — she's learning sewin' and readin' from the nuns, and as soon as she's baptized we're going to be married regular."

" Oh! " A sigh of relief escaped me. " Then you'll not need Rebecca for six months or so? "

" No; but you'll ask her? " pleaded Jack.

" If I'm here."

As they were going out Jack slipped back from the hallway to the fireplace, leaving Mizza outside.

" Ramsay? "

" Yes? "

" You think—it's—it's—all right? "

" What? "

" What I done about a mate? "

" Right? " I reiterated. " Here's my hand to you—blessing on the voyage, Captain Jack Battle! "

" Ah," smiled Jack, " you've been to the wilderness—you understand! Other folks don't! That is the way it happens out there! "

He lingered as of old when there was more to come.

" Ramsay? "

" Sail away, captain! "

" Have you seen Hortense? " he asked, looking straight at me.

" Um—yes—no—that is—I have and I haven't."

" Why haven't you? "

"Because having become a grand lady, her ladyship didn't choose to see me."

Jack Battle turned on his heel and swore a seaman's oath. "That—that's a lie," said he.

"Very well—it's a lie, but this is what happened," and I told him of the scene in the theatre. Jack pulled a puzzled face, looking askance as he listened.

"Why didn't you go round to her box, the way M. Radisson did to the king's?"

"You forget I am only a trader!"

"Pah," says Jack, "that is nothing!"

"You forget that Lieutenant Blood might have objected to my visit," and I told him of Blood.

"But how was Mistress Hortense to know that?"

Wounded pride hugs its misery, and I answered nothing.

At the door he stopped. "You go along with Radisson to Oxford," he called. "The court will be there."

CHAPTER XXVI

AT OXFORD

RIOTING through London streets or playing second in M. Radisson's games of empire, it was possible to forget her, but not in Oxford with the court retinue all about and the hedgerows abloom and spring-time in the air. M. Radisson had gone to present his reports to the king. With a vague belief that chance might work some miracle, I accompanied M. Radisson till we encountered the first belaced fellow of the King's Guard. 'Twas outside the porter's lodge of the grand house where the king had been pleased to breakfast that morning.

"And what might this young man want?" demanded the fellow, with lordly belligerence, letting M. Radisson pass without question.

Your colonial hero will face the desperate chance of death; but not the smug arrogance of a beliveried flunkey.

"Wait here," says M. Radisson to me, forgetful of Hortense now that his own end was won.

And I struck through the copse-wood, telling myself that chance makes grim sport. Ah, well, the toughening of the wilderness is not to be undone by fickle fingers, however dainty, nor a strong life blown out by a girl's caprice! Riders went clanking past. I did not turn. Let those that honoured dishonour doff hats to that company of loose women and dissolute men! Hortense was welcome to the womanish men and the mannish women, to her dandified lieutenant and foreign adventuresses and grand ambassadors, who bought English honour with the smiles of evil women. Coming to a high stone wall, I saw two riders galloping across the open field for the copse wood.

"A very good place to break foolish necks," thought I; for the riders were coming straight towards me, and a deep ditch ran along the other side of the wall.

To clear the wall and then the ditch would be easy enough; but to clear the ditch and then the wall required as pretty a piece of foolhardy horsemanship as hunters could find. Out of sheer curiosity to see the end I slackened my walk. A woman in green was leading the pace. The man behind was shouting "Don't try it! Don't try it! Ride round the end! Wait! Wait!" But the woman came on as if her horse had the bit. Then all my mighty, cool stoicism began thumping like a smith's forge. The woman was Hortense, with that daring look on her face I had seen come to it in the north land; and her escort, young Lieutenant Blood, with terror as plainly writ on his fan-shaped elbows and pounding gait as if his horse were galloping to perdition.

"Don't jump! Head about, Mistress Hillary!" cried the lieutenant.

But Hortense's lips tightened, the rein tightened, there was that lifting bound into air when horse and rider are one—the quick paying-out of the rein—the long, stretching leap—the backward brace—and the wall had been cleared. But Blood's horse balked the jump, nigh sending him head over into the moat, and seizing the bit, carried its cursing rider down the slope of the field. In vain the lieutenant beat it about the head and dug the spurs deep. The beast sidled off each time he headed it up, or plunged at the water's edge till Mistress Hortense cried out:

"Oh—please! I cannot see you risk yourself on that beast! Oh—please won't you ride farther down where I can get back!"

"Ho—away, then," calls Blood, mighty glad of that way out of his predicament, "but don't try the wall here again, Mistress Hillary! I protest 'tis not safe for you! Ho—away, then! I race you to the end of the wall!"

And off he gallops, never looking back, keen to clear the wall and meet my lady half-way up.

Hortense sat erect, reining her horse and smiling at me.

"And so you would go away without seeing me," she said, "and I must needs ride you down at the risk of the lieutenant's neck."

"'Tis the way of the proud with the humble," I laughed back; but the laugh had no mirth.

Her face went grave. She sat gazing at me with that straight, honest look of the wilderness which neither lies nor seeks a lie.

"Your horse is champing to be off, Hortense!"

"Yes—and if you looked you might see that I am keeping him from going off."

I smiled at the poor jest as a court conceit.

"Or perhaps, if you tried, you might help me to hold him," says Hortense, never taking her search from my face.

"And defraud the lieutenant," said I.

"Ah!" says Hortense, looking away. "Are you jealous of anything so small?"

I took hold of the bit and quieted the horse. Hortense laughed.

"Were you so mighty proud the other night that you could not come to see a humble ward of the court?" she asked.

"I am only a poor trader now!"

"Ah," says Hortense, questioning my face again, "I had thought you were only a poor trader before! Was that the only reason?"

"To be sure, Hortense, the lieutenant would not have welcomed me—he might have told his fellow to turn me out and made confusion."

And I related M. Radisson's morning encounter with Lieutenant Blood, whereat Mistress Hortense uttered such merry peals of laughter I had thought the chapel-bells were chiming.

"Ramsay!" she cried impetuously, "I hate this life—why did you all send me to it?"

"Hate it! Why——?"

"Why?" reiterated Hortense. "Why, when a king, who is too busy to sign death-reprieves, may spend the night hunting a single moth from room to room of the palace? Why, when ladies of the court dress in men's clothes to run the streets with the Scowerers? Why, when a duchess must take me every morning to a milliner's shop, where she meets her lover, who is a rope-walker? Why, when our sailors starve unpaid and gold enough lies on the basset-table of a Sunday night to feed the army? Ah, yes!" says Hortense, "why do I hate this life? Why must you and Madame Radisson and Lady Kirke all push me here?"

"Hortense," I broke in, "you were a ward of the crown! What else was there for us to do?"

"Ah, yes!" says Hortense, "what else? You kept your promise, and a ward of the crown must marry whom the king names——"

"Marry?"

"Or—or go to a nunnery abroad."

"A nunnery?"

"Ah, yes!" mocks Hortense, "what else is there to do?"

And at that comes Blood crashing through the brush.

"Here, fellow, hands off that bridle!"

"The horse became restless. This gentleman held him for me till you came."

"Gad's life!" cries the lieutenant, dismounting. "Let's see?" And he examines the girths with a great show of concern. "A nasty tumble," says he, as if Hortense had been rolled on. "All sound, Mistress Hillary! Egad! You must not ride such a wild beast! I protest, such risks are too desperate!" And he casts up the whites of his eyes at Mistress Hortense, laying his hand on his heart. "When did you feel him getting away from you?"

"At the wall," says Hortense.

The lieutenant vaulted to his saddle.

"Here, fellow!"

He had tossed me a gold-piece.

They were off. I lifted the coin, balanced it on my thumb, and flipped it ringing against the wall. When I looked up, Hortense was laughing back over her shoulder.

On May 17th we sailed from Gravesend in the Happy Return, two ships accompanying us for Hudson Bay, and a convoy of the Royal Marine coming as far as the north of Scotland to stand off Dutch highwaymen and Spanish pirates.

But I made the news of Jack Battle's marriage the occasion of a letter to one of the queen's maids of honour.

CHAPTER XXVII

HOME FROM THE BAY

'TWAS as fair sailing under English colours as you could wish till Pierre Radisson had undone all the mischief that he had worked against the Fur Company in Hudson Bay. Pierre Radisson sits with a pipe in his mouth and his long legs stretched clear across the cabin-table, spinning yarns of wild doings in savage lands, and Governor Phipps, of the Hudson's Bay Company, listens with eyes a trifle too sleepily watchful, methinks, for the Frenchman's good. A summer sea kept us course all the way to the northern bay, and sometimes Pierre Radisson would fling out of the cabin, marching up and down the deck muttering, "Pah! 'Tis tame adventuring! Takes a dish o' spray to salt the freshness out o' men! 'Tis the roaring forties put nerve in a man's marrow! Soft days are your Delilah's that shave away men's strength! Toughen your fighters, Captain Gazer! Toughen your fighters!"

And once, when M. Radisson had passed beyond hearing, the governor turns with a sleepy laugh to the captain.

" A pox on the rantipole! " says he. " May the sharks test the nerve of his marrow after he's captured back the forts! "

In the bay great ice-drift stopped our way, and Pierre Radisson's impatience took fire.

" What a deuce, Captain Gazer! " he cries. " How long do you intend to squat here anchored to an ice-pan? "

A spark shot from the governor's sleepy eyes, and Captain Gazer swallowed words twice before he answered.

" Till the ice opens a way," says he.

" Opens a way! " repeats Radisson. " Man alive, why don't you carve a way? "

" Carve a way yourself, Radisson," says the governor contemptuously.

That was let enough for Pierre Radisson. He had the sailors lowering jolly-boats in a jiffy; and off seven of us went, round the ice-pans, ploughing, cutting, portaging a way till we had crossed the obstruction and were pulling for the French fort with the spars of three Company boats far in the offing.

I detained the English sailors at the river-front till M. Radisson had entered the fort and won young Jean Groseillers to the change of masters. Before the Fur Company's ships came, the English flag was flying above the fort and Fort Bourbon had become Fort Nelson.

"I bid you welcome to the French Habitation," bows Radisson, throwing wide the gates to the English governor.

"Hm!" returns Phipps, "how many beaver-skins are there in store?"

M. Radisson looked at the governor. "You must ask my tradespeople that," he answers; and he stood aside for them all to pass.

"Your English mind thinks only of the gain," he said to me.

"And your French mind?" I asked.

"The game and not the winnings," said he.

No sooner were the winnings safe—twenty thousand beaver-skins stowed away in three ships' holds—than Pierre Radisson's foes unmasked. The morning of our departure Governor Phipps marched all our Frenchmen aboard like captives of war.

"Sir," expostulated M. de Radisson, "before they gave up the fort I promised these men they should remain in the bay."

Governor Phipps's sleepy eyes of a sudden waked wide.

"Aye," he taunted, "with Frenchmen holding our fort, a pretty trick you could play us when the fancy took you!"

M. Radisson said not a word. He pulled free a gantlet and strode forward, but the doughty governor hastily scuttled down the ship's ladder and put a boat's length of water between him and Pierre Radisson's challenge.

The gig-boat pulled away. Our ship had raised anchor. Radisson leaned over the deck-rail and laughed.

"Egad, Phipps," he shouted, "a man may not fight cowards, but he can cudgel them! An I have to wait for you on the River Styx, I'll punish you for making me break promise to these good fellows!"

"Promise—and when did promise o' yours hold good, Pierre Radisson?"

The Frenchman turned with a bitter laugh.

"A giant is big enough to be hit—a giant is easy to fight," says he, "but egad, these pigmies crawl all over you and sting to death before they are visible to the naked eye!"

And as the Happy Return wore ship for open sea he stood moodily silent with eyes towards the shore where Governor Phipps's gig-boat had moored before Fort Nelson.

Then, speaking more to himself than to Jean and me, his lips curled with a hard scorn.

"The Happy Return!" says he. "Pardieu! 'tis a happy return to beat devils and then have all your own little lies come roosting home like imps that filch the victory! They don't trust me because I won by trickery! Egad! is a slaughter better than a game? An a man wins, who a devil gives a rush for the winnings? 'Tis the fight and the game—pah!—not the thing won! Storm and cold, man and beast, powers o' darkness and devil, knaves and fools and his own sins—aye, that's the scratch!—The man and the beast and the dark and the devil, he can breast 'em all with a bold front! But knaves and fools and his own sins, pah!—death grubs!—hatching and nesting in a man's bosom till they wake to sting him! Flesh-worms—vampires—blood-suckers—spun out o' a man's own tissue to sap his life!"

He rapped his pistol impatiently against the deck-rail, stalked past us, then turned.

"Lads," says he, "if you don't want gall in your wine and a grub in your victory, a' God's name keep your own counsel and play the game fair and square and aboveboard."

And though his speech worked a pretty enough havoc with fine-spun rhetoric to raise the wig off a pedant's head, Jean and I thought we read some sense in his mixed metaphors.

On all that voyage home he never once crossed words with the English officers, but took his share of hardship with the French prisoners.

"I mayn't go back to France. They think they have me cornered and in their power," he would say, gnawing at his finger-ends and gazing into space.

Once, after long reverie, he sprang up from a gun-waist where he had been sitting and uttered a scornful laugh.

"Cornered? Hah! We shall see! I snap my fingers in their faces."

Thereafter his mood brightened perceptibly, and he was the first to put foot ashore when we came to anchor in British port. There were yet four hours before the post-chaise left for London, and the English crew made the most of the time by flocking to the ale-houses. M. Radisson drew Jean and me apart.

"We'll beat our detractors yet," he said. "If news of this capture be carried to the king and the Duke of York * before the shareholders

* The Duke of York became Governor of the Hudson's Bay Company after Prince Rupert's death, and the Company's charter was a royal favour direct from the king.

spread false reports, we are safe. If His Royal Highness favour us, the Company must fall in line or lose their charter!"

And he bade us hire three of the fleetest saddle-horses to be found. While the English crew were yet brawling in the taverns, we were to horse and away. Our horse's feet rang on the cobblestones with the echo of steel and the sparks flashed from M. Radisson's eyes. A wharfmaster rushed into mid-road to stop us, but M. Radisson rode him down. A uniformed constable called out to know what we were about.

"Our business!" shouts M. Radisson, and we are off.

Country franklins got their wains out of our way with mighty confusion, and coaches drew aside for us to pass, and roadside brats scampered off with a scream of freebooters; but M. Radisson only laughed.

"This is living," said he. "Give your nag rein, Jean! Whip and spur! Ramsay! Whip and spur! Nothing's won but at cost of a sting! Throw off those jack-boots, Jean! They're a handicap! Loose your holsters, lad! An any highwaymen come at us to-day I'll send him a short way to a place where he'll stay! Whip up! Whip up!"

"What have you under your arm?" cries Jean breathlessly.

"Rare furs for the king," calls Radisson.

Then the wind is in our hair, and thatched cots race off in a blur on either side; plodding workmen stand to stare and are gone; open fields give place to forest, forest to village, village to bare heath; and still we race on.

. . . . . .

Midnight found us pounding through the dark of London streets for Cheapside, where lived Mr. Young, a director of the Hudson's Bay Company, who was favourable to Pierre Radisson.

"Halloo! Halloo!" shouts Radisson, beating his pistol-butt on the door.

A candle and a nightcap emerge from the upper window.

"Who's there?" demands a voice.

"It's Radisson, Mr. Young!"

"Radisson! In the name o' the fiends—where from?"

"Oh, we've just run across the way from Hudson Bay!" says Radisson.

And the good man presently appears at the door with a candle in one hand and a bludgeon in the other.

"In the name o' the fiends, when did you

arrive, man?" exclaims Mr. Young, hailing us inside.

"Two minutes ago by the clock," laughs Radisson, looking at the timepiece in the hall. "Two minutes and a half ago," says he, following our host to the library.

"How many beaver-skins?" asks the Englishman, setting down his candle.

The Frenchman smiles.

"Twenty thousand beaver-skins and as many more of other sorts!"

The Englishman sits down to pencil out how much that will total at ten shillings each; and Pierre Radisson winks at us.

"The winnings again," says he.

"Twenty thousand pounds!" cries our host, springing up.

"Aye," says Pierre Radisson, "twenty thousand pounds' worth o' fur without a pound of shot or the trade of a nail-head for them. The French had these furs in store ready for us!"

Mr. Young lifts his candle so that the light falls on Radisson's bronzed face. He stands staring as if to make sure we are no wraiths.

"Twenty thousand pounds," says he, slowly extending his right hand to Pierre Radisson. "Radisson, man, welcome!"

The Frenchman bows with an ironical laugh.

"Twenty thousand pounds' worth o' welcome, sir!"

But the director of the Fur Company rambles on unheeding.

"These be great news for the king and His Royal Highness," says he.

"Aye, and as I have some rare furs for them both, why not let us bear the news to them ourselves?" asks Radisson.

"That you shall," cries Mr. Young; and he led us up-stairs, where we might refresh ourselves for the honour of presentation to His Majesty next day.

CHAPTER XXVIIII

REBECCA AND I FALL OUT

M. Radisson had carried his rare furs to the king, and I was at Sir John Kirke's door to report the return of her husband to Madame Radisson. The same grand personage with sleek jowls and padded calves opened the door in the gingerly fashion of his office. This time he ushered me quick enough into the dark reception-room.

As I entered, two figures jumped from the shadow of a tapestried alcove with gasps of fright.

" Ramsay! "

It was Rebecca, the prim monkey, blushing a deal more than her innocence warranted, with a solemn-countenanced gentleman of the cloth scowling from behind.

" When—when—did you come? " she asked, all in a pretty flutter that set her dimples atrembling; and she forgot to give me welcome.

" Now—exactly on the minute! "

"Why—why—didn't you give us warning?" stammered Rebecca, putting out one shy hand.

At that I laughed outright; but it was as much the fashion for gentlemen of the cloth to affect a mighty solemnity in those days as it was for the laity to let out an oath at every other word, and the young divine only frowned sourly at my levity.

"If—if—if you'd only given us warning," interrupts Rebecca.

"Faith, Rebecca, an you talk of warning, I'll begin to think you needed it——"

"To give you welcome," explains Rebecca.

Then recovering herself, she begs, with a pretty bobbing courtesy, to make me known to the Reverend Adam Kittridge.

The Reverend Kittridge shakes hands with an air as he would sound my doctrine on the spot, and Rebecca hastens to add that I am "a very—*old*—*old* friend."

"Not so *very* old, Rebecca, not so very long ago since you and I read over the same lesson-books. Do you mind the copy-heads on the writing-books?

"'*Heaven to find. The Bible mind. In Adam's fall we sinn'ed all. Adam lived a lonely life until he got himself a wife.*'"

But at that last, which was not to be found among the head-lines of Boston's old copy-books, little Rebecca looked like to drop, and with a frightened gesture begged us to be seated, which we all accomplished with a perceptible stiffening of the young gentleman's joints.

" Is M. Radisson back? " she asks.

" He reached England yesterday. He bade me say that he will be here after he meets the shareholders. He goes to present furs to the king this morning."

" That will please Lady Kirke," says the young gentleman.

" Some one else is back in England," exclaims Rebecca, with the air of news. " Ben Gillam is here."

" O-ho! Has he seen the Company? "

" He and Governor Brigdar have been among M. Radisson's enemies. Young Captain Gillam says there's a sailor-lad working on the docks here can give evidence against M. Radisson."

" Can you guess who that sailor-lad is, Rebecca? "

" It is not—no—it is not Jack? " she asks.

" Jack it is, Rebecca. That reminds me, Jack sent a message to you! "

" A message to me? "

" Yes—you know he's married—he married last year when he was in the north."

" Married? " cries Rebecca, throwing up her hands and like to faint from surprise. " Married in the north? Why—who—who married him, Ramsay? "

" A woman, of course! "

" But—" Rebecca was blushing furiously, " but—I mean—was there a chaplain? Had you a preacher? And—and was not Mistress Hortense the only woman——? "

" No—child—there were thousands of women—native women——"

" Squaws! " exclaims the prim little Puritan maid, with a red spot burning on each cheek. " Do you mean that Jack Battle has married a squaw? " and she rose indignantly.

" No—I mean a woman! Now, Rebecca, will you sit down till I tell you all about it? "

" Sir," interjects the young gentleman of the cloth, " I protest there are things that a maid ought not to hear! "

" Then, sir, have a care that you say none of them under cloak of religion! *Honi soit qui mal y pense!* The mind that thinketh no evil taketh no evil."

Then I turned to Rebecca, standing with a startled look in her eyes.

"Rebecca, Madame Radisson has told you how Jack was left to be tortured by the Indians?"

"Hortense has told me."

"And how he risked his life to save an Indian girl's life?"

"Yes," says Rebecca, with downcast lids.

"That Indian girl came and untied Jack's bonds the night of the massacre. They escaped together. When he went snow-blind, Mizza hunted and snared for him and kept him. Her people were all dead; she could not go back to her tribe—if Jack had left her in the north, the hostiles would have killed her. Jack brought her home with him——"

"He ought to have put her in a house of correction," snapped Rebecca.

"Rebecca! Why would he put her in a house of correction? What had she done that she ought not to have done? She had saved his life. He had saved hers, and he married her."

"There was no minister," said Rebecca, with a tightening of her childish dimpled mouth and a reddening of her cheeks and a little indignant toss of the chin.

"Rebecca! How could they get a minister a thousand leagues away from any church? They will get one now——"

Rebecca rose stiffly, her little lily face all aflame.

"My father saith much evil cometh of this—it is sin—he ought not to have married her; and—and—it is very wrong of you to be telling me this—" she stammered angrily, with her little hands clasped tight across the white stomacher.

"Very unfit," comes from that young gentleman of the cloth.

We were all three standing, and I make no doubt my own face went as red as theirs, for the taunt bit home. That inference of evil where no evil was, made an angrier man than was my wont. The two moved towards the door. I put myself across their way.

"Rebecca, you do yourself wrong! You are measuring other people's deeds with too short a yardstick, little woman, and the wrong is in your own mind, not theirs."

"I—I—don't know what you mean!" cried Rebecca obstinately, with a break in her voice that ought to have warned; but her next words provoked afresh. "It was wicked!—it was sinful!"—with an angry stamp—"it was shameful of Jack Battle to marry an Indian girl——"

There I cut in.

"Was it?" I asked. "Young woman, let

me tell you a bald truth! When a white man marries an Indian, the union is as honourable as your own would be. It is when the white man does *not* marry the Indian that there is shame; and the shame is to the white man, not the Indian——!"

Sure, one might let an innocent bundle of swans' down and baby cheeks have its foibles without laying rough hands upon them!

The next,—little Rebecca cries out that I've insulted her, is in floods of tears, and marches off on the young gentleman's arm.

Comes a clatter of slippered heels on the hall floor and in bustles my Lady Kirke, bejewelled and befrilled and beflounced till I had thought no mortal might bend in such massive casings of starch.

"La," she pants, "good lack!—Wellaway! My fine savage! Welladay! What a pretty mischief have you been working? Proposals are amaking at the foot of the stairs. O—lud! The preacher was akissing that little Puritan maid as I came by! Good lack, what will Sir John say?"

And my lady laughs and laughs till I look to see the tears stain the rouge of her cheeks.

"O—lud," she laughs, "I'm like to die! He tried to kiss the baggage! And the little saint jumps back so quick that he hit her ear by mistake! La," she laughs, "I'm like to die!"

I'd a mind to tell her ladyship that a loosening of her stays might prolong life, but I didn't. Instead, I delivered the message from Pierre Radisson and took myself off a mighty mad man; for youth can be angry, indeed. And the cause of the anger was the same as fretteth the Old World and New to-day. Rebecca was measuring Jack by old standards. I was measuring Rebecca by new standards. And the measuring of the old by the new and the new by the old teareth love to tatters.

Pierre Radisson I met at the entrance to the Fur Company's offices in Broad Street. His steps were of one on steel springs and his eyes afire with victory.

"We've beaten them," he muttered to me. "His Majesty favours us! His Majesty accepted the furs and would have us at Whitehall to-morrow night to give account of our doings. An they try to trick me out of reward I'll have them to the foot o' the throne!"

But of Pierre Radisson's intrigue against his detractors I was not thinking at all.

"Were the courtiers about?" I asked.

"Egad! yes; Palmer and Buckingham and Ashley leering at Her Grace of Portsmouth, with

Cleveland looking daggers at the new favourite, and the French ambassador shaking his sides with laughter to see the women at battle. His Royal Highness, the Duke of York, got us access to present the furs. Egad, Ramsay, I am a rough man, but it seemed prodigious strange to see a king giving audience in the apartments of the French woman, and great men leering for a smile from that huzzy! The king lolls on a Persian couch with a litter of spaniel puppies on one side and the French woman on the other. And what do you think that black-eyed jade asks when I present the furs and tell of our captured Frenchmen? To have her own countrymen sold to the Barbadoes so that she may have the money for her gaming-table! Egad, I spiked that pretty plan by saying the Frenchmen were sending her a present of furs, too! To-morrow night we go to Whitehall to entertain His Majesty with our doings! We need not fear enemies in the Company now!"

"I'm not so sure of that," said I. "The Gillams have been working against you here, and so has Brigdar."

"Hah—let them work!"

"Did you see *her*?" I asked.

"*Her*?" questions Radisson absently. "Pardieu, there are so many *hers* about the court now with no she-saint among them! Which do you mean?"

The naming of Hortense after such speech was impossible. Without more mention of the court, we entered the Company's office, where sat the councillors in session around a long table. No one rose to welcome him who had brought such wealth on the Happy Return; and the reason was not far to seek. The post-chaise had arrived with Pierre Radisson's detractors, and allied with them were the Gillams and Governor Brigdar.

Pierre Radisson advanced undaunted and sat down. Black looks greeted his coming, and the deputy-governor, who was taking the Duke of York's place, rose to suggest that "Mr. Brigdar, wrongfully dispossessed of the fort on the bay by one Frenchman known as Radisson, be restored as governor of those parts."

A grim smile went from face to face at Pierre Radisson's expense.

"Better withdraw, man, better withdraw," whispers Sir John Kirke, his father-in-law.

But Radisson only laughs.

Then one rises to ask by what authority the Frenchman, Radisson, had gone to report matters to the king instead of leaving that to the shareholders.

M. de Radisson utters another loud laugh.

Comes a knocking, and there appears at the door Colonel Blood, father of the young lieutenant, with a message from the king.

" Gentlemen," announces the freebooter, " His Majesty hath bespoke dinner for the Fur Company at the Lion. His Royal Highness, the Duke of York, hath ordered Madeira for the councillors' refreshment, and now awaits your coming! "

For the third time M. Radisson laughs aloud with a triumph of insolence.

" Come, gentlemen," says he, " I've countered. Let us be going. His Royal Highness awaits us across the way."

Blood stood twirling his mustaches and tapping his sword-handle impatiently. He was as swarth and straight and dauntless as Pierre Radisson, with a sinister daring in his eyes that might have put the seal to any act.

" Egad's life! " he exclaimed, " do fur-traders keep royalty awaiting? "

And our irate gentleman must needs haste across to the Lion, where awaited the Company Governor, the Duke of York, with all the merry young blades of the court. King Charles's reign was a time of license, you have been told. What that meant you would have known if you had seen the Fur Company at dinner. Blood, Senior, I mind, had a drinking-match against Sir George Jeffreys, the judge; and I risk not my word on how much those two rascals put away. The judge it was who went under mahogany first, though Colonel Blood scarce had wit enough left to count the winnings of his wager. Young Lieutenant Blood stood up on his chair and bawled out some monstrous bad-writ verse to "a fair-dark lady"—whatever that meant—"who was as cold as ice and combustible as gunpowder." Healths were drunk to His Majesty King Charles, to His Royal Highness the Duke of York, to our councillors of the Company, to our governors of the fur-posts, and to the captains. Then the Duke of York himself lifted the cup to Pierre Radisson's honour; whereat the young courtiers raised such a cheering, the grim silence of Pierre Radisson's detractors passed unnoticed. After the Duke of York had withdrawn, our riotous sparks threw off all restraint. On bended knee they drank to that fair evil woman whom King Louis had sent to ensnare King Charles. Odds were offered on how long her power with the king would last. Then followed toasts to a list of second-rate names, dancing girls and French milliners, who kept place of assignation for the dissolute crew, and maids of honour, who were no maids of honour, but adventuresses in the pay of great men to advance their interest with the king, and riffraff women whose names history hath done well to forget. To these toasts Colonel Blood and Pierre Radisson and I sat with inverted glasses.

While the inn was ringing to the shouts of the revellers, the freebooter leaned across to Pierre Radisson.

"Gad's name if they like you," he mumbled drunkenly.

"Who?" asked Radisson.

"Fur Company," explained Blood. "They hate you! So they do me! But if the king favours you, they've got to have you," and he laughed to himself.

"That's the way with me," he whispered in drunken confidence to M. Radisson. "What a deuce?" he asked, turning drowsily to the table. "What's my boy doing?"

Young Lieutenant Blood was to his feet holding a reaming glass high as his head.

"Gentlemen, I give you the sweet savage!" he cried, "the Diana of the snows—a thistle like a rose—ice that burns—a pauper that spurns——"

"Curse me if he doesn't mean that saucy

wench late come from your north fort," interrupted the father.

My hands were itching to throw a glass in the face of father or son, but Pierre Radisson restrained me.

"More to be done sometimes by doing nothing," he whispered.

The young fellows were on their knees draining bumpers; but Colonel Blood was rambling again.

"He gives 'em that saucy brat, does he? Gad's me, I'd give her to perdition for twopenny-worth o' rat poison! Look you, Radisson, 'tis what I did once; but she's come back! Curse me, I could 'a' done it neater and cheaper myself—twopenny-worth o' poison would do it, Picot said; but gad's me, I paid him a hundred guineas, and here she's come back again!"

"Blood . . . Colonel Blood," M. Picot had repeated at his death.

I had sprung up. Again M. Radisson held me back.

"How long ago was that, Colonel Blood?" he asked softly.

"Come twenty year this day s'ennight," mutters the freebooter. "'Twas before I entered court service. Her father had four o' my fellows gibbeted at Charing Cross. Gad's me, I swore he'd sweat for it! She was Osmond's only child—squalling brat coming with nurse over Hounslow Heath. 'Sdeath—I see it yet! Postillions yelled like stuck pigs, nurses kicked over in coach dead away. When they waked up, curse me, but the French poisoner had the brat! Curse me, I'd done better to finish her myself. Picot ran away and wrote letters—letters—letters, till I had to threaten to slit his throat, 'pon my soul, I had! And now she must marry the boy——"

"Why?" put in Radisson, with cold indifference and half-listening air.

"Gad's life, can't you see?" asked the knave. "Osmond's dead, the boy's lands are hers—the French doctor may 'a' told somebody," and Colonel Blood of His Majesty's service slid under the table with the judge.

M. Radisson rose and led the way out.

"You'd like to cudgel him," he said. "Come with me to Whitehall instead!"

CHAPTER XXIX

THE KING'S PLEASURE

My Lady Kirke was all agog.

Pierre Radisson was her "dear sweet savage," and "naughty spark," and "bold, bad beau," and "devilish fellow," and "lovely wretch!"

"La, Pierre," she cries, with a tap of her fan, "anybody can go to the king's *levee*! But, dear heart!" she trills, with a sidelong ogle. "Ta!—ta! naughty devil!—to think of our sweet savage going to Whitehall of an evening! Lud, Mary, I'll wager you, Her Grace of Portsmouth hath laid eyes on him——"

"The Lord forbid!" ejaculates Pierre Radisson.

"Hoighty-toighty! Now! there you go, my saucy spark! Good lack! An the king's women laid eyes on any other man, 'twould turn his head and be his fortune! Naughty fellow!" she warns, with a flirt of her fan. "We shall watch you! Ta-ta, don't tell me no! Oh, we know this *gâité de cœur*! You'll presently be *intime* o' Portsmouth and Cleveland and all o' them!"

"Madame," groans Pierre Radisson, "swear, if you will! But as you love me, don't abuse the French tongue!"

At which she gave him a slap with her fan.

"An I were not so *young*," she simpers, "I'd cuff your ears, you saucy Pierre!"

"So young!" mutters Pierre Radisson, with grim looks at her powdered locks. "Egad's life, so is the bud on a century plant young," and he turns to his wife.

But my Lady Kirke was blush-proof.

"Don't forget to pay special compliments to the favourites," she calls, as we set out for Whitehall; and she must run to the door in a flutter and ask if Pierre Radisson has any love-verse ready writ, in case of an *amour* with one of the court ladies.

"No," says Radisson, "but here are unpaid tailor bills! 'Tis as good as your *billets-doux*! I'll kiss 'em just as hard!"

"So!" cries Lady Kirke, bobbing a courtesy and blowing a kiss from her finger-tips as we rolled away in Sir John's coach.

"The old flirt-o'-tail," blurted Radisson,

"you could pack her brains in a hazel-nut; but 'twould turn the stomach of a grub!"

. . . . . .

'Twas not the Whitehall you know to-day, which is but a remnant of the grand old pile that stretched all the way from the river front to the inner park. Before the fires, Whitehall was a city of palaces reaching far into St. James, with a fleet of royal barges at float below the river stairs. From Scotland Yard to Bridge Street the royal ensign blew to the wind above tower and parapet and battlement. I mind under the archway that spanned little Whitehall Street M. Radisson dismissed our coachman.

"How shall we bring up the matter of Hortense?" I asked.

"Trust me," said Radisson. "The gods of chance!"

"Will you petition the king direct?"

"Egad—no! - Never petition a selfish man direct, or you'll get a No! Bring him round to the generous, so that he may take all credit for it himself! Do you hold back among the onlookers till I've told our story o' the north! 'Tis not a state occasion! Egad, there'll be court wenches a plenty ready to take up with a likely looking man! Have a word with Hortense if you can! Let me but get the king's ear—" And Radisson laughed with a confidence, methought, nothing on earth could shake.

Then we were passed from the sentinel doing duty at the gate to the king's guards, and from the guards to orderlies, and from orderlies to fellows in royal colours, who led us from an ante-room to that glorious gallery of art where it pleased the king to take his pleasure that night.

It was not a state occasion, as Radisson said; but for a moment I think the glitter in which those jaded voluptuaries burned out their moth-lives blinded even the clear vision of Pierre Radisson. The great gallery was thronged with graceful courtiers and stately dowagers and gaily attired page-boys and fair ladies with a beauty of youth on their features and the satiety of age in their look. My Lord Preston, I mind, was costumed in purple velvet with trimming of pearls such as a girl might wear. Young Blood moved from group to group to show his white velvets sparkling with diamonds. One of the Sidneys was there playing at hazard with my Lady Castlemaine for a monstrous pile of gold on the table, which some onlookers whispered made up three thousand guineas. As I watched my lady lost; but in spite of that, she coiled her bare arm around the gold as if to hold the winnings back.

"And indeed," I heard her say, with a pout, "I've a mind to prove your love! I've a mind not to pay!"

At which young Sidney kisses her finger-tips and bids her pay the debt in favours; for the way to the king was through the influence of Castlemaine or Portsmouth or other of the dissolute crew.

Round other tables sat men and women, old and young, playing away estate and fortune and honour at tick-tack or ombre or basset. One noble lord was so old that he could not see to game, and must needs have his valet by to tell him how the dice came up. On the walls hung the works of Vandyke and Correggio and Raphael and Rubens; but the pure faces of art's creation looked down on statesmen bending low to the beck of adventuresses, old men pawning a noble name for the leer of a Portsmouth, and women vying for the glance of a jaded king.

At the far end of the apartment was a page-boy dressed as Cupid, singing love-songs. In the group of listeners lolled the languid king. Portsmouth sat near, fanning the passion of a poor young fool, who hung about her like a moth; but Charles was not a lover to be spurred. As Portsmouth played her ruse the more openly a contemptuous smile flitted over the proud, dark face of the king, and he only fondled his lap-dog with indifferent heed for all those flatterers and foot-lickers and curry-favours hovering round royalty.

Barillon, the French ambassador, pricked up his ears, I can tell you, when Chaffinch, the king's man, came back with word that His Majesty was ready to hear M. Radisson.

" Now, lad, move about and keep your eyes open and your mouth shut! " whispers M. Radisson as he left me.

Barillon would have followed to the king's group, but His Majesty looked up with a quiet insolence that sent the ambassador to another circle. Then a page-boy touched my arm.

" Master Stanhope? " he questioned.

" Yes," said I.

" Come this way," and he led to a tapestried corner, where sat the queen and her ladies.

Mistress Hortense stood behind the royal chair.

Queen Catherine extended her hand for my salute.

"Her Majesty is pleased to ask what has become of the sailor-lad and his bride," said Hortense.

"Hath the little Puritan helped to get them married right?" asked the queen, with the soft trill of a foreign tongue.

"Your Majesty," said I, "the little Puritan holds back."

"It is as you thought," said Queen Catherine, looking over her shoulder to Hortense.

"Would another bridesmaid do?" asked the queen.

Laughing looks passed among the ladies.

"If the bridesmaid were Mistress Hillary, Your Majesty," I began.

"Hortense hath been to see them."

I might have guessed. It was like Hortense to seek the lonely pair.

"Here is the king. We must ask his advice," said the queen.

At the king's entrance all fell back and I managed to whisper to Hortense what we had learned the night before.

"Here are news," smiled His Majesty. "Your maid of the north is Osmond's daughter! The lands young Lieutenant Blood wants are hers!"

At that were more looks among the ladies.

"And faith, the lieutenant asks for her as well as the lands," said the king.

Hortense had turned very white and moved a little forward.

"We may not disturb our loyal subject's possession. What does Osmond's daughter say?" questioned the king.

Then Hortense took her fate in her hands.

"Your Majesty," she said, "if Osmond's daughter did not want the lands, it would not be necessary to disturb the lieutenant."

"And who would find a husband for a portionless bride?" asked King Charles.

"May it please Your Majesty," began Hortense; but the words trembled unspoken on her lips.

There was a flutter among the ladies. The queen turned and rose. A half-startled look of comprehension came to her face. And out stepped Mistress Hortense from the group behind.

"Your Majesties," she stammered, "I do not want the lands——"

"Nor the lieutenant," laughed the king.

"Your Majesties," she said. She could say no more.

But with the swift intuition of the lonely

woman's loveless heart, Queen Catherine read in my face what a poor trader might not speak. She reached her hand to me, and when I would have saluted it like any dutiful subject, she took my hand in hers and placed Hortense's hand in mine.

Then there was a great laughing and handshaking and protesting, with the courtiers thronging round.

"Ha, Radisson," Barillon was saying, "you not only steal our forts—you must rifle the court and run off with the queen's maid!"

"And there will be two marriages at the sailor's wedding," said the queen.

It was Hortense's caprice that both marriages be deferred till we reached Boston Town, where she must needs seek out the old Puritan divine whom I had helped to escape so many years ago.

Before I lay down my pen, I would that I could leave with you a picture of M. Radisson, the indomitable, the victorious, the dauntless, living in opulence and peace!

But my last memory of him, as our ship sheered away for Boston Town, is of a grave man standing on the quay denouncing princes' promises and gazing into space.

M. Radisson lived to serve the Fur Company for many a year as history tells; but his service was as the flight of a great eagle, harried by a multitude of meaner birds.

THE END